The Lesser Light

The Lesser Light

Lights of the Collapse
Book 1

Millie Copper

Written by Millie Copper

Edited by Ameryn Tucker

Proofread by MDC Proofreading

Cover design by Dauntless Cover Design

Also by Millie Copper

The Havoc in Wyoming Series

When a series of coordinated attacks devastate the United States, the people of Bakerville, Wyoming, must come together to survive. Unfortunately, not everyone has the town's best interest at heart. Some are striving for personal gain during the apocalypse.

The Montana Mayhem Series

A group from Bakerville, Wyoming strikes out on their own while searching for the desires of their heart. Unfortunately, the road will not be easy, and sometimes the heart is hardened and deceitful. When things don't work out as they hoped, will they become stranded in the wilderness? Or will each be able to find their way home?

The Dakota Destruction Series

After a series of coordinated attacks devastate the United States, Katie and Leo sacrifice everything to help their country. But some things aren't as they seem. Is it time to go home and start fresh, or can something good come out of this terrible situation?

Wyoming Fall Series (In The October Fall World)

In the blink of an eye, an EMP changed everything for Lauren and her family. Now they are in a fight for survival, trying to keep their loved ones alive as society collapses around them. Their once peaceful town of Cody, Wyoming has turned into a powder keg. And with law enforcement a thing of the past, evil lurks around every corner.

Nonfiction Books

Millie has penned seven nonfiction, traditional food focused books, sharing how, with a little creativity, anyone can transition to a real foods diet without overwhelming their food budget. Many of her books also include preparedness and food storage tips.

Find these titles at:
MillieCopper.com

Join My Reader's Club!

Receive a complimentary copy of *Starborn: A Lights of the Collapse Short Story Prequel*. As part of my reader's club, you'll be the first to know about new releases and specials. I also share info on books I'm reading, preparedness tips, and more. Please sign up at:

MillieCopper.com/Freebie

Chapter 1

Maddie flopped onto her bed, her phone held above her face as she scrolled mindlessly through her social media feed. The afternoon sun streamed through her window and cast a warm glow across her room, but she barely noticed.

Her plans for the day had evaporated when her friends canceled their mall trip at the last minute. Not that it really mattered. The mall was lame, with more stores closed than open. But still, it was something to do.

"Ugh!" She tossed her phone aside. The ceiling fan spun overhead, its gentle whirring the only sound in the quiet house. Her grandma was out of town, her mom was at work, and her brother was at a friend's house, leaving Maddie alone with her boredom.

She rolled off her bed, wandered into the family room, and plopped on the couch. The remote felt heavy in her hand as she flicked through streaming services, but nothing caught her interest. Even her favorite shows seemed dull today.

With a sigh, Maddie turned off the TV and grabbed a book from the nearby shelf. She'd been meaning to read it for weeks, but now, as she stared at the first page, the words swam before her eyes. After a few minutes of trying to focus, she snapped the book shut and tossed it aside.

Her gaze drifted to the corner of the room where her brother Jackson's VR sat. The headset and controllers gleamed in the afternoon light, almost beckoning her. Maddie bit her lip, considering.

Their dad had given them the two-person set a few months ago, insisting it was for both of them, but she'd never really been interested in gaming. Jackson had wanted to take it up to his room, but their grandma said since it belonged to both of them, it should remain in the family room.

"Well," she muttered to herself, "it's not like I have anything better to do."

She ran her fingers over the smooth surface of the headset. She'd seen Jackson use it countless times, but she'd spent little time with it herself. He'd tried to show her how to use it by playing some silly game where they worked in a fast-food restaurant. She kept dropping the hamburgers on the floor, much to Jackson's amusement. Maddie didn't think it was funny and quit playing.

Maybe today, without her brother nagging at her, she could get the hang of it. With a shrug, she slipped on the headset and grabbed the controllers.

The world around her disappeared as the game booted up. Maddie gasped as she found herself standing in a vibrant, colorful landscape. *This definitely isn't the restaurant game*, she thought. *What has Jackson been playing?* The graphics were incredible, more realistic than she'd imagined. She could almost feel the virtual breeze on her skin.

A menu appeared before her, floating in mid-air. Maddie reached out hesitantly, her virtual hand moving in sync with her real one. Suddenly, she was in a bustling city square. Avatars of other players moved around her, some chatting, others engaged in what looked like quests. She took a tentative step forward, marveling at how natural it felt to move in the virtual world.

When she pressed the help button, an avatar approached her and offered a tutorial. She accepted and followed the guide through the basics of movement, interaction, and combat. She found herself grinning as she successfully completed her first mini-quest. It consisted of collecting a set of magical artifacts scattered around the city.

Time seemed to fly by as she explored the game world. She joined a group of other players to tackle a dungeon, her heart racing as they fought off waves of monsters. The teamwork and strategy required were surprisingly engaging, and she found herself getting caught up in the excitement.

As she emerged from the dungeon, flush with victory and newfound confidence in her gaming abilities, a bright orange ball popped up in the bottom corner. Wondering where that would take her, she was just about to click on it when a notification covered her field of view—a message from player BreveBravo.

"Hey, JackAttack! Didn't expect to see you on this early. How's it going, cuz?"

Maddie froze, her virtual avatar standing stock-still in the bustling square. JackAttack was her brother's gamer name. She probably should have signed off as him and on as herself before getting so far into the game. The player messaging her must be their cousin, Eddie, who often played with Jackson. She hesitated, unsure how to respond.

Another message appeared: *"Earth to Jackson! You there, dude?"*

Maddie's fingers hovered over the virtual keyboard, torn between pretending to be Jackson and coming clean. Just as she was about to decide, the orange ball in the corner of the screen began to pulse gently, growing larger with each beat. Its glow was mesmerizing, almost magnetic, drawing her gaze and pulling her focus. Her hand twitched involuntarily toward it, the urge to click on it nearly irresistible.

"Hey! Why are you touching my stuff?" Jackson's voice boomed from behind her. Before she could react, he yanked the VR from her face, sending it flying.

Maddie swatted his arm in frustration. "Knock it off! It's not just yours. Dad said it was for both of us. Dork." She reached out to reclaim the headset, but Jackson swiveled away, keeping it just out of her grasp.

"If Grandma were here, you wouldn't do that." She narrowed her eyes at her younger brother. "Why are you home? I thought you were at Billy's place?"

"I was at Bobby's." He muttered something under his breath about how his dumb sister couldn't ever remember his friends' names. "*She* called. Said I need to get home."

"Mom? Mom called you? From work?"

He shook his head. "I don't— " His lips stretched in a tight line.

"You don't what?"

"I don't think she was at work. The noise wasn't right. Too loud." He tilted his head and lowered his voice to a whisper. "I think she was in a bar."

Maddie closed her eyes and rubbed her fingers along her forehead. "I'll call her. It's been over a year. She's been doing good. Great, even. Staying on her medication and . . . and . . . Grandma wouldn't have gone on her trip if she didn't think Mom was okay. I mean, she almost canceled her trip because of the weird stuff going on. She wouldn't have left us if she thought mom was going to . . . to . . . you know."

Jackson gave an exaggerated shrug. "Call her. Don't call her. I don't care. I'm going to play *my* game."

"Whatever. That dumb VR gives me motion sickness, anyway." But even as she said it, Maddie couldn't help but think of the orange ball. It had been so magnificent, almost hypnotic. For a moment, she felt a strange longing to see it again.

He smirked. "Too bad for you, Maddie. You just don't know what you're doing."

She stuck her tongue out at him before spinning on her heel. When she reached the kitchen, she turned back. "Why'd she tell you to come home?"

"I don't know. Who cares? Bobby's was boring, anyway. His mom's all freaked. Said she heard on TV that there might be martial law or something."

"What? What do you mean martial law?" Maddie leaned against the breakfast bar, her mind racing from this news.

"How should I know? You're supposed to be the smart one." He slid into the headset and turned his back toward her.

"Yeah. Whatever. Fine," she muttered on her way out of the room. When she entered the living room at the front of the house, she pulled her phone from her pocket and sank onto the sofa. Sure enough, there was a missed call from her mom.

She tried calling her back, but it went directly to voicemail without even ringing—typical for when she was working. She was a certified nursing assistant at a rehabilitation facility and wasn't allowed to have her phone with her when she was on the floor. *Maybe Jackson got it wrong and Mom was just on break when she called?* Maddie thought. *She really has been doing fine.*

Leaning back on the sofa, Maddie ran a hand through her hair, feeling the need for a shower. She gave her armpits a quick sniff and grimaced. Definitely. If her grandma were home, she'd be nagging both siblings to take their daily showers.

You'd think that at almost seventeen and thirteen, they'd be able to remember on their own. During the school year, it was no problem and was part of their daily routines. Maddie always showered as soon as she got out of bed each morning, while Jackson preferred to shower at night. She thought that said a lot about their personalities. She had no trouble waking up in the morning, but Jackson was always a slug, preferring to stay up way too late.

With summer here and her grandma away on an Alaskan cruise with her friends, their routines had completely fallen apart. She had been gone for the past week and would be away for about five weeks in total, accounting for a leisurely road trip to and from, plus the twenty-four-day cruise.

Her grandma had called it the trip of a lifetime and had been as giddy as a teenager about the whole adventure. She never would have left if she'd even thought that Heather, Maddie's mom, was struggling with her medication.

Maddie jumped at the ring of the phone. Glancing at the display, a smile crept over her face. "Hey, Dad. What's up?"

"Maddie? Where are you?" His tone was urgent. Concerned.

"Um . . . home?"

"What about Jackson? Is he with you?"

"Uh, yeah. Playing that stupid game."

Dad let out a noisy sigh. "Okay. Good. Your mom?"

"At work." *I think.* "Why all the questions?"

"You didn't hear? About the explosion in Casper?"

"What explosion?" Maddie switched her phone to speaker so she could open her favorite social media app. It took only a minute of scrolling to find posts about the trouble.

Her dad was still talking. "It happened at a pub near the mall. I'm surprised you didn't hear it."

"At the mall?" Her eyes went wide as she considered how she was supposed to go there today. One of the photos in a post showed the building before the explosion. She immediately recognized the restaurant. It wasn't exactly at the mall but was on Second Street, between the mall and where her mom worked. "I didn't hear anything. It looks bad. Is it . . . do you think . . ."

"Is it part of the attacks? I don't know. I hope not."

"Attacks? No one's calling them attacks, Dad. Oh, except Grandpa Dick. I forgot he thinks they're part of some sort of conspiracy. But I saw an interview about it. It isn't a conspiracy, but maybe an illness. Like hay fever or something."

Her dad, Brian Reynolds, gave a snort. "Yeah, right. I saw that movie. 'The plants made them do it.' It's science fiction, Maddie. I think my dad is right about this. I know he can come up with some weird ideas, but this time, there are too many strange things happening for them not to be some kind of coordinated attack.

"But to answer your question about the explosion, I don't know. Not for sure. There isn't enough info yet. It could've been a gas leak or something. I hope it's only that building that is affected. It's way too close to where your mom works."

Maddie stifled a sigh. "I'm sure she's fine. But, Dad? Have you heard anything about martial law?"

"What about martial law?"

"You know Jackson's friend Bobby? I guess his mom said she heard we might get martial law."

"In Wyoming?"

"Uh . . . I don't know. Jackson didn't say." Maddie continued scrolling as they talked. There was more about the explosion at the pub, but she didn't see anything about martial law.

She considered telling her dad about the weird phone call Jackson received from their mom but decided against it. He didn't need to know about stuff like that. It only upset him when their mom had an episode, and then he'd talk about trying to gain custody again.

Not that Maddie wouldn't want to live with her dad, but she didn't want to leave Casper and her friends, and especially not Grandma Bea. Besides, Jackson didn't always pay attention. Maybe he just didn't understand their mom's call. "So . . . we're fine, Dad. Is any weird stuff happening up there? Everything normal at the lodge?"

"Normal?" He scoffed. "It's tourist season. There's not much normal this time of year. We've got a full house, with every room and cabin rented. Your grandpa and grandma even rented out those two new cabins."

"The one we stayed in last summer? It doesn't have any electricity."

"Right! Seems there's a market for off-grid living. Who knew? I guess people like the idea of roughing it for a few days, then they can appreciate their television and computers even more when they go back home. It's good, though. Since it's a mile hike to get to them, they don't get breakfast delivery. They're welcome to pick up a basket the night before, but they have to order in advance so we know they want it. Then they can walk down and join us for dinner. Have you heard from Bea? How's her trip going?"

"Grandma Bea called the night before they boarded . . . um, embarked? I think that's what they do on a ship? Embark and disembark?"

"Okay, sure. You haven't heard from her since then?"

"*Daaaad.* She's on vacation. She's supposed to be having fun. We're fine. Jackson's good. I'm good." Maddie hesitated before adding, "Mom's good."

"Is she? She's doing okay with your grandma gone?"

"She's fine, Dad."

"I should've insisted on you and Jackson staying up here with me while Bea's gone. I'd feel better about everything."

"I told you, we're fine." Maddie rolled her eyes. "Look. I, uh . . . thanks for calling me about the explosion. No problems here. I'm going to take a shower."

"Okay, Maddie. Take care of your brother. Tell your mom I called. Ask her if she can give me a call if she has a minute."

"Sure, Dad. I'm sure she'll be happy to call you." Not. While Heather didn't badmouth her former husband these days, she didn't really talk to him either. When arrangements were made to visit her dad and his parents at the lodge they owned and operated near Yellowstone National Park, Grandma Bea usually handled it.

Grandma Bea got along okay with Maddie's dad. She had hated him for a while, blaming him for some of the troubles with Heather, but she seemed to respect him for sobering up and doing well now. Brian lived in a cabin at his parents' lodge up the North Fork, about an hour from the town of Cody and minutes from the East Gate entrance to Yellowstone.

After they said their goodbyes, which included a warning to "be careful," Maddie went back to scrolling on her phone. Updates about the Casper explosion dominated the news, along with speculation linking it to other recent incidents.

It all started a few weeks ago with a random event. A girl around Maddie's age attacked people on the New York subway with a knife, resulting in several deaths. The girl was stopped and seemed completely out of it, probably on drugs or something. Or maybe, like Maddie's mom, she had voices in her head telling her to do things.

Since then, there had been more unsettling stories—a guy stole a semitruck and drove it down a sidewalk in Atlanta, leaving dozens dead. He seemed completely out of his mind.

Then there were a couple of mass shootings where the shooters acted disoriented, as if they weren't aware of their actions.

Earlier today, a girl around Maddie's age stole a small airplane and crashed it into a hangar—like she was driving a car, not flying a plane. Six people died.

Maddie heard an interview with a doctor who thought it was some kind of mass illness or psychosis making people do those things. He was even supposed to get the CDC to review the information and do . . . well, she wasn't entirely certain what they were supposed to do. Maybe make a vaccine or something to get people to stop killing? Wouldn't that be some kind of great invention?

Chapter 2

At the shelf by the back door, Maddie picked up the binoculars her grandma used for birding and then stepped out onto the deck. She moved against the rail, pushing her mother's much-too-full ashtray to the side. "So gross," she muttered.

She didn't need the binoculars to see the column of smoke rising in the hot, windless sky. Even with the lenses, it was hard to make out much more detail. The buildings remained obscured, nestled in an office district with several restaurants and businesses near the care center where her mom worked. Still . . . it did seem awfully close to the care center.

According to social media, there was a suspicion that nearby buildings might have been affected as well. With the clock just shy of one in the afternoon, Maddie couldn't help but wonder how many people had been inside the restaurants during the explosion.

She wrinkled her nose, catching a faint whiff of smoke. It was surprisingly mild, likely due to the still air—a rarity in Casper—keeping it from drifting their way. She set the binoculars down on the picnic table and wiped her forehead with the back of her hand. It was only early June and already much too hot.

Picking up the binoculars again, Maddie turned her gaze westward from the smoke column. She could just make out the tree line along the North Platte River. Continuing to scan, she searched for Lake McKenzie—a modest water spot but perfect for leisurely activities.

While showering would have been practical, Maddie decided to head to the lake. Last Christmas, Grandma Bea surprised them all with paddleboards. Maddie had fallen in love with paddleboarding after borrowing a friend's board last year, prompting her to ask for her own.

For some reason, Grandma Bea thought it'd be a great family activity and had bought boards not only for Maddie but also for Jackson, Heather, and herself, along with wetsuits suitable for Wyoming's never-warm waterways.

They had enjoyed several outings over Memorial Day weekend, starting at Lake McKenzie before venturing out to Alcova Reservoir, about thirty miles from Casper, for a bigger water adventure.

Before leaving for the lake, she needed to try her mom again. If nothing else, just so she could tell Jackson that everything was fine. He pretended like he didn't care how she acted, but Maddie knew that was a lie. She should also tell him about the explosion.

Maddie called her mom, pacing nervously on the back deck. Still no answer. She left a brief voicemail, trying to keep her voice steady. "Hey, Mom. It's Maddie. Just checking in. There was some kind of explosion. Can you see it? It's close to your work. Call me back when you can, okay?" She hesitated, then added, "Love you."

She slipped her phone into her pocket and headed back inside. Jackson was exactly where she'd left him, completely absorbed in his VR world.

"Jackson," she called. No response. "Jackson!"

He jumped, nearly toppling over as he yanked off the headset. "What?"

"There was an explosion near Mom's work."

His eyes widened. "What? Is she okay?"

"I can't reach her, but I'm sure she's fine. Probably working and doesn't have her phone. You know how it is." Maddie bit her lip. "Look, I'm taking the paddleboard to the lake. I need to clear my head. You coming?" Where did that come from? She had no intention of inviting him to go along with her. Surely, he'd say no.

Jackson hesitated, glancing back at his game. "I guess. Yeah, okay."

"Really? Um, okay."

As they gathered their gear, she filled Jackson in on what little she knew about the explosion.

His face grew more worried with each detail. "You don't think . . . ." His voice trailed off.

"Think what?"

"That it's like those other things? The subway attack, the truck thing?"

She shrugged, trying to appear nonchalant. "Probably just an accident—a gas leak or something."

They loaded the paddleboards into the back of her car and set off for Lake McKenzie. The streets were conspicuously quiet. Usually, on a summer afternoon like this, kids would be out playing and people would be walking their dogs or working in their yards.

But today, curtains were drawn, and a stillness hung in the air. The few people they did see outside were standing in groups, talking and pointing in the direction of the explosion.

As they neared the interstate to take them toward Bryan Stock Trail, the road that led to Lake McKenzie, a faint acrid smell reached them.

"Pew!" Jackson rolled up his window and reached for the buttons to control the air conditioner.

"It doesn't work." Maddie shook her head as she batted his hand away from the knobs. "You know that. Just leave the window down."

"But it stinks."

"Get used to it. It'll probably stink for days. Just like when there are wildfires around and the smoke settles in."

Jackson grumbled about something that Maddie chose to ignore. When they arrived at the lake, which was really nothing more than a duck pond, they found it deserted. On a normal day, there would be at least a few other people around, fishing or lounging on the small beach. Today, it was just them and the ducks.

They inflated their boards in silence. As Maddie was about to push off from shore, Jackson spoke up. "What if Mom was in the explosion?"

Maddie's stomach clenched. She'd been trying not to think about that possibility. "She wasn't," she said firmly. "She was at work. The care center's up the road."

"But what if— "

"She wasn't there, Jackson. Now come on, let's paddle."

Out on the water, some of her tension eased. The rhythmic motion of paddling, the sun on her face, the gentle lapping of water against her board—it all helped calm her churning thoughts. She paddled from her knees, not yet having the core strength necessary to stand up.

Jackson, however, popped right up and gave her a saucy grin before quickly losing his balance and splatting into the water.

"Ha!" she laughed. "Not as smooth as you thought."

Jackson shook the water from his hair and wiped his face. "Yeah, yeah," he retorted with a playful smirk. "At least I got up. What's your excuse?"

She rolled her eyes, but a smile tugged at her lips. "Oh, please. I'm just savoring the moment."

"Sure you are." Jackson splashed water in her direction before pulling himself back onto his board with ease. "Maybe, by the end of the summer, you'll be able to stand up without looking like a baby giraffe."

Maddie splashed him back, laughing. "Baby giraffe? Seriously?"

He shook his head, still grinning, as he got back into position and smoothly stood up again. "Watch and learn, Maddie. Watch and learn."

Surrounded by laughter and teasing, her worries melted away, even if just for a little while. The world beyond the shore seemed distant and insignificant compared to the here and now, under the sun and sky, with Jackson's sass keeping her grounded in the moment.

They'd been out for about twenty minutes when a distant rumble made them both pause.

"What was that?" Jackson asked, his voice tight.

"Probably just a truck or something," Maddie said, but she wasn't convinced. It sounded more like an explosion.

Sirens began to wail. So many sirens. Too many. Even the town warning siren was going off.

Another deafening boom, this time bigger, created ripples across the water.

"Maddie!" Jackson almost lost his balance as he pointed in the direction of their home. "What is that?"

She whipped around, her eyes wide with fear and disbelief. This was big. Bigger than anything she'd ever faced.

Chapter 3

Across the landscape, a colossal fireball churned and roared. Its metal frame glowed crimson, shedding flaming debris in its wake. Heat waves shimmered around it and ignited patches of dry grass. A thick plume of black smoke trailed behind, casting a brief shadow over the terrain.

"Maddie . . ." Jackson's voice quivered. "What is that?"

"I think it's a semitruck or something. It must have exploded and . . . and wow. Just wow." She cleared her throat. "It's okay." She tried to remain calm, but her heart was racing. "Let's head back."

Jackson nodded before shifting to sit on his board, looking like a serious paddler. As they paddled toward shore, their fun was replaced by a sense of urgency, Maddie's phone buzzed in its waterproof pouch. In her haste to check it, she nearly fell off her board.

It was a text from her mom: *"Stay home. Do not leave the house under any circumstances. I'll be home as soon as I can."*

Maddie exhaled, but her relief evaporated as another explosion shattered the air, closer this time. She flinched, and her eyes darted toward the noise. Beyond the trees, in the direction of the city dump, a dark plume of smoke curled toward the sky.

"What's happening?" Jackson whispered.

Maddie and Jackson reached the shore and stared at the ominous smoke plumes rising all around them. The sirens hadn't stopped wailing, and now a multitude of car horns joined the chorus.

"We should go home," Jackson said, his voice small and uncertain.

Maddie nodded. "Mom sent a text telling us to stay home."

"She doesn't know we're here?"

"I couldn't reach her, and . . ." Maddie shrugged. When their mom was at work, they pretty much spent their days as they wished. They checked in with each other, and Grandma Bea when she was home, but that was all. To say their mom put little effort into parenting would be an understatement. Even telling them to stay home was out of character.

"She must be worried if she sent that text."

Just then, Jackson's phone buzzed. "It's her." Seconds later, he thrust the phone in Maddie's direction so she could see the screen. "She told me to get home and stay there. I guess we should do it."

Maddie hesitated. While she truly wondered what was happening, especially with so many explosions and sirens going crazy, her first instinct was to ignore the texts. *What gives her the right to order us around?* she thought. *It's not like she acts like a mom.*

Years ago, she had insisted that Maddie call her Heather instead of mom, though Maddie still often used the latter. Jackson never referred to her as mom to her face and rarely when talking about her. Grandma Bea was more of a mother to both of them than Heather had ever been.

"I guess." She sighed as she glanced around. "This is kind of boring, anyway."

"And dangerous," Jackson muttered, and Maddie nodded in agreement.

They deflated their boards and loaded them into the back of the car before setting off toward home. The acrid smell of smoke grew stronger as they passed an auto parts store that was on fire. The streets were no longer empty. People were rushing about, some throwing belongings into cars, others running on foot.

"Where's everyone going?" Jackson pointed out the window.

Maddie shook her head as her mind raced. *What if we can't get home? What if something happens to us on the way? What if Mom comes home and finds the house empty?*

Her thoughts were interrupted by a scream. A man stumbled out of a house. His lanky frame moved in erratic jerks, tattoos visible on his arms and back as his T-shirt rode up. A woman appeared in the doorway, her blond ponytail matted with blood from a gash above her eyebrow.

"Help!" the woman cried. "He's trying to kill me!"

The man whirled around at the sound of her voice. A low, animal-like sound rumbled from his throat as he lunged, his hands outstretched toward the woman.

Maddie's foot hovered over the gas pedal.

Jackson leaned forward, his seatbelt straining. "We have to do something."

"Not our fight." Maddie accelerated, taking the corner sharply. In the rearview mirror, the couple's struggle became a blur.

Their street came into view. A man who lived at the beginning of the street was loading boxes into his pickup truck. His wife emerged from their spacious beige home, a floral suitcase in one hand with their pig-tailed daughter balanced on her hip.

"Looks like the Burkes are leaving too."

Leave it to Jackson to remember their names. He seemed to know everyone in the neighborhood.

Maddie pulled her car into the garage and hit the button as soon as her trunk was clear of the door. "Leave the boards. I'll grab them in a bit. Let's make sure all the doors are locked."

"Why lock the doors?" Jackson's voice trembled. "It's inside the garage."

"I-I don't know. It just seems like the right thing to do."

"Why was that man attacking that woman? Do you think he has the sickness? Whatever it is? I thought people just attacked groups?"

"We hear about the groups, but . . ." She shook her head. "I don't know. I've read a few articles that said domestic abuse has increased over the last few weeks and may be related to whatever is happening."

"Domestic abuse? Is that when husbands and wives fight?"

"Mm-hmm. Let's get inside and get everything locked up. I'll text Mom and tell her we'll stay put."

Whatever was happening, whatever those "attacks" really meant, Maddie had a sinking feeling things would never be the same. All she could do was keep herself and Jackson safe until their mom got there. She really wished Grandma Bea was home. Dealing with this without someone they could count on was the worst.

Her fingers flew across her phone screen as she typed out a quick message to her mom: *"We're home. Everything okay?"*

She hit send, then stared at the screen, willing a response to appear. Nothing.

"Did she answer?" Jackson asked, peering over her shoulder.

"Not yet. I'm going to try calling."

She dialed her mom's number, but it went straight to voicemail. "Uh, hey, it's Maddie. We're home like you said. Call us back, okay?"

"Maybe her phone died," Jackson suggested.

"Yeah, maybe," Maddie muttered, unconvinced. She started scrolling through her feed. Her eyes widened as she took in the flood of posts.

"Wow," she whispered.

"What?" Jackson asked, trying to see her screen.

"It's not just Casper. Look at this." She angled the phone so Jackson could see. "There were bombings in, like, fifty other cities today. And some protest in Chicago turned into a full-on riot."

"What were they protesting?"

Maddie skimmed the article. "I don't know. Something about . . . wait, that can't be right."

"What is it?"

"It says they were protesting against 'government mind-control experiments.' That's crazy talk."

Jackson's eyes went wide. "Do you think that's what's causing all this? All the attacks and stuff?"

Maddie rolled her eyes. "No, dummy. That's just conspiracy theory stuff."

But a tiny part of her wondered if maybe, just maybe, there was something to it. She pushed the thought away.

"Hey, look." Jackson pointed at the screen. "The president's talking about a nationwide curfew."

Maddie frowned as she read the article. "That's stupid. How's a curfew going to help? The bombs are going off during the daytime. And remember that kid who crashed the truck into the parade and killed all those people? That was in the morning."

"Maybe it's for the protest or to prevent rioting?"

"I guess. But it feels like they're just doing something to look like they're in control." Maddie tossed her phone onto the couch in frustration. "This is so messed up."

Jackson flopped down next to her. "What do we do now?"

"I don't know. Wait for Mom, I guess." She picked up her phone again and called the care center where their mom worked. A loud noise sounded, and a computerized message played, "We're sorry, all circuits are busy. Please try your call again later."

Maddie muttered under her breath.

"You said a bad word," Jackson said with a hint of a smirk on his face.

"Oh, shut up," she snapped. "This isn't funny, Jackson."

His face fell. "I know. I'm just . . . I'm scared, Maddie."

Her expression softened. "Yeah. Me too." She reached out and squeezed his hand. "But we'll be okay. We just have to stick together, all right?"

Jackson nodded. "Can we try calling Grandma Bea?"

"Good idea." She dialed their grandmother's number, but again, the call wouldn't go through.

"Can you call Dad?"

"Maybe. I talked to him earlier— "

"You did? When?"

Oops. She hadn't thought of mentioning the call to Jackson. "Before. When you were playing your game."

"You didn't tell me."

"Sorry." She stared at the phone, avoiding her brother's glare as she pulled up her dad's number. The computerized message played again. "I think the phone system is overloaded or something. Nothing seems to be working."

"What if something happened to them?" Jackson's voice quavered.

"Don't say that," Maddie said sharply. Then, more gently, she said, "Grandma said we wouldn't be able to reach her, remember? She didn't get the internet package to use her phone while on the ship. And Dad . . . I'm sure they're fine. Really. Why wouldn't they be?"

They sat in silence for a moment, and the weight of the situation pressed down on them.

"I'm hungry," Jackson said finally.

Maddie glanced at the clock. It was nearly four. Their mom had a day shift that ended at two-thirty. She should've been home already. "Yeah, okay. Let's see what we've got."

They headed to the kitchen and rummaged through the cabinets and fridge. Grandma Bea had bought plenty of groceries before she left, filling up the pantry and fridge. But nothing sounded good.

"Mac and cheese?" Jackson suggested, holding up a box.

"I guess."

As she boiled the water and stirred the pasta, Maddie's mind raced. *What if Mom doesn't come home? What if something had happened to her? To Grandma Bea? To Dad?*

She pushed the thoughts away and focused on the simple task at hand. She was being silly. Just because she couldn't call them, it didn't mean they weren't fine.

"Hey, Maddie?" Jackson's voice broke into her thoughts.

"Yeah?"

"What if . . . what if she doesn't come home from work?"

Maddie's hand tightened on the spoon. "She'll be back soon."

"But what if she's not? What do we do?"

Maddie turned to face her brother, seeing the fear in his eyes. She wanted to tell him everything would be fine, but the words stuck in her throat. Instead, she said, "Then we figure it out. Together. Okay?"

Jackson nodded but didn't look convinced.

As they ate their mac and cheese in front of the TV, watching news reports of the chaos unfolding across the country, the distant sound of the town's emergency whistle drifted through the air, faint but unmistakable. The responsibility hit her, hard and uninvited. She was only sixteen, but right now, she was all Jackson had. And she had no idea what to do next.

The news anchor's voice droned on, listing city after city affected by the day's events. Maddie tried to focus, but the information blurred together in her mind.

"Maybe we should call the police," Jackson suggested between bites of mac and cheese.

"And tell them what? That Mom's not home from work yet? They've got bigger problems right now."

"But what if she's hurt? What if she needs help?"

Maddie set down her bowl, her appetite gone. "Look. I'm worried, too, okay?"

"I'm not worried." He shook his head, but the look on his face said otherwise. Jackson went out of his way to pretend he didn't like their mom, but Maddie knew the truth. He longed for her love and attention, just like she did.

"Her text said she'd be home when she could. She's probably just stuck at work or something."

Jackson pushed his food around with his fork. "You really think so?"

"Yeah, I do," Maddie said, trying to sound more confident than she felt. "Remember when that big snowstorm hit last winter? She had to stay at the care center for two days."

"I guess," Jackson mumbled.

Maddie stood up and grabbed their bowls. "Come on, let's clean up and then figure out what to do next."

As they washed dishes, a loud bang from outside made them both jump. Her hand froze mid-scrub, and soap suds dripped onto the floor.

Jackson's eyes widened. "What was that?" he whispered.

Maddie strained to listen. The neighborhood had fallen unnaturally still.

Then came another bang, louder this time.

She moved toward the front window, her heart pounding. She reached for the curtain, hesitated, then slowly pulled it aside.

Her breath caught in her throat.

Chapter 4

Maddie's tension melted into a surprised chuckle. "It's just a deer."

Jackson crowded next to her at the window. A young mule deer stood in their yard, its ears twitching nervously. As they watched, it lowered its head to nibble at their flowerbed. Their grandma wouldn't be happy about that.

"How'd it make that loud bang?" Jackson whispered, still wary.

Maddie pointed to their overturned metal garbage can. "Must've knocked that over. Probably spooked itself in the process."

She let the curtain fall back, her shoulders dropping with relief. "Those city deer are getting bolder every year." Maddie knew she should go outside and shoo the deer away, but she couldn't bring herself to leave the safety of their home.

"Yeah," Jackson agreed, but his voice remained tense. "Think it means anything? Like, maybe it's running from something?"

Maddie paused, then shook her head. "Let's not jump to conclusions. If it was running from something, do you think it'd be eating Grandma's roses?"

Jackson nodded, but he seemed unconvinced. "What if the bad guys come here?"

"What bad guys?"

"You know, the ones doing all the bombings and stuff."

"Jackson, there aren't 'bad guys' running around. It's not like in your video games. This is . . . complicated."

"But people are getting hurt," Jackson insisted. "Someone's doing it."

"Yeah, but . . ." Maddie trailed off, unsure how to explain. How could she make sense of it for her brother when she didn't understand it herself? "Look, we're safe here, okay? We've got food and water, and the doors are locked. We just need to wait it out."

Another bang from outside made them both flinch.

"It's probably that dumb deer again," Maddie said, but she wasn't sure she believed it. "Or maybe someone loading up their car. You know, like the Burkes were."

"If you say so," Jackson muttered as they returned to the kitchen.

They finished the dishes in tense silence, both jumping at every little noise from outside. When they were done, Maddie grabbed her phone and refreshed her social media feeds. In the background, the town whistle echoed faintly, a reminder that something was off—something they couldn't escape.

"Anything new?" Jackson asked.

"Nothing good. More reports of attacks, and riots are spreading to other cities." She paused a moment while she picked at a piece of skin on her thumb. "Maybe we should . . . I don't know, prepare or something?"

"Prepare how?"

Maddie thought back to movies she'd seen. "We should probably gather supplies. You know, just in case."

They spent the next half hour raiding the pantry, pulling out boxes of cookies and granola bars, bags of chips, and bottles of water. They grabbed a first aid kit from the bathroom and blankets out of the linen closet.

As they worked, Maddie kept checking her phone, hoping for some word from their mom, dad, or grandma.

She'd sent dozens of messages and tried calling over and over. Nothing.

"Should we board up the windows?" Jackson asked as they surveyed their stockpile.

Maddie shook her head. "No, that would just freak out the neighbors. And Mom, too, when she gets home."

"*If* she gets home," Jackson whispered.

"She will," Maddie snapped, more harshly than she intended. She softened her tone. "Sorry. I'm just . . . this is scary for me, too, you know?"

Jackson nodded and looked down at his feet. "I wish Grandma Bea was here."

"Me too, bud." Maddie pulled him into a hug. He resisted at first before yielding, his tense shoulders relaxing against her embrace. "But hey, we've got each other, right? And we're Reynolds. We're tough."

He managed a small smile. "Yeah, I guess we are. You sure we shouldn't board up the windows?"

"How? It's not like we have a bunch of boards hanging out in the garage."

"There's some stuff in the shed out back. Things the old owners left behind, plus the wood Grandma bought when she had the garden beds made."

"That'd be too much hauling and hammering."

"We could put blankets over the windows."

"Why would we do that?"

"I don't know. I just thought . . ." Jackson turned back toward the television.

Maddie was surprised he'd been sitting with her for so long. Usually, he'd be in the corner playing his video games, or even upstairs in his room chatting on the computer.

He and their cousin, Eddie, who lived in Oregon, were almost the same age and often played games together. Even though they were separated by many miles, the two had a strong bond. Eddie's dad, Rich, was their dad's older brother. Rich wasn't close to Brian or the rest of the Reynolds family, so it was kind of surprising how well the cousins got along.

Eddie's older sister, Alyson, wasn't nearly as friendly with Maddie as their younger siblings were with each other. In fact, the two girls, only eighteen months apart in age, rarely spoke and had little in common.

Last summer, they'd all gone up to their grandparents' lodge for a visit at the same time. To say it was awkward would be an understatement. Jackson and Eddie were great together, but not Alyson and Maddie. Even all the adults had strained relations. It was definitely a vacation Maddie had no intention of repeating.

As evening approached, the street outside grew quieter. The Burkes had left, along with a few other neighbors. Those who remained had battened down, curtains drawn and lights low. And, thankfully, the banging noises had stopped, and the deer had moved on to destroy someone else's flowers.

Maddie tried calling her mom again, and then her dad and grandma for good measure. Her heart rate accelerated when her dad's phone rang instead of giving the all-circuits-are-busy message. But neither he nor his voicemail picked up. After over a dozen rings, she reluctantly hung up.

"Maybe we should try to get some sleep," she suggested, eyeing Jackson's drooping eyelids. "It's almost ten."

He shook his head stubbornly. "I'm not tired. Besides, that stupid whistle keeps going off."

"Well, I'm tired," Maddie lied. "And we should conserve our energy, just in case."

"In case of what?"

She shrugged. "I don't know. Anything. Come on, we can camp out here in the living room."

They dragged blankets and pillows from their beds, with Maddie setting up on one couch and Jackson on the other. Maddie left the TV on low, more for the comforting background noise than for any actual information.

As they settled in, Jackson spoke up. "Maddie?"

"Yeah, bud?"

"Do you really think everything's going to be okay?"

Maddie was quiet for a long time. She wanted to reassure him, to say, "Yes, of course, everything will be fine." But she couldn't bring herself to lie. Not about this.

"I don't know, Jackson," she said finally. "But whatever happens, we'll stick together. And we're going to get through it. Okay?"

"Okay," he whispered.

As Jackson's breathing evened out into sleep, Maddie lay awake, staring at the ceiling. The weight of responsibility pressed down on her and made it hard to breathe. She was just a kid herself, really. How was she supposed to handle all this? And exactly where was their mother? Was Jackson right about her being at a bar?

It had been a while, but their mom had lost track of time more than once. Not just hours—days. Maddie still remembered the time her mom left her alone with baby Jackson and didn't come back for two nights. If her mom was off on a bender, she'd . . . she didn't know what she'd do, but it would be something big.

She looked over at her sleeping brother and knew she'd do whatever it took to keep him safe. He could be a major pain, but he was still her responsibility. Just like he'd been all those years ago. She'd had a break since Grandma Bea took them in, but Maddie knew she had to protect Jackson. Their mom sure wouldn't, so it was up to her.

With that thought, Maddie finally drifted off into an uneasy sleep, the low murmur of the TV providing a soundtrack to her troubled dreams.

Maddie jolted awake to a noise at the front door. Her heart pounded in her chest as she sat up, straining to hear. It came again—a faint, persistent knock. She glanced at Jackson, who was still sound asleep, his face calm and untroubled.

Carefully, she slipped out from under the blankets, grabbed a golf club from her grandma's bag in the front closet, and tiptoed toward the door. Every creak of the floorboard made her wince, but she couldn't afford to not be cautious. If someone dangerous was out there . . .

With a shaky breath, she peered through the peephole. Her pulse quickened at the sight of a shadowy figure standing on the porch.

Chapter 5

Relief and anger collided when Maddie recognized her mother standing there, looking haggard and worn, with dried blood streaking her cheek and cuts lining her arms.

Maddie yanked the door open. "Mom! What the—?" she hissed, trying to keep her voice low so as not to wake Jackson. "You couldn't call or text? We've been worried sick!"

Her mother stepped inside, her pale face etched with exhaustion and something else—fear. "I couldn't, Maddie. The phones are out. The care center was hit by one of the blasts. People were injured. We had to help with triage. It's a mess. My car was destroyed in the explosion."

Maddie's gaze flicked to the gash on her mom's face and the blood staining her sleeves. She knew she should comfort her, make sure she was okay, but her anger flared. "You could have found a way to let us know! Do you have any idea what it's been like here, not knowing where you were or if you were okay?"

Her mom looked away, guilt clear on her face. "I stayed to help as long as I could, but I knew I had to get home. With Grandma gone, I knew you and Jackson needed me."

"Humph. As if." But her eyes lingered on her mom's injuries, her worry betraying her words.

At that moment, Jackson stirred and sat up, rubbing his eyes. "What's happening?" he mumbled, blinking at the sight of their mother. Relief crossed his face as a small smile began to form. He quickly schooled his expression into a more neutral expression. "We're fine. Maddie took care of everything."

Maddie noticed a flicker of disappointment cross her mom's face before she said, "Of course she did. I knew she would. My friend Glenda gave me a ride home. We uh . . ." She shook her head. "Anyway, they evacuated our work. The building's a mess. I might be out of a job. They told us to call corporate in a few days. Maybe there'll be something at one of the other facilities."

Maddie tried to swallow her frustration, but it bubbled over. "Great, just great. Now we have even more to worry about."

Her mom's eyes filled with tears. "There's nothing I can do about this, Maddie. I'm sorry."

"Sorry isn't enough! You should act like a mom and not a baby!" She turned on her heel and stormed off to her room, slamming the door behind her.

She plopped on her bed, fuming, trying to calm down. The responsibility of taking care of Jackson and the uncertainty of their situation weighed heavily on her. She knew her mom was trying, but it didn't feel like it was enough. Not now, not when everything was falling apart.

Needing a distraction, Maddie powered on her laptop. She started searching for any updates on the attacks. Her screen was soon filled with headlines:

"Multiple Cities Hit by Coordinated Bombings."

"Thousands Dead."

"Casualties Mount as Chaos Unfolds Across the Country."

The news was grim. Each article painted a picture of widespread panic and destruction. A knot tightened in her stomach as she read about the severity of the situation. There were reports of overwhelmed hospitals, power outages, and disrupted communication networks. The government was urging people to stay indoors and conserve resources.

In many ways, it reminded her of the worldwide pandemic they'd experienced years before. The entire world was on lockdown then.

Maddie leaned back in her chair and rubbed her temples as the gravity of the situation sank in. The parallels to the pandemic were unsettling, but this felt different—more immediate, more violent.

She thought about how young she and Jackson had been during the lockdowns and how Grandma Bea did her best to shield them from everything happening. School had been canceled, and they couldn't go to their friends' houses. They spent a lot of time in their large backyard. Her grandma had ordered yard games off the internet, and they played badminton and croquet.

This was before their mom had completed her training to be a CNA. She was working at Albertsons then. As an essential worker, she worked long hours and came home grumpy and tired. She'd stopped taking her meds and fell off the wagon that summer. Not that it was very surprising. Maddie knew her mom didn't do well under stress.

When she didn't show up for work for several days in a row, she was fired. She hadn't come home over those days either. She'd just disappeared, as she often did during a binge, and no one knew where she was. When she did reappear, Grandma Bea wouldn't allow her back into the house.

She spent a few days doing who knows what before she showed up again, saying she needed help. She went to an inpatient treatment facility, again, and sobered up and got back on her meds.

It was while in there she decided to get her nursing training. She seemed to like the work and even talked about going to college to become a registered nurse. Maddie doubted that would happen. Her mom was all talk with little to no follow-through.

The most likely scenario, considering what happened today, was her mom would start drinking . . . again. They didn't keep alcohol in the house, but she could easily get it.

Maddie furrowed her brow. She said her car was destroyed in the explosion. They lived many blocks from the nearest liquor store. She'd have to walk. Or take either Maddie's or Grandma Bea's car. Maddie had her car keys, but Grandma Bea left a spare set of keys in the kitchen.

She let out a sigh and shook her head. Chances were good her mom would disappear. That was fine. She and Jackson would probably be better off without her bothering them, anyway.

She scrolled through more articles, her eyes widening at the scope of the attacks. Major cities like New York and LA were having trouble, as were small cities like Casper. But not just those. Even tiny little towns were being affected. There was a town of only three thousand people in Kansas that was burning. The loss of life was estimated to be over 50 percent of the residents.

A thought struck her, and she quickly opened a new tab to check the local news. She knew about the explosions and the chaos she and her brother had experienced earlier, but was that the end of it?

Her breath caught in her throat as she saw images of familiar streets in chaos. Something had happened downtown, not a fire but maybe a riot of some sort. Windows were shattered in many buildings.

The west side Walmart also looked terrible. Something similar to downtown must have happened.

The Events Center had been one of the places where a bomb, or something, had gone off. The photos showed the building blown in half.

The care center where her mom worked was barely recognizable, its facade blackened and crumbling. Maddie's anger softened slightly as she imagined the terror and confusion of the scene.

Even the mall had been hit. Her heart rate went up a few notches as she realized she could have been there. Been right in the middle of the destruction.

She thought about her friends, scattered across Casper. *Are they safe? Were any of them near the blast sites? The riots?* Maddie popped off messages on her TalkZap app to her closest friends, figuring they were likely asleep but would respond at a reasonable hour.

It was almost five in the morning. Would her dad be up? She tried calling him and got the all-too-familiar circuits are down message. She sent him a text, asking him to contact her as soon as he could.

When he did, she was going to make him set up an account on Chum Fun or TalkZap so they could easily chat. Chum Fun would probably be smart. That's the platform her grandma preferred. She could set up a group chat.

She took a deep breath, trying to center herself. What would her dad do in this situation? He'd always been the calm one, the planner.

Maddie glanced around her room, mentally cataloging their resources. She and Jackson had made a cursory inventory, which essentially amounted to pulling out all the snack food from the cabinets.

Even though Grandma Bea always kept a well-stocked pantry, Maddie knew they should go to the grocery store and buy more. Not just junk either. Real food. If it was like before, during the pandemic, there'd be shortages. She didn't want Jackson to be hungry. She didn't want to be hungry either.

With her mom potentially out of a job, and probably planning a binge, along with the world in chaos, Maddie knew she'd have to step up even more.

She thought about the part-time job she'd been considering for the summer. Grandma Bea had told her she'd rather she not find work; since her grandma would be gone, Maddie needed to be home for Jackson.

Grandma Bea had left a stash of cash that only Maddie knew about so they could be well taken care of. Plus, her dad had given her a credit card for emergencies. Still, a job might be smart. Would that even be an option now?

A muffled sound from the living room caught her attention. It was her mom's voice, low and urgent. Was someone in the house?

She moved to her bedroom door, straining to listen. The floor creaked beneath her feet. Then the room went dark.

Chapter 6

Maddie stood completely still as she strained to make out the sounds coming from below. She reached out her hand and searched for the doorknob in the dark.

Had the power simply gone out, or had something worse happened? A chill ran down her spine as her imagination conjured up unsettling possibilities.

As she opened the door and stepped out into the dark hallway, the lights flickered back on. The sudden brightness momentarily blinded her, and she blinked rapidly to adjust her vision. Still, Maddie breathed a sigh of relief.

Her brother's voice drifted up. His words were mumbled, but the stomping up the stairs made it clear he was in a hurry. "She's impossible," he muttered as he brushed by her, his face a mask of frustration.

Seconds later, she heard his bedroom door slam shut. The sound echoed through the house, a punctuation mark to his anger. Their mom probably said or did something to upset him.

Despite Jackson's attempts to appear tough, his sensitivity was evident. Their mom had an uncanny knack for pressing his emotional buttons. Sometimes, Maddie thought she did it on purpose. After all, she seemed to go out of her way to press Maddie's buttons too.

Maddie leaned against the wall, her fingers tracing the familiar texture of the wallpaper as she hesitated, considering what to do. Should she go downstairs and see if her mom was okay? Find out if she knew why the power went out?

Maddie let out a snort. Of course, she wouldn't know why the power went out. She'd be even more in the dark than Maddie. She let out a laugh at her play on words.

The house settled into an uneasy quiet, broken only by the muffled sounds of Jackson's music bleeding through his closed door. Shaking her head, she went back into her room, softly closed the door, and retreated into her own sanctuary.

Rearranging herself on her bed, she went back to navigating social media, hoping to find more personal accounts and updates. Her feed was flooded with frantic posts from acquaintances and celebrities she followed, all sharing their own fears and experiences. Some were looking for missing loved ones, some offered thoughts and prayers, while others shared their knowledge of resources.

Maddie's heart ached as she scrolled. The world felt like it was unraveling, and she was just one small person amid it all.

A notification popped up on her screen, a message from her cousin Eddie in Oregon. She quickly opened the chat window.

Eddie: *Maddie, are you guys okay?*

Maddie: *We're fine, I guess. Mom just got home. What about you? Why are you up so early? It's what . . . 4 in the morning there?*

Eddie: *Almost. My dad and Alyson just got home. We're fine now. He was at a meeting in Portland yesterday when there was an accident on I-205. He was stuck in traffic for hours. He picked up Alyson. Some bad stuff happened in Portland.*

Maddie: *Are they okay?*

Eddie: *I don't know. She's pretty shaken up. But . . . yeah, she'll probably be fine. Astoria is quiet compared to what my dad said was happening in Portland. But it's still a little weird here. They got a flat and had to walk home. Dad said there were people patrolling the neighborhoods.*

Maddie: *Casper's a mess too. There were explosions. One of them was near my mom's work. Jackson and I saw a semitruck on fire. It was like a big rolling fireball. I don't know exactly what's going on. It's scary.*

Eddie: *Yeah, my parents are freaking out. My dad's even been trying to call his parents and Uncle Brian. Especially since there was an explosion in Cody.*

Maddie: *Cody? I didn't hear.*

Eddie: *Yep. Yesterday. The Irma Hotel. The building was destroyed.*

Maddie felt a pang of worry for her dad, Eddie's Uncle Brian. She knew he wasn't in Cody yesterday, or hadn't been when she spoke to him, but her Uncle Rich must be concerned if he was trying to get in touch with his folks. They didn't get along very well. They tried, but it was always uncomfortable when they got together. She'd experienced that firsthand last summer.

Maddie: *I tried calling my dad last night. No luck. The phones are messed up. He's not on social media, so I can't message him.*

Eddie: *Same here. Internet's spotty too. My dad says it's going to be like it was before, with the lockdowns.*

Maddie: *It might.*

There was a long pause before Eddie wrote back.

Eddie: *This is scarier though. Have you seen the videos of the bombings and other attacks?*

Maddie hesitated before responding. She'd seen some things in her social media feed, and hours earlier on the television, but she hadn't specifically searched for videos.

Her curiosity got the better of her. She searched for footage of the attacks and found countless clips showing explosions, destroyed buildings, shootings, and chaos in the streets. It was overwhelming.

Maddie: *Just saw some. It's bad. Really bad.*

Eddie: *I know. But hey, it'll probably be fine. My mom says the government is acting as they should.*

Maddie wanted to believe him. She needed to believe him.

Maddie: *Yeah, probably so.*

Eddie: *Agreed. Is Jackson up? I haven't seen him online.*

Maddie: *I'm not sure. I think he went to his room. When our mom got home, she woke us both up, but he may have gone back to sleep. I think I'm going to do the same thing. It's too early.*

Eddie: *Same. Talk to you later.*

Maddie closed the chat window, then leaned back and stared at the ceiling. The conversation with Eddie had given her a small sense of connection and comfort, but the uncertainty of their situation still loomed large.

She took a deep breath and looked at her phone, hoping for new messages or updates. The unknown pressed down on her, but she knew she had to stay strong for Jackson and herself.

She crawled back into bed as the early morning light filtered through her window. Eddie was right. It was good the government was acting so quickly. Whatever was happening would probably be resolved within a day or two.

Still . . . it was odd that so many cities were being affected at once. What could cause something like that? Maddie's thoughts swirled with possibilities, each more unsettling than the last.

As she finally drifted off to sleep, a nagging feeling persisted in the back of her mind: this was just the beginning, and the true danger was still out there, lurking in the shadows.

Chapter 7

The sizzle of bacon filled the kitchen as Maddie stood at the stove, carefully flipping pancakes. Jackson sat at the table with his eyes fixed on his phone.

"Any news?" Maddie asked, keeping her voice low to avoid waking their mother.

Jackson shook his head. "Nothing new since last night. It's weird, though. Usually, there'd be updates by now."

Maddie slid a pancake onto a plate. "Maybe the news sites are overwhelmed. Remember how it was during the pandemic?"

"I don't know." Jackson frowned. "I didn't have a phone then, remember? And Grandma hardly let me watch TV. This is just . . . chaos."

Maddie sighed and turned off the stove. "What are your friends saying? Have you heard from anyone?"

"A few. Matt's family is talking about leaving town. And Rebecca said her dad—you know, the one who works at the hospital? He hasn't been home since yesterday."

Maddie brought the plates to the table and sat across from her brother. "I'm worried about Dad," she admitted. "The cabins are pretty far out of town, but if something happened in Cody . . ."

Jackson's face was etched with concern. "Maybe we should try calling him again."

"I did. Right before I started cooking. I still can't get through. Let's eat." Maddie pushed a plate toward him. "Then we can try reaching Dad and Grandma Bea. Maybe . . . maybe I can even try messaging Grandpa Dick through their cabin booking system. Grandma Ruth has alerts set up on her phone to be notified when someone tries to contact her there."

Maddie smiled, pleased with the option of another way to reach their dad. She knew her grandparents wouldn't ignore a potential customer. Not that she felt her dad was ignoring her, but it was still frustrating.

They ate in silence for a few moments, the situation hanging over them.

"Maddie?" Jackson said suddenly, his voice small. "What if . . . what if this doesn't get better? What are we going to do?"

Maddie reached across the table and squeezed her brother's hand. "Hey, we're going to be okay. We've got each other, and we're smart. We'll figure it out."

Jackson nodded but didn't look entirely convinced. "But what about Mom? You know how she gets when things are stressful. And with Grandma Bea gone . . ."

"I know." Maddie's jaw tightened. "But we can handle it. We've done it before, right?"

"Yeah, I guess. I just wish— "

He was cut off by a simultaneous buzz from both their phones. Maddie grabbed hers, and her heart raced as she read the alert.

"Jackson, are you seeing this?" she asked, her voice tight with concern.

His face paled. "Yeah. State of Emergency for Natrona County. What's going on?"

Maddie scrolled through the alert. "It's not just us. There have been incidents in Laramie, Sheridan, Gillette, and Cody."

Jackson's head snapped up. "Cody? Besides the hotel you said blew up? Dad— "

"Hold on," Maddie cut him off, already dialing their father's number. The call wouldn't go through. She muttered under her breath while trying again.

"Is it something new? Is Dad okay?"

"Check your phone. See what you can find out. I'll do the same." Maddie was pulling up her favorite news site.

"I don't see anything. Just the Irma Hotel and Restaurant from yesterday . . . oh, and something happened at a doctor's office too. But nothing big. You find anything?"

"No, nothing else."

"Try Grandma," Jackson suggested, his own fingers flying over his phone screen.

"She won't know anything about what's happening in Cody. She's on a cruise ship, remember?"

"Please? Can you just call her?"

"I can try. But we probably won't reach her, anyway."

Maddie switched to her grandmother's contact info. Again, nothing but an error message. Panic started to build in her chest. "No change. Either the lines are still overwhelmed or there's something wrong with the cell towers."

Just then, they heard a shuffling sound from the hallway. Their mother appeared in the doorway, her eyes red-rimmed and puffy.

"Mom?" Maddie said, surprised to see her up. "We just got an alert about— "

"I know," her mom interrupted, her voice trembling. "I've been trying to call your father and Grandma Bea for the last hour. Nothing's getting through."

Maddie exchanged a worried glance with Jackson. Their mother looked like she was on the verge of tears, and Maddie felt a mixture of frustration and concern. She needed to take charge of the situation before it spiraled out of control.

"Okay, let's not panic," she said, trying to keep her voice steady. "I'm going to try texting Dad and Grandma. Maybe data is working even if calls aren't."

Her fingers flew across her phone screen as she typed out messages to both her father and grandmother. When those didn't seem to go through, she hesitated for a moment before opening Chum Fun.

"What are you doing?" Jackson asked, peering over her shoulder.

"Trying Chum Fun. I messaged Grandma on it last night." She shook her head. "She hasn't read it yet. Let me . . . Let me try again."

As she navigated the app, a notification caught her eye. The Wyoming governor just made a post. Maddie's stomach dropped as she read it aloud:

"In light of the ongoing crisis, I have issued an executive order declaring an emergency response for all affected counties. We are working tirelessly to address these unprecedented events and to ensure the safety of all Wyoming residents."

The kitchen fell silent as the gravity of the situation sank in. Maddie looked from her brother's worried face to her mother's tear-streaked one.

"What do we do now?" Jackson asked.

Before Maddie could respond, their mother burst into tears. "Oh, God! Oh, God," she sobbed, collapsing into a chair. "Your father . . . your grandmother . . . what if something happened to them?"

Maddie felt a flash of irritation. This was exactly what she'd been afraid of—her mother falling apart when they needed her the most. She took a deep breath and forced herself to stay calm.

"Mom, we don't know anything yet. We can't assume the worst. Right now, we need to focus on what we can control."

Jackson nodded, seeming to draw strength from Maddie's composure. "Yeah, Mom. Dad's smart. He'll be okay."

Her sobs quieted to sniffles, but she still looked devastated. Maddie exchanged a glance with Jackson, silently communicating their shared worry and frustration.

"Okay, let's think this through," Maddie said, taking charge. "We already sorted out a few things yesterday, but we're going to need to get more groceries and stuff. Jackson, do you want to start a list?"

Jackson nodded, grateful for the task.

"Mom, I need you to pull yourself together," she said, her voice gentle but firm. "Can you try calling your corporate office? See if you can find out more information about what's happening. Maybe, since they're not local, the call will go through. I know they said to check in a few days, but they might have more info now." Maybe if her mom could work, she'd be able to keep herself together. It was worth a try. Anything to keep her from going on a binge again.

Her mom nodded weakly and wiped her eyes. "Y-yes, I can do that. I'd like to find out about my patients, and they did have some information yesterday. Not much, but someone knew someone who said the CDC was involved."

Maddie rolled her eyes. "That's old news. Everyone's saying the CDC is involved."

She turned back to Chum Fun, scrolling through a feed packed with panic: posts about power outages, looting, and wild theories about the attacks.

"It was bad yesterday," her mom said softly. "I can't even believe how bad things were. At the rehab center and then . . . later."

"Mm-hmm," Maddie muttered, only half listening as she scrolled.

Her mom kept talking, voice all wobbly, like she was the only one who'd had a rough time. She hadn't even bothered to ask them if they were scared being home all alone.

"Maddie?" Jackson called from the pantry. "We've got a decent amount of canned stuff and other pantry things, but we're low on fruit, vegetables, and milk. And we need more cookies."

Maddie made a mental note. "Good to know. I'm going to the store later today."

Just then, their mother let out a frustrated groan. "I can't get through to anyone at work. The lines are all busy."

"Keep trying," Maddie encouraged. "In the meantime, let's turn on the TV. Maybe we can get some more information from the news."

As Jackson grabbed the remote, Maddie's phone buzzed. Her heart leaped, hoping it was a response from her dad or grandma. Instead, it was a message from her best friend, Sonja: *"Maddie, are you guys okay? Things are crazy here. My parents are talking about leaving town. Call me if you can."*

Maddie quickly typed out a response, letting Sonja know they were safe for now and asking her to keep in touch. As she hit send, she realized she hadn't checked TalkZap to see if she'd had any responses. The thought of coordinating communication with everyone while also managing her family's situation felt overwhelming.

The TV flickered to life, showing scenes of chaos from various cities across the country. The news anchor's voice was grim as he reported on the widespread attacks and the government's struggle to respond.

"Oh no," her mom whispered, her eyes glued to the screen. "It's worse today than yesterday even. And yesterday was terrible. The things— "

"Shh," Maddie said. "I want to hear this."

She felt fear bubbling up inside her but forced it down. Panicking wasn't an option—not when her family needed her to stay strong.

When the report was finished Maddie took a breath. "Okay," she said, her voice steadier than she felt. "Here's what we're going to do. Jackson, finish checking our supplies. Mom, keep trying to reach your work and see if you can get through to any of the neighbors. I'm going to make a list of what we might need if we have to stay inside for a while."

"I need to tell you about yesterday," their mom said, her voice cracking as she spoke. "I need to tell you what happened."

"Later, Mom," Maddie dismissed her. "We have things to do."

Her mom looked ready to argue but gave a reluctant nod.

As her family moved to follow her instructions, Maddie's mind raced. She thought about her dad and grandma, hoping they were safe. She thought about her friends and their families, wondering if anyone else was planning to leave town. And she thought about the uncertain future stretching out before them, filled with unknowns and potential dangers.

But most of all, she thought about Jackson. He was here, and he needed her. Whatever was happening in the world, whatever challenges lay ahead, Maddie knew one thing for certain: she would do anything it took to keep Jackson safe.

She glanced at her mom. Heather was trying her phone, tears streaming down her face. As usual, she'd be little to no help.

As she began jotting down a list of supplies, Maddie glanced out the front window. The street outside looked deceptively normal; the sun was shining, and a gentle breeze rustled the leaves. It was hard to believe that just beyond their peaceful neighborhood, the world as they knew it might be falling apart.

"Maddie?" Jackson's voice pulled her from her thoughts. "I found some batteries and flashlights in the pantry. Candles too."

"Good thinking. Bring anything you think might be useful to the kitchen table."

As Jackson disappeared back into the walk-in pantry, their mother let out a frustrated sigh. "I still can't get through to anyone. What if the phones never work again? What if— "

"Mom," Maddie cut her off. "We can't think like that. We have to stay focused on what we can do right now."

"You're right. You're so much stronger than me, Maddie. I don't know what we'd do without you."

Maddie felt a complex mixture of emotions at her mother's words—pride, frustration, and sadness. She wished she didn't have to be the strong one all the time, but now wasn't the moment to dwell on that.

"We're fine." Maddie hoped she sounded more confident than she felt. "Now, let's see if we can— "

A loud crash sounded, accompanied by shattering glass. All three of them froze, exchanging alarmed looks.

"What was that?" Jackson whispered, emerging from the pantry with an armful of supplies.

Maddie rushed to the window. Across the street, the neighbors were locked in a violent struggle on their front lawn.

Chapter 8

The wife, dressed in a business suit, was moving erratically, her actions jerky and uncoordinated. The husband was backing away, and his hands were raised defensively.

"Oh no," Maddie gasped. "It's the people across the street, that snooty woman. Something's wrong. She's . . . she's attacking her husband!"

"The attorney?" Her mother asked. "Charla Weber?"

Jackson joined her at the window, his eyes wide with fear. "It's like that couple we saw yesterday," he whispered.

Their mother came up behind them, her face pale. "We have to help him."

Maddie nodded, already pulling out her phone. "I'm calling 9-1-1."

She dialed the number, and to her relief, the call went through. But her relief quickly turned to frustration when she was met with a recorded message. "Due to the high volume of calls, wait times may be longer than usual. If this is not an emergency, please hang up and . . ."

"No, no, no." Maddie ended the call and tried again.

Outside, the situation was escalating. Mrs. Weber had a hammer. She swung it at her husband and hit him on the arm. His scream pierced the air.

"Maddie, we have to do something!" Jackson cried.

Maddie shook her head while her mom said, "I . . . I don't know if we should go out there. Can you tell if she's singing? If she is, it's too dangerous."

"Is she singing?" Maddie looked at her mom and made a face. *What is she talking about?* "I'm going to try to help him. Mom, keep trying 9-1-1. Jackson, stay inside no matter what, okay?"

Her mom reached out to stop her, but Maddie slipped by. She sprinted to the front door and grabbed the golf club she'd left there the night before. As she stepped outside, the warm morning air hit her face, a stark contrast to the chilling scene unfolding before her.

"Mrs. Weber!" she called out, her voice stronger than she felt. What was the first name her mom used? "Uh, Charla? Is something, um, wrong?"

Brilliant, Maddie. Of course, something's wrong, she thought. *She has the sickness, whatever it is, that causes people to go nuts. And now she's going to set her sights on you instead of her poor whimpering husband.*

Charla Weber's head snapped toward Maddie, her eyes unfocused and wild, yet a pleasant, almost serene smile rested on her face. She lowered the hammer.

Her husband took the opportunity to turn tail and run back into the house, slamming the door with extra force. The woman's entire body seemed to shake, reminding Maddie of a wet dog attempting to dry itself.

Her focus seemed to clear as her shoulders dropped. "What is going on?" Mrs. Weber asked, her voice barely above a whisper. She glanced down at the hammer. "Why? Oh . . . no." She shook her head. "No. Not me. Not— "

The unmistakable growl of an approaching diesel engine filled the air. Both Maddie and Mrs. Weber looked toward the pickup accelerating down the street.

Mrs. Weber straightened her shoulders and dropped the hammer as she sprinted toward the neighborhood street.

"No! Don't do it," Maddie cried. Everything seemed to slow as the truck barreled toward them. Maddie felt a surge of panic as she watched Mrs. Weber run into the street,

intent on only one thing. The pickup showed no signs of
slowing.

The next moment was a blur. Mrs. Weber reached the
middle of the street just as the truck hit her, sending her
tumbling across the pavement. Maddie screamed and
dropped the golf club as she ran to Mrs. Weber's side, her
heart pounding.

"Call 9-1-1!" Maddie shouted to Mr. Weber, who had
opened the door as he realized what his wife intended to
do. Like Maddie, he'd probably seen the videos on the
internet of similar incidents of violence, followed by
confusion and regret.

She kneeled beside Mrs. Weber, who lay motionless,
blood seeping onto the asphalt. Maddie's hands shook as
she checked for a pulse, relieved to find one but terrified
by how weak it was.

The driver, pale and shaking, stumbled out of the truck
and stared in horror at what he'd done. "I didn't see her,"
he kept repeating, his voice barely a whisper.

Maddie didn't look up. She focused on Mrs. Weber,
praying help would arrive in time.

"Maddie!" her mother's voice called from their
doorway. "I got through! The police and ambulance are
on their way! Get back inside, now! Was she . . . was she
singing?"

"What? Singing? No." Maddie shook her head.

"Still. Go inside. She might . . . she might still be
dangerous."

Maddie's next-door neighbor rushed over with a first
aid kit in hand. He dropped to his knees beside Mrs. Weber
and quickly assessed her injuries, talking to her as he told
her what he was doing.

Mr. Weber, cradling his injured arm close to his chest, kneeled beside his wife with tears streaming down his face. "She didn't know who I was. She was . . . she was out of her mind. Just like . . . like . . ."

"She's a Star Bright," the neighbor with the first aid kit declared matter-of-factly.

"A Star Bright?" Maddie's mom asked as she stood behind her.

"She's not. She can't be," Mr. Weber said. "Besides, that's just a rumor. Conspiracy— "

"Does your wife usually take a hammer to you?" The neighbor motioned toward Mr. Weber's arm. "Looks like she broke it."

"Go inside the house, Maddie," her mother said, her voice strong and controlled. "Stay with Jackson."

"No, I can help here."

"Go to the house."

Maddie hesitated, torn between obeying and wanting to stay and help. The intensity in her mother's eyes made her decision. It was a look she couldn't recall ever having seen before.

She ran back to the house, worry gnawing at her insides. As she reached the doorway, she glanced back to see the neighbor and her mom working together to keep Mrs. Weber stable.

The chaos and fear of the moment lingered in the air, but Maddie knew she had to stay strong for Jackson, who would be just as scared as she was.

The pickup driver had sunk to his knees, his face buried in his hands. Was he praying? Mr. Weber was openly weeping.

Her brother met her as she went inside the house. "Is she— "

Maddie shook her head. "She doesn't look good."

"She has the sickness," Jackson said. "It's like . . . it's like that movie where that guy wakes up from a coma and everyone wants to kill everyone else."

"When did you see that movie?" she asked as they moved toward the window, where they could watch.

"Last night. Some of it, anyway. People were talking about it online. They say that's what the CDC is trying to find a vaccine to fix."

"You shouldn't be watching movies like that. It'll just scare you."

"This scares me." He gestured to the scene in front of their house. Jackson's voice dropped to a whisper. "You have blood on you." He indicated the sleeve of her hoodie. It was also on her hands.

"I'll go wash. Are you going to— " She motioned toward the window.

"She seems to know what she's doing, huh?" he asked as Maddie headed toward the guest bathroom.

"Mom? I guess."

Maddie closed the bathroom door with her hip and stared into the mirror as she took several deep breaths. She carefully peeled off her hoodie, making sure not to transfer any more blood onto her body or clothing.

She turned on the water and scrubbed her hands vigorously, watching the pink-tinged water swirl down the drain. Her stomach churned as she remembered Mrs. Weber's broken body on the pavement. She splashed cold water on her face, trying to compose herself before facing Jackson again.

It *was* like that movie. She'd seen it last winter over at a friend's house. That one and the sequel. She hated both of them. Movies like that were not her preference. Give her a romantic comedy any day.

She went to the laundry room and set her hoody to soak in the washing sink. When she returned to the living room, Jackson was still glued to the window. "The ambulance is here," he reported, his voice tight with anxiety.

Maddie joined him and watched as paramedics swarmed around Mrs. Weber. Their mother stood to the side, talking to a police officer. Mr. Weber sat on the curb, cradling his injured arm, looking shell-shocked, as an EMT tended to him.

"What made her do that?" Jackson asked softly.

"I don't know. It's like . . . it's like she wasn't herself anymore."

"Like those other attacks we've been hearing about," Jackson said. "The ones they're calling Star Brights. Like the movie about the rage."

A chill ran down Maddie's spine. She'd seen references to Star Brights online but hadn't paid much attention, dismissing it as another internet rumor. Now, she wasn't so sure.

"What do you know about them?" she asked, turning to face her brother.

Jackson's eyes were wide. "Not much. Just what I've seen online. People saying that sometimes, out of nowhere, someone will just . . . change. Start attacking people, singing nursery rhymes or old pop songs. They call them Star Brights because— "

"Because of the songs," Maddie finished, remembering what she'd read. "Twinkle, twinkle, little star. Star light, star bright . . ."

"Even the Star-Spangled Banner," Jackson added.

"But that's just a theory, right? It can't be real. Besides, Mrs. Weber wasn't singing."

Jackson shrugged, looking uncertain. "I don't know. It seemed crazy before, but after what we just saw . . ."

They fell silent, watching as the paramedics loaded Mrs. Weber into the ambulance. They helped her husband in too. The man driving the truck and the neighbor who'd administered first aid were still standing in the street. Their mother was walking back toward the house, her face set in a grim expression.

"Get away from the window," Maddie said suddenly, pulling Jackson back. "We don't want Mom to think we've been spying."

"I'm sure she knows we were watching."

Even so, they retreated to the couch, trying to look casual as their mother entered.

She paused in the doorway and studied them for a moment before speaking. "Are you both all right?"

Maddie nodded. "Yeah, we're fine. How's Mrs. Weber?"

She sighed and sunk into an armchair. "It's . . . not good. They're taking her to the hospital, but . . ." She trailed off and shook her head.

"Um, is she . . ." Jackson said hesitantly. "Was Mrs. Weber a . . . a Star Bright?"

Their mother's head snapped up, her eyes narrowing. "Where did you hear that term?"

"Online," Jackson mumbled. "People have been talking about it."

Her mom was quiet for a moment. When she spoke, her voice was low and serious. "I don't know what's happening out there. But whatever it is, it's dangerous. We need to be careful. Very careful."

Maddie felt a surge of frustration. "But what does that mean, Mom? What are we supposed to do?"

"For now, we stay inside. We don't go out unless it's absolutely necessary. We keep the doors locked and the curtains closed. And we stay together."

"But what about our friends?" Maddie protested. "What about— "

"Everything's been canceled. All public gatherings and events are shutting down."

Maddie and Jackson exchanged worried glances. The situation was escalating faster than they'd realized.

"What about Dad?" Jackson asked. "And Grandma Bea?"

Her mom's face softened. "I'm going to keep trying to reach them. But for now, we have to focus on keeping ourselves safe. Okay?"

"Can I at least text my friends?" Maddie asked.

"Yes, but be careful what you say. There's no reason to mention the incident with Mrs. Weber. We don't want to spread panic. And don't be spreading rumors about her being a Star Bright. That's a stupid term, anyway." Her mom paused before taking a deep breath. "I saw some of them last night."

"Saw some of what?" Jackson leaned forward.

"The singers. The Star Brights. There was . . . there was a man at the hospital and then a whole group of them. Glenda and I . . . they . . . they stopped her car and attacked us."

"They attacked you? Is that how you got the cut on your face?"

"No, that was from earlier. In the explosions. I'm fine." She paused a moment while she rubbed her shoulder. "But they took the car. We had to run to get away."

Maddie leaned back and crossed her arms across her chest. "I thought you said Glenda drove you home?"

Heather nodded. "She did. But we had to go to her house and get her husband's car. We left hers on Yellowstone."

Pursing her lips, Maddie said, "Sounds like quite the story."

"You don't believe me?"

"I don't know, Mom. Should I?"

Her mom's face tightened, a mix of frustration and hurt. "Maddie, I'm telling you the truth. Why would I make this up?"

Maddie shrugged, her arms still crossed. "It just sounds . . . I don't know, over the top. A whole group of them attacking you and stealing Glenda's car? Why haven't I heard about this happening to anyone else?"

Heather rubbed her temples. "I don't care if it sounds crazy. It happened. I'm just glad we got away."

Jackson glanced between them, his voice hesitant. "Mom, did you tell the police?"

"They're swamped, Jackson. They're dealing with explosions, injuries, and chaos everywhere. And besides, what would I even tell them? That some crazed singers attacked us and stole a car? They'd probably think I was losing it."

Maddie's expression softened, though doubt still lingered in her tone. "So, what now? Are they just out there somewhere, roaming around?"

Heather met Maddie's gaze, her voice steady but grim. "I don't know. But if they are, we need to be careful. I'm not sure why it happens. The neighbor said he thought Charla Weber was one, but I'm not sure. She wasn't acting the same as the people I saw."

Jackson leaned forward, a flicker of unease crossing his face. "How was it different?"

Heather hesitated, her eyes distant as if replaying the events in her mind. "Their eyes. The way they moved. It was like they weren't even human anymore."

Silence settled over the room, broken only by the sound of Maddie's phone vibrating on the table.

As Maddie checked it, she noticed her hands were shaking. She took a deep breath and tried to steady herself. "Another news alert. No changes. Just more of the same."

"Maddie?" Jackson said, his voice tense. "What if . . . what if one of us becomes a Star Bright?"

The question hung in the air, heavy and terrifying.

Their mom paled but quickly composed herself. "That's not going to happen. We're going to be fine. We just need to stay calm and stick together."

Maddie wanted to believe her, but doubt gnawed at her. She thought about Mrs. Weber, how she'd been confused and violent, breaking her husband's arm with a hammer. Could that happen to any of them?

As she typed out messages to her friends, the reality of it all crashed over her, impossible to ignore. Whatever lay ahead, she knew she had to stay strong—for Jackson, for herself, and even for her mom.

A rustle caused her to look up. "Are you okay?" her mother asked as she kneeled beside her and placed a hand on her forearm. "That was incredibly brave, Maddie. And incredibly foolish. You could have been hurt."

Maddie stiffened at her touch. Taking the hint, her mom withdrew her hand.

Maddie nodded, unable to form words. The reality of the situation was sinking in. Whatever was happening in the world had just landed on their doorstep. The safe, familiar neighborhood that she'd lived in for several years suddenly felt alien and dangerous.

A knock at the door made them all jump. "Police," a voice called. "We need to ask you some questions."

Maddie's mother stood up, straightening her shoulders. She looked determined and in control. "I'll handle this. Take Jackson to the kitchen. Both of you get a drink of water."

Jackson and Maddie exchanged surprised glances. Maddie gave a slight nod and followed her mother's instructions, with Jackson right behind her. At that moment, Maddie sensed a flicker of hope. Maybe, just maybe, they could face this crisis together after all.

As she turned on the faucet, Maddie couldn't shake the nagging fear in the pit of her stomach.

If this was happening here, in their quiet neighborhood, what else was unfolding across the city? Across the country?

And where were her father and grandmother in all this chaos? Was her grandma safe on the cruise ship? Was her dad safe at the isolated lodge?

The world as they knew it was changing. Once again, Maddie had a sinking feeling that this was only the beginning.

Chapter 9

Maddie and Jackson huddled in the kitchen, straining to hear their mother's conversation with the police officer. The muffled voices from the living room were too low to make out clearly, but the tone seemed serious and urgent.

"What do you think they're talking about?" Jackson whispered, his eyes wide with concern.

She glared at him. "What do you think? Mrs. Weber, of course."

Jackson nodded, but his furrowed brow betrayed his anxiety. "Do you think they'll want to talk to us too?"

"Probably not you. But maybe . . ." She shrugged.

"Maybe you?"

Before Maddie could answer, their mother's voice rang out, slightly louder than before. "I appreciate your concern, officer, but my daughter is still shaken up. You already have my statement. Isn't that enough?"

The officer's voice returned in a mumble, too low to make out.

"Perhaps you could come back tomorrow?" her mom suggested.

After a pause, the officer's deep voice, now sounding closer to the kitchen, replied, "I understand, ma'am. But it's important we get all the information we can while it's still fresh. Are you sure she can't spare just a few minutes?"

Maddie's heart raced. Part of her wanted to go out there, to tell the officer everything she had seen. Tell him how Mrs. Weber was hitting her husband, how she seemed crazy out of her mind.

But another part of her, the part that still couldn't quite believe what had happened, wanted to hide away and pretend it was all a bad dream. That this entire thing was a bad dream.

Maybe she could go to sleep and when she woke up, Grandma Bea would be home, and her mom's work would still be fine and . . . she sighed as she shook her head.

"I'm sure." Her mom's voice was strong. "My daughter's well-being is my priority right now. We'll be happy to cooperate fully tomorrow."

There was another pause, longer this time. Finally, the officer spoke again. "All right, Mrs. Reynolds. I'll try to come by tomorrow. But please, if you or your daughter remember anything important, don't hesitate to call the station."

"Are the phones working now? It took me ten minutes to get through to 9-1-1, and I haven't been able to reach my husband— " She cleared her throat. "The children's father. We get a call-can't-be-completed message, or it just goes dead."

"Communications are spotty right now. Some cell companies are more reliable than others. You might try email. In fact, email the station tomorrow. Someone will get back to you. Let me give you the address to use."

"Of course, Officer. Thank you for understanding."

Maddie and Jackson exchanged glances as the front door closed. A moment later, their mother appeared in the kitchen doorway, her face a mixture of exhaustion and determination.

"Is everything okay?" Maddie asked tentatively.

"Yes, everything's fine. The officer just had some additional questions about what happened. I told him you weren't up for talking right now."

Maddie felt a surge of gratitude toward her mother. It was rare moments like these, when she stepped up and acted like a real parent, that made Maddie wonder if things could be different, if they could be a normal family.

"Thanks," Maddie murmured.

"Of course, honey. Now, why don't we all go sit in the living room? I think we could use a little family time after all that excitement."

As they settled onto the couch, Jackson spoke up. "That was pretty cool, how you handled that cop."

Her mom looked surprised, then pleased. "Oh, well, I just wanted to make sure you both felt safe and comfortable."

Jackson nodded, then asked hesitantly, "Do you think . . . do you think I could make you a grilled cheese sandwich? You probably haven't eaten yet."

The question hung in the air for a moment, the offer of nurturing so unexpected from Jackson that it caught them all off guard. Her mom's eyes welled up with tears, but before she could respond, there was another knock at the door.

"It's probably just the officer again. I'll handle it."

Jackson and Maddie exchanged curious glances and shared a silent agreement. Trying to be as quiet as possible, they tiptoed after their mother to the door. They pressed themselves against the wall, peering around the corner with wide eyes.

When she opened the door, it wasn't the police officer standing there. It was their next-door neighbor, the one who helped with Mrs. Weber. He smiled nervously.

"Hi there," he said. "I just wanted to check in and see how you all were doing after . . . well, after everything that happened."

"That's very kind of you. Please, come in." Her mom glanced back at them, then shook her head and motioned them to move into the living room.

As the neighbor entered, Maddie studied him curiously. He had moved in over the winter, and while they had exchanged waves, they had never really spoken.

He was tall and lean, with a neatly trimmed silver beard. The fine lines around his eyes and the subtle creases at the corners of his mouth suggested a life marked by laughter.

"I'm Tom." He extended his hand to their mother. "We haven't been properly introduced."

"Heather." She shook his hand. "And these are my children, Maddie and Jackson."

Tom nodded at them both. "Nice to meet you all. I just wanted to make sure everyone was okay. That was . . . quite an intense situation out there." He looked directly at Maddie. "I wanted to make sure you were handling things okay."

Maddie lifted her shoulders. "I guess."

Jackson nodded slightly in acknowledgment of their neighbor's concern.

"Something like that . . . it can be very traumatic to witness," Tom said.

"My daughter is strong. Won't you sit down?" Her mom motioned to the side chair in the front room.

"Thank you."

As Tom moved toward the chair, Maddie and Jackson engaged in a silent tug-of-war for the corner spot on the couch—the best seat for both comfort and a clear view of their visitor.

Maddie, being older and slightly quicker, managed to claim it first. Jackson shot her a look of mock outrage before reluctantly settling for the middle cushion.

Maddie couldn't help but smirk at her small victory. It was a familiar, almost comforting moment of sibling rivalry amid the chaos of the day. She nudged Jackson with her elbow, a silent apology and reassurance rolled into one gesture.

He rolled his eyes but gave her a tiny smile in return, their momentary squabble already forgotten in the face of more pressing matters.

Oblivious to their silent exchange, her mom perched on the arm of the couch nearest Tom's chair, her attention fully focused on him. She fidgeted slightly, and her eyes darted to Tom's face more often than necessary. "We're fine, thank you. And how are you holding up? You were right in the thick of it too."

Tom sighed and ran a hand through his hair. "I'm all right. It's not the first emergency I've dealt with. I used to be an EMT, years ago. But this . . . this was different."

He paused, looking thoughtful. "Have you heard the latest news? My ex-wife—we're divorced but still in touch—she's in California on business. Apparently, the governor there is grounding all flights."

"What?" Maddie exclaimed. "Can a governor do that?"

Tom nodded grimly. "They're saying it's for public safety while they investigate these incidents. It's causing quite a stir—lawsuits, protests, you name it. And rumor has it the president is considering similar measures on a national level."

Maddie's mother leaned forward, her interest clearly piqued. "That's . . . wow. Do they really think that will help?"

"Hard to say," Tom replied. "But they're grasping at straws, trying to contain whatever this is." He motioned toward the front door and the street beyond. "But obviously, things can happen anywhere. Yesterday was crazy. The explosions here and in other parts of Wyoming. Even the Irma Hotel in Cody."

"Our dad lives near Cody," Jackson said. "Is it as bad as here?"

Tom shrugged. "I saw the report on the Irma, but they were still investigating. Said it may have been a gas leak. But with everything else . . ." He shook his head. "The various explosions must be intentional. Either a mass terrorist event or like what happened out there with the Webers. Some folks are saying it might be some kind of virus causing people to go berserk."

As Tom continued to share what he had heard, he didn't give any information that was different from what Maddie and Jackson had already discussed. Maddie couldn't help but notice how attentively her mother was listening, how she seemed to hang on to his every word. It was a stark contrast to her usual disinterest in most conversations.

The discussion continued, touching on various aspects of the unfolding crisis: the government's response, the public's reaction, the spreading fear and uncertainty, and the Star Bright rumors.

Through it all, Maddie observed the subtle interplay between her mother and Tom, the way they seemed to gravitate toward each other, finding common ground in their shared concern and confusion.

As the conversation wound down, Tom stood to leave. "Well, I should get going. But please, don't hesitate to come over if you need anything. We neighbors need to stick together in times like these."

"Thank you, Tom," her mom said warmly. "We really appreciate it."

After Tom left, there was a moment of silence. Then Jackson spoke up, his voice tinged with a mixture of curiosity and skepticism. "So, what do you think about all that?"

Her mom sighed and sunk back onto the couch. "I don't know what to think anymore. Everything's happening so fast, it's hard to keep up."

Maddie nodded in agreement. "Yeah, it's like the whole world's gone crazy overnight."

As they sat there, each lost in their own thoughts, she couldn't shake the feeling that their lives were balancing on a knife's edge. The familiar routines and certainties of yesterday seemed to be slipping away, replaced by a new reality filled with danger and uncertainty.

But as she looked at her mother, who still seemed fully present and engaged, and her brother, who had offered to make their mom a sandwich in a rare display of care, Maddie felt a glimmer of hope.

Maybe, just maybe, this crisis would bring them closer together. Maybe it would force them to become the family they always had the potential to be. The family she always wished she could have.

With a sigh, their mom popped to her feet. "I'm going to the store. We need to stock up on groceries, just in case things get worse."

Maddie and Jackson exchanged a quick, worried look. They both knew what her sudden errands could mean.

"I'll come with you," Maddie offered, already standing. "I can help carry stuff."

"Yeah, me too," Jackson chimed in. "We can get more if we all go."

"No, you two need to stay here where it's safe. We don't know what's going on out there, and I don't want to risk anything happening to you."

A knot formed in Maddie's stomach. She'd heard this kind of talk before, and it rarely ended well. "Mom, are you sure? Maybe we should all just stay home . . ."

"I'll be fine," she insisted, avoiding eye contact. "I won't be gone long. Just . . . stay inside and keep the doors locked, okay?"

As she grabbed her purse and the spare key for Grandma Bea's car, Maddie and Jackson shared another look, this one filled with understanding and resignation. They both recognized the signs—the nervous energy, the flimsy excuses, the insistence on going alone.

"She's going to the liquor store, isn't she?" Jackson muttered under his breath, low enough that only Maddie could hear.

Maddie nodded slightly, her jaw clenched. "Probably," she whispered back. "So much for handling the crisis."

They watched in silence as their mother walked out the door, her promises to return soon ringing hollow in their ears.

"Come on," she said to Jackson, trying to keep her voice light. "Let's make those grilled cheese sandwiches you mentioned. Mom might be . . . delayed."

Jackson nodded; his expression was a mixture of disappointment and resignation. "Yeah, okay. Only I'd rather have those frozen pizzas Grandma left us."

As they headed to the kitchen, Maddie couldn't help the anger and frustration swirling inside her. Just when they needed their mother the most, it seemed she was falling back into old, destructive patterns. She'd been sober for over a year. Taking her medication. Doing so well.

But Maddie pushed those feelings aside. She had to focus on taking care of Jackson and keeping them both safe in this increasingly uncertain world.

As the midday sun streamed through the window, casting bright patterns across the living room floor, Maddie made a silent promise to herself. No matter what challenges lay ahead, no matter how dark and frightening the world became, she would do everything in her power to keep Jackson safe.

Her mom would do whatever she did. That was on her. But Maddie knew how to care for her brother.

Little did she know, the true tests of her resolve were only just beginning.

Chapter 10

Maddie and Jackson had spent the last couple of hours alternating between watching the news, checking their phones for updates, and peering out the window for any sign of their mother's return.

They'd discussed going to their church youth group, which met on Wednesday evenings, but when Maddie checked the church's website, she discovered the groups were canceled. Sunday service was still planned, but that could change, depending on the situation by then.

Maddie checked the time again; her impatience grew with each passing minute. Jackson shifted restlessly beside her, and the two exchanged glances—an unspoken acknowledgment of their shared unease.

Would she even bother to come back today? Or, like so many times in the past, would she go on another binge and return days later, sick and in desperate need of a shower?

At the unmistakable sound of the garage door opening, they both exhaled. "She's back," Jackson said with both relief and apprehension in his voice.

Maddie steeled herself for whatever state her mother might be in. They both moved toward the door to the garage, arriving just as it swung open.

Their mother stepped in, her arms laden with grocery bags, looking flushed but sober. "Can you two give me a hand?" she asked, her voice strained but steady.

Maddie and Jackson exchanged a puzzled look before moving to help. As they unloaded the car, Maddie held in her comments about the items she had purchased.

Instead of practical items, the kind of things Grandma Bea always bought, the bags were filled with junk food— packages of cookies, brownies from the bakery, cans of soda, and bags of chips.

"I thought we should have a few comfort foods," her mom explained as she pulled out boxes of mac and cheese. "Things are getting pretty crazy out there."

Maddie watched her closely, searching for any signs of intoxication, but found none. Instead, she seemed upset and preoccupied, her movements jerky and her gaze distant.

"Are you okay?" Jackson asked, concern evident in his voice.

Her mom paused, a can of soup in her hand. "I'm fine. It's just . . . it's a mess out there. People are panicking and are buying everything in sight. I couldn't even get the brands I prefer." She pointed toward the garage. "There's more in the car. More soda and bottled water and . . ." She snickered slightly. "Toilet paper."

Maddie smiled, remembering the debacle over toilet paper in the early days of the pandemic. Grandma Bea had almost come to blows with a woman who tried to steal a package out of their cart. At least her mom had recalled the trouble, too, and brought home a few smart things.

As they continued to unpack, her mom kept up a steady stream of chatter, detailing the chaos she'd witnessed in town. She talked about long lines, empty shelves, and heated arguments breaking out between shoppers. All the while, she moved efficiently around the kitchen.

Maddie watched this display of maternal competency with growing confusion and, if she was honest with herself, a twinge of resentment. Where was this responsible, caring mother when they needed her before? Why did it take a crisis for her to step up?

"We should inventory what we have," her mom said. "Maddie, can you check the pantry? Jackson, you take the freezer. I'll work on organizing these new supplies."

"Since when do you care about being organized?" Maddie muttered. The words were out of her mouth before she could stop them.

Her mom froze with a package of ramen in her hand. "Excuse me?"

Maddie knew she should back down, but something inside her snapped. All the fear, frustration, and confusion of the past few days came bubbling to the surface. "You heard me. This whole responsible mom act—where's it coming from? You've never cared about being prepared before. You've never cared about anything before. Especially not us." Maddie pointed from herself to her brother.

"Maddie," Jackson hissed, his eyes wide with alarm.

Her mom put down the ramen, her face a mask of hurt and surprise. "I'm just trying to take care of us, Maddie. I thought that's what you wanted."

"What I wanted?" Maddie's voice rose. "What I wanted was a mother who cared enough to do this stuff all the time, not just when the world's falling apart!"

"That's not fair! I've always cared about you two. I'm doing my best here."

"Your best? Your 'best' usually involves disappearing for days on end or passing out on the couch. Excuse me if I'm a little skeptical of this sudden change."

"Maddie, stop it," Jackson interjected, moving to stand between them. "She's trying. Can't you see that?"

She stared at her brother in disbelief. "Are you kidding me? You're taking her side?"

"I'm not taking sides. I just think we should be grateful she's here and is trying to help." He pointed to the counter. "She bought your favorite cookies."

The betrayal Maddie felt at that moment was overwhelming. She'd always been the one to take care of Jackson, to shield him from their mother's shortcomings. And now he was defending her?

"Fine," Maddie spat, grabbing her car keys from the hook near the garage door. "If you two want to play happy family, go right ahead. I'm out of here."

"Maddie, wait!" her mother called, but Maddie was already storming out of the kitchen.

She ignored the shouts behind her as she yanked open the door and ran to her car. Her hands were shaking as she jammed the key into the ignition. She hit the garage door opener and was moving as soon as it lifted.

As she peeled out of the driveway, she caught a glimpse of her mom and Jackson in the rearview mirror, standing there with matching expressions of shock and concern. But she didn't care. She needed to get away. She needed to clear her head.

Without really thinking about it, she found herself heading toward Casper Mountain. She had only gotten her license last fall, on the day of her sixteenth birthday, and she could practically hear Grandma Bea's voice warning her about driving while upset. But right now, the familiar route up the mountain pulled her like a magnet.

The winding road had always been her go-to place when she needed to escape, even before she could drive. She remembered countless times when Grandma Bea had driven her up here, understanding without words that

Maddie needed the perspective that only altitude could provide.

Now, with her hands gripping the steering wheel, perhaps a bit too tightly, she felt a bittersweet pang. She wished Grandma Bea were here now, to offer wisdom or even just a comforting presence.

As she navigated the curves, each turn taking her farther from home and the suffocating weight of her family responsibilities, her mind raced. *Why does she have to choose now to start acting like a parent? Where was this concern, this preparedness, when I was a little girl, before Grandma Bea stepped in to save us, and I was expected to be the adult in the house time and time again?*

And Jackson—how can he not see through this sudden change? How can he not realize bringing home junk food is only a Band-Aid? Soon, she'll do what she always does and fall apart, leaving us to fend for ourselves.

Angry tears blurred her vision, but she blinked them away, forcing herself to focus on the road ahead. She was keenly aware of her inexperience behind the wheel, especially on this challenging road. The last thing she needed was to end up in a ditch because she couldn't keep her emotions in check.

The sun had set completely now, and the darkening sky matched her mood perfectly. The shadows of the pine trees stretched across the road like grasping fingers, and she suppressed a shiver. She'd never driven up here alone at night before, and the familiar landscape suddenly seemed alien and foreboding.

Still, she pressed on, each mile putting more distance between her and the scene in the kitchen. She replayed the argument in her head, wincing at the harshness of her own words.

Part of her knew she'd been unfair, that she should've been grateful for her mother's efforts. But a larger part, the part still raw from years of disappointment and neglect, couldn't let go of the resentment so easily.

As the road climbed higher, Maddie felt her breathing start to even out. The cool mountain air flowing through the open window helped clear her head, and she found herself loosening her death grip on the steering wheel.

Maybe this drive was exactly what she needed to calm down and figure out how to handle the situation back home.

She glanced around, trying to get her bearings as she slowed the car. She realized she was at the Casper Mountain Trails Center, set up for cross-country skiers.

Last winter, one of her friends held a birthday party at the Trails Center building. They had a great time playing in the snow. Some of the others brought cross-country skis to use on the numerous groomed trails, but Maddie didn't have any.

She'd wished she had rented some until her friend Sonja, who was borrowing skis from someone else, mentioned that it was more hard work than fun, especially when trying to ski uphill.

As Maddie pulled into the Trails Center parking lot, she was so lost in her thoughts that she almost missed the figure stumbling onto the road ahead of her. She slammed on the brakes, her heart pounding as her car screeched to a halt just inches from the person.

She stared at the figure illuminated by her headlights. The woman looked disheveled, her clothes torn and dirty, as if she'd been wandering in the woods for days. Her wild hair framed a face etched with distress, and she stumbled slightly as she moved toward the car.

"Help me," the woman called out, her voice trembling. "Please, I've been lost for hours. Longer maybe."

Maddie hesitated, her hand on the door handle. Every instinct screamed at her to drive away, but she couldn't bring herself to abandon someone who might genuinely need help. Wasn't that why she'd always stepped up for her family, after all?

"Are you hurt?" she called through the window, not quite ready to get out of the car.

The woman shook her head and moved closer. "No, I just . . . I got turned around on one of the trails." She motioned toward the multitude of trails used for both cross-country skiing and summer hiking or biking. "My phone died. I've been trying to find my way back to the parking lot."

Maddie nodded. "Well, I guess you're here now." She glanced around but didn't see any other cars in the lot. "I can call someone for you," she offered, her unease growing. "Maybe. The phones are unpredictable."

The woman was at the car now, her hands gripping the door frame. Up close, Maddie could see a sheen of sweat on her forehead, despite the cool night air. "No, no, I just need a ride. Can you take me down the mountain?"

Maddie had to think fast. She was alone in a dark parking lot on a mountain, face to face with a stranger who was acting increasingly erratic. Memories of Charla Weber wielding the hammer replayed through her head.

At that moment, as fear began to grip her heart, she wished more than anything that she had stayed home. But it was too late for regrets now. She had to figure out how to handle this situation and get herself to safety.

"I'm sorry," she said, trying to keep her voice steady. "I'm not supposed to give rides to strangers. But I can definitely call someone to help you." She hit the button to roll up the window.

The woman's expression shifted, going from desperation to something entirely different. A smile appeared, but it wasn't one of relief or gratitude. It was wide and unnatural, stretching her lips too far and showing too many teeth. Her hands shifted from the door frame to the window, pressing firmly as it slowly ascended.

"Oh, sweetie," the woman said, her voice taking on a sing-song quality that sent chills down Maddie's spine. "Don't you know? There are no strangers anymore. We're all friends now."

Maddie's hand flew to the gear shift, ready to throw the car into reverse. But before she could make a move, the woman's face contorted further. Her eyes rolled back slightly, and she began to sing in a chilling, off-key voice. "When You Wish Upon a Star."

Chapter 11

Maddie's blood ran cold as the woman's out-of-tune singing filled the air. The seemingly innocent lullaby took on a sinister quality in the woman's unnatural voice.

She'd read some of the internet rumors about the Star Brights and their unpredictable, violent behavior. But up until now, she wasn't sure they were true. Charla Weber wasn't singing but did have the same vacant and confused look as this woman.

Without hesitation, she slammed the car into reverse. The sudden movement caught the woman off guard, and she stumbled back, her hand slipping from the window. The tires screeched against the pavement as she backed up, her heart pounding.

The woman's singing stopped abruptly, replaced by an inhuman shriek that sent shivers down Maddie's spine. The woman sprinted toward the car. Her movements were smooth and purposeful, and her pace quickened with every step.

Maddie's hands shook as she shifted into drive, her foot heavy on the accelerator. The car lurched forward, and the tires spun against the loose gravel at the edge of the road. For a terrifying moment, she thought she might not get traction, but then the car shot forward, leaving the screaming woman behind.

As she sped down the mountain road, her mind whirled with panic and confusion. She glanced in her rearview mirror, half expecting to see the woman chasing after her car. The road behind her was empty, but the woman's chilling song still echoed in her ears.

"Oh, no! Oh, no!" Her knuckles were white on the steering wheel. She needed to calm down, to think clearly. The winding mountain road was treacherous enough in daylight; in the dark, with her limited driving experience, it was downright dangerous.

She forced herself to take deep breaths, trying to slow her racing heart. "You're okay," she told herself aloud. "You're okay. You're safe in the car. She can't catch you. Just focus on driving."

As she navigated a particularly sharp turn, her phone rang. The sudden noise in the quiet car made her jump, and the vehicle swerved dangerously close to the edge of the road. She overcorrected, the tires skidding on the loose gravel.

For a heart-stopping moment, she thought she was going to lose control completely. But then the tires found traction, and she managed to straighten out the car. She let out a shaky breath and pulled over at a wide spot on the side of the road. Her legs felt like jelly, and her hands trembled as she put the car in park.

The phone was still ringing. She glanced at the screen; it was Jackson. She hesitated for a moment, tears stinging her eyes, before answering.

"Maddie?" Jackson's voice was tight with worry. "Where are you? Are you okay?"

She opened her mouth to respond, but a sob escaped instead. Now that the immediate danger had passed, the full weight of what had happened hit her.

"Maddie?" Jackson's voice rose in pitch. "What's wrong? Are you hurt?"

"I'm okay," Maddie finally managed. "I'm not hurt. I just . . . something happened. Someone . . . I think I saw a Star Bright."

There was a sharp intake of breath on the other end of the line. "Where are you?"

"On Casper Mountain." She wiped her eyes. "I'm pulled over on the side of the road. I . . . I don't know if I can drive right now. My hands won't stop shaking."

After a muffled conversation, her mom came on the phone. "Stay there. We're coming to get you."

The concern in her mother's voice brought fresh tears to Maddie's eyes. "I'm not hurt. I'm just scared. Mom, it was terrible. She seemed normal at first, but then . . ."

"Shh, it's okay. You're safe now. We're on our way. Just stay in the car, lock the doors, and we'll be there as soon as we can. Do you know where you are?"

She did her best to describe where she was, even though there was little doubt her mom wouldn't easily see her little red hatchback parked on the side of the mountain.

After hanging up, she sat in silence, jumping at every sound from the dark forest around her. She kept reliving the encounter in her mind, second-guessing her actions.

Should I have tried to help the woman? Could I have done something differently? Why did she sing? What makes the Star Brights do that? What makes them Star Brights in the first place?

Maybe it really was a virus, and the CDC needed to make some kind of vaccine. Of course, the last time they put out a rushed vaccine . . .

The wait seemed endless, but finally, headlights approached. She tensed, afraid the Star Bright woman had found her car and was tracking her down.

But then she recognized her grandma's SUV. Relief washed over her as the vehicle pulled up next to her. Her mom rolled down her window, and Maddie did the same.

"I'm going to go up and turn around. There's enough room for me to pull in behind you. I'll be right back."

Within moments, headlights appeared behind Maddie as the SUV pulled up. Her mother and Jackson hurried over to her. Maddie unlocked the doors, and suddenly she was enveloped in her mother's embrace.

"Oh, sweetheart," her mom murmured as she stroked Maddie's hair. "I'm so glad you're okay."

Jackson hovered nearby, his face pale with worry. "What happened?" he asked as their mom released Maddie.

She took a shaky breath and described what had happened.

"You did the right thing," her mom said when Maddie finished. "You got yourself out of a dangerous situation. That's what matters."

Jackson nodded in agreement. "Yeah, who knows what could have happened if you'd tried to help her. We did some internet searches on the Star Brights. They are . . ."

"Unpredictable," her mother finished his sentence as both of them bobbed their heads.

Maddie felt a surge of gratitude for their understanding. The argument from earlier seemed trivial now, in the face of what had just happened.

"I'm sorry," Maddie said, looking at both of them. "I shouldn't have run off like that. It was stupid and dangerous."

"Yes, it was. But let's not worry about that now. The important thing is that you're safe. Come on, let's get you home." Her mom motioned toward her grandma's car, and the passenger door opened. Tom, the next-door neighbor, stepped out.

"Tom will drive your car home. You can ride with me."

"Um . . . okay?" Maddie felt a wave of unease as this person she barely knew walked toward her. Surely, he must have heard about how she threw a fit and ran off. Embarrassment washed over her.

Maddie gave a reluctant nod. It was a good idea, but something about it felt wrong. Off.

As Tom approached, she couldn't shake the feeling of unease that settled in her stomach. His concerned expression seemed genuine, yet there was an undercurrent she couldn't quite place. She wondered if she was just being paranoid or if there was more to his sudden helpfulness.

When he reached for the car door, Maddie caught a faint, almost imperceptible smile on his lips. She couldn't tell if it was meant to be reassuring or if it hinted at something more sinister. Was he a Star Bright too?

Chapter 12

Maddie glanced at her mom, whose face still held a shy smile, then looked at Tom. His eyes were on her mom.

Is he attracted to her? That thought made Maddie squirm. Sure, her mom wasn't ugly, but she wasn't exactly someone you'd notice in a crowd. Years of struggle had taken its toll, and Maddie couldn't help but feel embarrassed. The idea that someone like Tom might find her mom appealing was hard to stomach.

Tom had never shown interest before. He'd give a friendly wave when he was outside and they drove by, but as far as Maddie knew, he'd never even spoken to her mother. In fact, usually, Tom was waving at Grandma Bea.

He was, based on his hair color and the lines on his face, probably closer to her grandmother's age than her mom's. Maybe he was one of those gross old men who liked younger women. Or perhaps he thought Heather Reynolds was older than she truly was, another effect of the years of alcohol abuse and neglect in her appearance.

"Okay." Maddie nodded. "That's fine."

As they drove back down the mountain, with Maddie in the passenger seat of Grandma Bea's SUV while Tom followed in Maddie's car, the adrenaline wore off. Exhaustion set in, and Maddie found herself fighting to keep her eyes open.

"Mom?" she said quietly.

"Yes, Maddie? What is it?"

"I'm sorry about what I said earlier. About you not caring. I know you've always cared. It's just . . ."

Her mom reached over and squeezed her hand. "I know, Maddie. And you were right, in a way. I know I haven't been the mother you and Jackson deserved. I was so grateful when Grandma Bea stepped in to help, and I allowed her to take on the role of parent. But I'm trying to do better now. I must do better. I hope you can give me another chance."

Maddie nodded, too tired to say more. She leaned back in the seat and closed her eyes. When she opened them, they were pulling into the garage.

"Wait a minute, and I'll help you inside," her mom said as she opened her door.

Tom was pulling Maddie's car into the third bay, her usual parking spot. The large garage looked almost empty without her mom's car in its spot.

"You okay?" Jackson asked as he opened the back door to slide out.

"I guess. Tired."

"She's being awfully . . . nice," he said, his voice low.

"Mm-hmm," she muttered as she watched her mom speak with Tom.

As Maddie watched them, her mind raced. *Are Dad and his parents okay? Is Grandma Bea safe on the cruise ship? What about Eddie and his parents in Oregon?*

She even wondered if the insurance would replace her mom's car that was lost in the explosion yesterday. Phones needed to work reliably for that. Maybe her mom already filed an online claim? She hadn't thought to ask.

Tom waved and headed outside, and then Jackson pressed the button to lower the garage door.

Her mom came to her side. "Ready?"

As they walked into the house, she leaned heavily on her mother. The events of the day had left her drained, both physically and emotionally.

Inside, her mom helped her to the living room. "How about a cup of tea? Jackson, can you put on the kettle?"

Maddie managed a small smile and sunk into the couch. "Thanks."

As her mother and Jackson hurried around, making tea and gathering blankets, she couldn't shake the realization of how quickly everything had shifted.

Yesterday, despite the awful explosions in Casper, she had felt a sense of security in their close-knit neighborhood. Now, the danger had reached their doorstep. And to her regret, she had foolishly ventured out in search of trouble.

"Here." Her mother placed a steaming mug on a coaster on the side table. "Drink this. It'll help you feel better."

Maddie wrapped her hands around the warm mug and inhaled the comforting scent of chamomile. "What are we going to do?" she asked. "If there are Star Brights here in Casper now . . ."

Her mother sat down beside her. "We'll figure it out. We'll be careful, stay informed, and look out for each other. That's all we can do for now."

Jackson nodded in agreement. "Yeah, and maybe we should set up some kind of neighborhood watch thing. Strength in numbers, right?"

She took a sip of her tea and let the warm liquid soothe her. Despite the fear and uncertainty, she felt a glimmer of hope. A neighborhood watch was a good idea, but how could they be sure another neighbor wouldn't freak out on them and put them in danger?

Mr. Weber had said his wife was fine one second and was hitting him the next. Maddie still wasn't sure the whole Star Bright thing was true. What if some people just used it as an excuse? Maybe Charla Weber was in an unhappy marriage and just snapped.

As she finished her tea, she felt her eyelids growing heavy. The events of the day had taken their toll, and exhaustion was setting in fast.

"Come on," her mother said gently, helping her up. "Let's get you to bed. Things will look better in the morning."

As she climbed the stairs, leaning on her mother for support, she heard Jackson's voice behind them. "Sleep tight, Maddie. Don't let the Star Brights bite."

Despite everything, she couldn't help but let out a small laugh. Trust Jackson to find humor even in the darkest situations.

In her room, her mom helped her into bed, tucking her in like she used to when Maddie was little. As she drifted off to sleep, she heard her mom and Jackson talking in low voices in the hallway.

"You think she'll be okay?" Jackson asked.

"Your sister is strong," her mother replied. "She'll be fine. We all will be."

Her last conscious thought before sleep claimed her was one of gratitude. Despite all their problems, despite the danger lurking outside, she had her family. And for now, that was enough.

Chapter 13

Maddie woke to the sound of hushed voices outside her door, followed by footsteps on the stairs. For a moment, she was disoriented, the events of the previous night feeling like a distant nightmare. But as she sat up, the reality of what had happened on Casper Mountain came rushing back.

She glanced at her phone. It was just past eleven. She never slept that late. She had spent almost twelve hours in bed, yet she still felt exhausted. Rubbing her eyes, she swung her legs over the side and padded to the door, curious about what was happening.

After a quick stop in the bathroom, she descended the stairs. She could make out her mother's voice and Jackson's excited whispers. The TV volume was low, but she could hear a stern voice speaking about "unprecedented events" and "public safety measures."

"Mom? Jackson?" Maddie called out as she entered the living room.

Her mother and brother were huddled on the couch, their eyes glued to the TV. Jackson looked up, his face a mixture of excitement and worry.

"Maddie, you're up," her mom said, patting the space next to her on the couch. "Come sit. The CDC is about to make an announcement."

She settled onto the couch and pulled her knees up to her chest. On the screen, a serious-looking man in a suit stood at a podium adorned with the CDC logo.

"We believe the recent spate of seeming terrorist attacks may be medically related," the CDC spokesperson began.

"There's evidence indicating that some, but not necessarily all, of the perpetrators were in a catatonic state. We also have reason to believe this condition is spreading."

A chill ran down Maddie's spine as she remembered the vacant look in the woman's eyes on Casper Mountain.

The CDC representative continued, explaining they had formed a task force to investigate how the condition was spreading. "At the moment, we think it may be some sort of bacteria or microbe, possibly a virus. The condition seems to affect mainly teens and those in their twenties to early thirties, though there have been a handful of older adults affected as well."

Charla Weber was probably in her midthirties. The lady on the mountain was younger than that, but the man and woman she and Jackson had seen arguing when they were driving home from paddleboarding were older, maybe in their forties or fifties.

The CDC spokesperson went on to appeal for public help. "If you or a family member or friend experiences anything being described as a sensation of losing time, you're asked to call the special hotline that has been set up to take reports. If you feel the urge to do harm to yourself or others, call 9-1-1 immediately.

"Many states, cities, and towns are enacting state of emergency procedures in light of recent events. We're providing guidance on how these efforts can best help with our directive of finding out the cause and ending it. Please follow your local mandates. It's highly possible there will be other efforts enacted to contain the spread of this unknown condition."

As the CDC briefing ended, the camera cut to the president, who stepped up to the podium. He thanked the CDC representative and then addressed the nation directly.

"As Dr. Thompson said, we require your assistance in getting to the bottom of this situation. At the same time, while our esteemed doctors are conducting their research, I have instructed federal law enforcement to do everything necessary to stop these vicious attacks.

"We are preventing all flights originating in other countries from landing at our airports or boats from entering our seaports. US citizens returning home from travels abroad will be provided assistance at the embassy."

Maddie's mother gasped. "I worry this could be a problem for your grandmother."

"Alaska is in the United States," Jackson said with a shrug.

"Her cruise begins and ends in Vancouver, Canada," Maddie said. "Remember? They drove to Seattle, left the car in a long-term parking place, then took the ferry to Canada to get on the cruise ship."

"Maybe . . . maybe this will be over by the time she's ready to come home? Maybe everything on the ship is normal and this isn't affecting her."

"I pray so," their mom muttered.

Before Maddie could respond, the president continued, "To help with our protection measures, we are either closing or limiting access to all federal buildings and property. This list includes, but is not limited to, post offices, military bases, government complexes, national parks, and more."

"National parks?" Her mom shook her head. "Just like before. Don't let people go outside and get fresh air."

"While you may still receive mail, you will not be able to go to the post office," the president explained. "Those of you who rent post office boxes, contact your local post office for guidance on retrieving your mail. Civilians working on military bases will be furloughed until further notice. Families of service members living on US bases will remain on base."

The president's words hung heavy in the air. Maddie looked at her mother and brother, seeing her own shock and disbelief mirrored in their faces.

"Other details of these measures are available on the White House website. As this press conference ends, I highly recommend you check with your state and local government for any announcements they have about specific measures to take."

He went on to mention that California had enacted a travel ban, allowing only residents to return home and facilitating the orderly departure of nonresidents.

"You should expect other states to follow this forward-thinking approach," the president warned. "While the temptation will be high to ignore these directives, they are being enacted for your safety and the safety of your family, friends, and neighbors. We expect these to be temporary measures while the task force determines the cause of these violent attacks."

As the president's address ended, a local news anchor appeared on screen. "We've just been informed that the governor of Wyoming will be addressing the state shortly. In the meantime, let's discuss what we've just heard from the CDC and the president."

The co-anchors began to dissect the announcements, assuring viewers that these measures would likely be short term while the authorities figured out exactly what was happening. They also cautioned against believing the conspiracy theories circulating on the internet.

"Humph," Jackson scoffed. "Sounds like Grandpa was right. He said it was just like last time, some kind of virus let loose by a foreign government to weaken us so they can come in and take over."

Maddie turned to her brother, surprised. "When did you talk to Grandpa Dick?"

Jackson looked sheepish. "Well, I didn't. Eddie told me. They managed to get through to them on their website. He heard his parents talking about what a nut Grandpa is."

She grabbed her phone. She'd completely forgotten she'd sent an email via the lodge's website. She navigated to the email she'd sent. Sure enough, there was a reply from East Gate Lodge and Cabins. Maddie let out a squeal. "It worked!"

"What worked?" her mom asked.

"I emailed the lodge yesterday and told them we couldn't get through by phone. There's a reply." Her fingers shook as she opened the email and quickly skimmed it.

"It's Dad! He says they're fine. Grandpa Dick has closed the place down. The guests that were scheduled have been canceled. Those who were there have already left or will be leaving soon. They're all sticking close to home and aren't going into Cody.

"He mentions the explosion at the Irma Hotel and says there was something that happened at a doctor's office, but they aren't sure if they're related to the troubles others are experiencing. They still want to be careful. He asks . . ."

Her eyebrows shot up. "He wants us to go up there. He says it'll be safe since we'll be so far from people."

Her mom scrunched her eyes closed as she shook her head. "What about all the people in Yellowstone?"

"The president just said they were closing Yellowstone," Jackson reminded them.

"Exactly. They're going to be leaving in droves."

"It's a five-hour drive. Even if we left right now, most of the people would be gone by the time we reached the lodge."

Her mom shrugged. "I don't know. Let me think about it. While I know you'd like to be with your dad and your grandpa . . ." She shook her head.

It was no secret that Maddie's mom didn't think much of her former father-in-law, and the feeling was mutual on Dick Reynold's end. He'd spent a lot of time blaming Heather for the troubles his son had encountered with the law.

It was finally Brian who'd told his dad that the troubles were of his own making and while Heather had issues, she wasn't responsible for his choices.

Even though Maddie's parents weren't friends, her dad never spoke badly of his former wife. Her mom used to talk badly about him, but Grandma Bea would put a stop to it whenever she heard it happening.

These days, Grandma Bea and her dad co-parented. Bea had even suggested Maddie and Jackson stay at the lodge the entire time she was gone on her cruise, but Jackson was playing baseball through the rec center and didn't want to miss it.

Instead, their dad planned to come down for a week in July to visit. Now, baseball was canceled. There wasn't any reason they couldn't, or shouldn't, go up to the lodge.

Before Maddie could respond, the news anchor announced that the governor was ready to address the state. The family fell silent as the governor appeared on screen, dressed in his usual cowboy hat, Wranglers, and boots.

He began by reiterating the points made by the CDC and the president, but then he diverged. "Wyoming isn't going to be taking the extreme measures of some other states. Not only is California locking their borders, but so are Oregon and Washington, as well as several states in the east."

"Another problem for Grandma, right?" Jackson interrupted. "What do you think Alaska is doing?" He grabbed his phone and started scanning.

The governor continued outlining Wyoming's approach. "What is going to happen in Wyoming is going to be on a lesser scale than the other states, who are not only locking their borders and not allowing anyone in or out, but are also enacting a shelter-in-place law. They're closing all businesses effective immediately, including stores, restaurants, bars—you name it.

"Wyoming is not going to take such drastic measures," he assured. "Instead, we will close only what the CDC deems necessary, not the full recommendations. We will leave our borders open, allowing travel on all interstates and state highways. Until we have proof this is an airborne virus, we are not going to close necessary facilities. Hospitals, gas stations, and grocery stores will all remain open."

The governor went on to list the businesses that would be closed: beauty salons, massage parlors, non-emergency doctors' offices, office buildings, and more.

Her mom scoffed. "Just like before."

"These will be closed under the emergency management directives given to me by the Wyoming constitution." The governor paused as he stared into the camera and assumed a neutral expression.

"I'm not going to lie to you. We don't know exactly what is happening. This time, we're not going to tell you it's only going to last for two weeks. The truth is, we don't know. We just don't know." He let out a breath. "Trust me when I tell you, I'll share more as more information becomes available."

As the governor spoke about working on compensation for those affected by the closures, Maddie's mother muttered, "Sure we can. How this guy was elected by the people of Wyoming, I'll never understand. He should just— "

Maddie shushed her mom as the governor continued speaking. When the address finally ended, her mom sat there, looking dumbfounded. She started wringing her hands. "I don't know what we'll do. I've already lost my job when the building was destroyed. Will there be compensation for me?"

Maddie felt a surge of irritation at her mother's reoccurring defeatist attitude, but before she could say anything, Jackson chimed in.

"It'll be fine," he said confidently. "And I googled— Alaska is still okay. Grandma should be fine." He paused, then added hopefully, "Maybe you can even play the game with me later?"

"The game?" their mom asked.

"The one I was telling you about this morning. With the VR sets. You'll love it. Everybody who plays it does. That's why it's the most popular game in the country—in the world."

Her mom nodded absently. "Maybe later." She got up and headed to the kitchen.

As Maddie watched her mother go, she couldn't shake the feeling that, despite the governor's assurances, things were far from fine. The world as they knew it was changing rapidly, and she wasn't sure any of them were prepared for what was coming.

Chapter 14

Maddie followed her mom into the kitchen and watched as she grabbed a package of cookies and a glass of milk. The familiar sight of her mom turning to food for comfort was both frustrating and oddly reassuring in its normalcy.

"Mom," Maddie began cautiously, "what do you think about going to Cody? To Dad's place?"

Her mom waved her hand dismissively and bit into a cookie with unnecessary force.

She shook her head, feeling her frustration mount. "We need to talk about this. If nothing else, Dad says we should plan for a long lockdown. I know you bought groceries yesterday, but should we buy more?"

She purposely avoided mentioning how the groceries her mom brought home weren't really what she'd consider suitable for the "end of the world."

While she may not know much about being ready for things, she'd spent enough time at her grandparents' lodge to know how they shopped. They routinely purchased big bags of beans and rice, along with noodles and lots of canned goods.

Her mom shot her a dirty look before taking another deliberate bite of her cookie.

"If we're not going to the lodge, then we need to buy more groceries," Maddie pressed on. "But honestly, I think we'd be dumb not to leave Casper."

As she turned to walk out of the kitchen, irritated by her mother's silence, her phone rang. Her heart leaped when she saw who it was.

"Dad!" she answered, unable to keep the relief out of her voice. "I'm so glad you reached me."

"Hey, sweetheart," her dad said, his voice tinged with worry. "How are you guys? Is everything okay? Jackson?"

At Maddie's squeal, Jackson had come running from the living room. "Is it really Dad?"

She nodded as she said, "We're fine, um . . . we're okay. Jackson's here. Mom too. We're all together."

Her dad let out a noisy sigh. "I'm so glad. So, so glad. Did you get my email about coming up to the lodge?"

"Yeah, we did, but . . ." She glanced at her mother, who was studiously ignoring the conversation. "We haven't really discussed it yet."

"Well, we need to make a decision soon. Things are getting worse by the hour. Can I talk to your mom?"

Maddie held out the phone to her mother. "Dad wants to talk to you."

Her mom shook her head and bit into another cookie with defiance.

Maddie put the phone back to her ear. "She doesn't want to talk right now, Dad."

"All right, then I'll come there myself. I'll load you up and— "

"I don't know if that's a good idea," she said hesitantly.

"What's not a good idea?" her mom suddenly spoke up.

"Dad says he'll come here if you don't talk to him."

Her mother's face hardened. "Give me the phone," she demanded, snatching it from Maddie's hand.

"You are not coming here! You left us to fend for ourselves years ago. This changes nothing." She paused, listening. "No. No. Don't come here. You're not welcome." Her mother's face grew redder with each passing moment. "What? Fine. Tell me what it is you think is happening. Because I watched the news too. I know exactly what is going on."

Another pause. "No. No. That's not true. I do not have my head in the sand. And believe me, if what you're going to tell me is some of that end-of-the-world stuff your folks are always spouting off about, I'm not interested. Jackson told me he talked to Eddie. Your brother and sister-in-law were the smart ones to cut ties with your crazy folks. Though, I guess your dad still calls them and gets them all wound up."

Maddie could hear her father's voice on the other end, but she couldn't make out the words.

"Oh really? You think so, huh?" her mom said sarcastically. "Fine. Fine. I'll put the phone on speaker so Maddie can hear too. And she is not more mature than me." She paused. "Really? That sure sounded like what you said. Let me tell you what your ultra-mature daughter did last night."

"Mom," Maddie hissed and shook her head.

"No. Fine. I'll let Maddie tell you herself."

Her mom took a deep breath and placed the phone on the table. "Go ahead. She can hear you."

"Maddie," her father's voice came through the speaker, "your mom says you all will be fine on your own— "

"We will," her mom interjected, meeting Maddie's gaze with a defiant nod.

Maddie rolled her eyes. "Yeah. We're fine. Why wouldn't we be?" she said, not entirely convincingly.

"I think things could get weird. I need you and your mom to go to the store. Take Jackson too. Don't leave him home alone. None of you should go anywhere alone."

"Humph." Her mom snorted. "You should have told your daughter that yesterday."

"Why? What happened yesterday?"

Maddie met her mom's gaze. The anger was still there, but she could see her mom's expression soften slightly as she said, "It's . . . it's not important right now."

"Okay, fine. Listen, Heather. I spoke with your mom."

"You did?" her mom asked, her voice tinged with both interest and relief while Maddie added, "When?"

Jackson quickly followed with, "You talked to Grandma Bea? Is she okay?"

"Not long ago. And yes, she's okay. Someone has a phone on the cruise ship that works . . . well, it works better than others. He was charging twenty dollars a minute to make calls, whether they connected or not. She'd already spent $120 trying to reach you guys when she tried me. It was a miracle it connected. Anyway, she agrees with me that you'd be safer here."

"Is she safe?" Heather asked, her voice full of concern for her mother.

"She said she's fine. They aren't going into ports, just anchored somewhere waiting for further instructions. Everything is okay right now. They have enough food for a few more days."

"And then what?" Jackson asked.

"She didn't say. We only had a minute to talk. She said to message her on Chum Fun when you're on your way up here. Then we'll message her when you arrive. She's on a list to use the internet. Everything is just weird right now. Bea really believes you should come up here."

Maddie and Jackson looked at their mother, who closed her eyes and shook her head. "I don't think it's that serious. Not yet, anyway. Remember how you said the children needed to go up there during the pandemic? That ended up not being necessary."

"I think this is different. They had an idea what they were dealing with then, a virus. This time, we don't really know what's causing the troubles and turning people into— "

"Star Brights," Jackson interjected. "We saw one yesterday. Our neighbor beat up her husband with a hammer. And last night, Maddie— "

Maddie popped her brother on the arm as she shook her head. "Shh!"

"Last night Maddie, what? You keep bringing up last night. What happened?"

"Never mind about that right now," her mom said, much to Maddie's relief and surprise.

There was a pause before her dad asked, "So, will you come up here?"

"No. Not right now." Her mom said, but her voice sounded less sure than it had only a few minutes prior. Maddie suspected knowing Grandma Bea thought their going up there was a good idea was causing her to be unsure of herself.

She could practically hear her dad shaking his head. "If you're not going to do what is best, then at least make sure you have what you need to hunker down. I've already sent money to that credit card I gave you, Maddie."

"What credit card?" her mom asked sharply.

Maddie gave her a look. "I'll tell you later."

"It's nothing, just something I gave her to use for any emergency she or Jackson might have. This qualifies. Go buy whatever you can. I sent plenty of money, so don't worry about the cost. Go now. Things could get weird. Weirder than they already are."

There was a pause, and then her dad asked hesitantly, "Does, um . . . does Bea still keep cash on hand?"

"How do you know about that?"

"Really, Heather? It's not like I'm going to forget something like that. If she does, get it too. Just in case there's a problem with the card. I'll pay her back for you."

"I can handle my own money. I don't need you to pay my bills. Besides, you think I don't have any cash?"

"That's fine. Pay attention to the news. Set up alerts on your phone so you can be notified of changes to the situation. The governor said he isn't going to do what they did in California and other states, but nothing would surprise me."

"We'd never stand for it," her mom said. "Even though he's a transplant, he's smart enough to know how Wyomingites are."

"We followed along before during the pandemic, remember?"

"And that right there is why the children and I are not going up there. You and your parents are convinced everything is a conspiracy. They're not all out to get us, you know."

"Are you sure?"

Heather's lips went tight and she let out a sigh. She looked like she wanted to say something more but stayed quiet.

"What about Eddie and Uncle Rich and Aunt Beth? Eddie said you guys talked to them?" Jackson chimed in.

"By email. We told them the same thing I'm telling you. They should leave Oregon. Especially considering the rules in place on the West Coast. Things could get interesting. They should leave and hightail it here. I don't think they will, though. They're stubborn too."

A tense silence settled over the group as they absorbed the information.

"You guys need to go now. Get food. Take Bea's car. It'll hold more than either of the others."

Maddie looked at her mom. They hadn't spoken to her dad since the explosion that destroyed her mother's car.

"Buy everything you can. Don't worry about the brands, Heather."

Her mom snorted and shook her head.

"Get lots of dry foods and canned goods. Fill the car with gas while you're out. In fact, you should fill them all. Call me when you get home. If you can't get through, email me."

As the call ended, Maddie looked between her mother and her brother. The tension in the room was unmistakable.

"We should go to Dad's," Jackson said.

"We're fine here," her mom insisted.

"Well," Maddie said, trying to sound more confident than she felt, "if we're not going up there, we should at least do what he suggested. Shop. Fill up the cars with fuel. Anything else we can think of."

"Maybe we should get more boards for the windows, like we talked about," Jackson suggested.

"What boards?" her mom asked.

Maddie waved her hand. "Never mind."

"Fine. But we're not panicking. We'll think this through rationally."

"I still think we should go to Cody," Jackson said. "Even Grandma Bea thinks so."

Maddie looked at her mother, waiting for her response.

Her mom's face was a mix of emotions—fear, stubbornness, and uncertainty. "I . . . I don't know. It's a big decision. We can't just pack up and leave on a whim."

"Why not?" Jackson asked.

"But Dad seems pretty sure it's the right thing to do," Maddie argued.

"Your father isn't always right, you know. He's been listening to your grandparents' doomsday theories for too long."

"But, Mom," Jackson said, "what if he is right this time? What if things do get really bad here?"

"Look, I know you two think I'm being difficult. But this is our home. We can't just abandon it because of some . . . some flu or whatever this is."

"It's not a flu." Jackson shook his head. "Not like any flu anyone has ever heard of, anyway. Not in real life. It's like a horror movie."

Maddie sat down next to her mother. "Mom, I get it. I don't want to leave either. But we need to at least consider it. Maybe we can make a list of pros and cons?"

"Okay. That's . . . that's reasonable. We can do that."

"Okay. But we need to be quick about it. If we're going to leave, we need to get going. If we're going to stay, we need to go shopping. I'm setting a timer."

For the next seven minutes, they debated the merits of staying versus going to Cody. Jackson pulled up news reports on his tablet, reading out updates on the spread of the Star Bright condition and the increasing restrictions in other states.

As they talked, Maddie could see her mother's resolve weakening. The reality of the situation was sinking in, and the idea of being stuck in Casper if things got worse was clearly unsettling to her.

Finally, her mom held up her hands. "All right, all right. I'm not saying yes . . . but I'm not saying no either. Let's sleep on it. We'll go ahead and do the shopping, buy supplies like your father suggested. We can always take them with us. If things look worse, we'll consider going to Cody. Besides, I'd feel better going up there with a carload of groceries. I don't want your grandpa accusing us of being freeloaders."

Maddie and Jackson exchanged glances. It wasn't a firm commitment, but it was progress.

"Okay," Maddie agreed. "That sounds fair. We should probably make a list of what we need to buy."

"Make it a quick list," Jackson urged. "Dad said we need to shop right away."

As they started compiling their shopping list, Maddie couldn't shake the feeling that their lives were balancing on a knife's edge. Whatever decision they made in the coming days would shape their future in ways they couldn't even imagine.

She just hoped they were making the right choice.

The store's automatic doors slid open with a mechanical whoosh, welcoming Maddie, Jackson, and Heather into the fluorescent-lit expanse of the supermarket. The cart rattled as Maddie pushed it through the aisles, noting the bare shelves that hinted at the growing unease in the community.

Despite the sparse selection, they managed to load the cart with an assortment of groceries. Boxes of pasta, canned goods, and other essentials filled the cart to the brim.

"This is getting a bit silly." Her mom's voice was tinged with uncertainty as she looked at the overflowing cart. "Do we really need all of this? And look at this." She picked up a small package of pasta. "I've never even heard of this brand."

"Me neither, but there were plenty on the shelf. I'm sure it's fine," Maddie said, her expression resolute.

"Besides, it's not like any of this stuff will go to waste. We've got things we can use for weeks. Did you see how many people are here now? Lots more than when we first arrived. I think we should go back down some of the aisles. Get more of this pasta. More beans and rice. Canned goods. We'll have plenty of room in Grandma's car."

Bouncing up and down on his toes, Jackson chimed in, "Dad says there's plenty of money on the credit card. We should buy anything we want. Everything. Maybe more cookies too." He glanced at his mom, who had polished off an entire bag of cookies on her own earlier. "A few bags."

Her mom wrung her hands, hesitating for a moment before nodding. "I guess a little more wouldn't hurt. Like you said, we'll eat it. And if I'm out of work . . . Okay. Let's do it."

They grabbed an empty cart for their second trip through the store and filled it with more indulgent purchases: cookies, toaster pastries, chips, and other fun snacks, along with soda pop, electrolyte drinks, and bottles of water. Whatever they thought sounded good. Many times, there was only one or two of something left on the shelf, and rarely was it a name brand, but they bought it anyway. They also stopped by the pharmacy aisle to pick up a ready-made medical kit and other supplies.

"Well, that should do it," her mom said, shaking her head. "With the price of groceries these days, it's going to cost plenty. Sure hope your dad was right."

"Let's go past the meat counter," Maddie suggested. "Even though Dad said to buy shelf-stable things, the fridge and freezer still work. We could at least get something good for dinner."

"Maybe steaks?" Jackson suggested. "And potatoes. I'll go grab a bag of potatoes."

"Grab a bag of apples too," her mom said. "They'll keep well, and the fiber will be good."

While Maddie and her mom went to the meat counter, Jackson weaved his way to the produce department.

"We should have stayed together," her mom mumbled as they walked. "Let's follow Jackson. We'll grab him, then we'll all go get the steaks. Maybe a chicken for tomorrow night too. Oh, and how about that crab dip we like? We'll buy some crackers and . . ." Her voice trailed off as they caught up with Jackson as he was looking over the bags of potatoes.

"We didn't want to leave you alone," Maddie said in answer to the question on his face.

"Oh, okay. Which ones? These big ones are for baking, right?"

"Grab those and we'll take these little fingerlings. I decided we'll roast a chicken tomorrow night. These will be perfect."

With their additional selections handled, they made their way to the front of the store, where the banks of check stands waited. When their mom had worked there, she'd been a backup checker. She'd enjoyed the job, to a point, but did seem to like working at the care center better.

As they stood in line at the checkout, an employee passed by, pushing a cart laden with toilet paper, paper towels, charcoal, and other barbecue supplies.

"Eww. What's that smell?" Jackson asked, scrunching up his nose.

"Smells like lighter fluid," the cashier replied, glancing at the other employee. "Hey, Lottie. You're leaking something. It's dripping out of the cart."

Lottie smiled and waved but kept moving, a small hum escaping her lips. A man in the next checkout line started humming, too, leaving his cart to join Lottie.

"Are they singing?" Heather whispered, her face turning pale.

Maddie watched with growing unease as Lottie handed him a bottle of lighter fluid. The cashier gave Maddie the total, and she quickly inserted the credit card, her eyes fixed on the growing group.

At least six others had joined in, and the humming had increased. It was an old song that she should know but couldn't place. Jackson's face turned pale as he muttered, "Star Brights. They've . . . they've got the sickness. We need to get out of here."

Her heart raced as she realized Jackson was right. But how could they leave? Lottie and her group were blocking the exit.

Chapter 15

The cashier turned and shouted at Lottie. "Get back to work! We're too busy for your shenanigans! And put that toilet paper back on the shelves. People are waiting for it."

Lottie started moving toward them, singing now instead of humming. "*And the star-spangled banner in triumph shall wave . . .*" Still smiling, she held both hands behind her back. The other singers stayed by the carts, stacking the toilet paper near the exit door.

Heather's voice grew urgent. "We need to leave. Now."

The tension in the store was slow to build. People exchanged nervous looks, but no one said anything at first. Whispers started up, quiet and unsure, but soon they were everywhere. Moms yanked their kids closer, and older people messed with their carts like they didn't know what else to do. Some looked at the exit, but the Star Brights were right there. If they could run, exactly how would they get out with the exit blocked?

"We've got to go," Jackson urged, his voice trembling. "Finish paying. We need to leave."

Maddie hit the button to finalize the transaction, deciding she didn't need a receipt. They needed to get out of there.

Lottie stopped a few feet away, and the cashier insisted again that she needed to get back to work. But where the cashier had been firm before, there was now a quiver in her voice.

Lottie swung her left arm. A stream of liquid shot out and soaked the cashier. With horror, Maddie realized it was lighter fluid.

"Go, Maddie! Go! Jackson, move!" Her mom pushed them, turning their filled cart away from the exit and toward the pharmacy.

Maddie stood there, frozen, as Lottie's right arm lifted, a lighter in her hand. The flame caught the soaked clothing, and the cashier let out a scream.

The other singers raised their voices. *"And the star-spangled banner in triumph shall wave . . ."* They lit their lighters and ignited the paper products drenched in fluid. The store erupted into chaos as people started screaming, and then gunfire rang out.

Maddie flinched and ducked behind the checkout stand. The smell of burning clothes and hair assaulted her nostrils.

"Move, Maddie! Move! Stay low!" Her mom yanked her arm, dragging her as she pushed the cart. Jackson was next to her, duck-walking as they rounded the bank of registers. The fire sprinklers activated and covered them in a mist of water.

"Run to the back!" her mom commanded. "We're going to the stockroom near the meat section. Don't stop until we go through the flapping doors. I'll use the cart to clear the path. Stay right behind me. Hold on to each other."

The screaming and shooting continued as they moved away from the front of the store. Her mom used the cart like a battering ram, knocking an unattended cart out of the way. She told a lady cowering on the side to get behind them and follow.

Jackson held the hem of their mom's shirt, Maddie held onto Jackson's, and the lady held onto Maddie's. The smell of smoke was awful, gagging them as they hustled down the aisle, picking up several other scared people along the way.

They reached the door to the stockroom, where a crush of people were trying to get inside, hoping for another exit.

"Ram them!" the lady behind Maddie yelled. Her mom considered it but instead skidded to a stop. "Stay in the middle," she ordered. In seconds, the way cleared enough for her to push the doors open with the cart.

Inside the stockroom, people stood wide-eyed and crying. Her mom wasted no time heading for the exit. When they reached the out-of-the-way door, tucked behind a large pallet of groceries, she pushed through, moving a brick to prop it open.

"Tell them, Maddie. Tell them how to get out," she ordered as she continued pushing the cart.

"The exit is here!" she yelled. The lady behind her scurried around and ran outside. As others saw where Maddie was and began to follow, her mom said, "It's time to go. They'll find their way."

Still pushing the cart, their mom told Jackson and Maddie to grab hold again. They formed their cart train and moved toward their SUV. The entrance of the building was a mess, flames licking at the outdoor displays of plants and picnic items. The off-key singing of *The Star-Spangled Banner* echoed loudly.

Maddie opened Jackson's door and helped him inside as their mom hurriedly packed the groceries into the car. "Leave them, Mom! We need to go!"

"Your dad's right. We need this food. We lost the few things we had in the second cart. They're going to close this store down." She plopped the rest of the groceries inside and jumped into the front seat, not even buckling her seatbelt before pulling out of the parking spot.

Maddie's breath was ragged, the distant sounds of police and fire sirens piercing the air. She hoped they'd send an ambulance, or ten, too. She had no idea how many people were hurt. Definitely the cashier. She might have even died.

The shooting—was it the Star Brights or someone else? Guns were common in Wyoming; it wouldn't be surprising if several people were armed.

Her mom gripped the steering wheel, her foot pressing down hard on the gas as she shot anxious glances in the rearview mirror at the chaotic scene they were leaving behind. "We're safe now," she murmured, more to herself than to anyone else.

Jackson, still pale, looked out the window. "Mom, what are we going to do if they close all the stores?"

"We'll figure it out, Jackson." Her voice was steady, despite the fear etched on her face.

Maddie leaned back in her seat, her heart still pounding. The Star Brights were getting bolder, more dangerous. She suspected this was only the beginning. But they'd stuck together, and her mom took the lead and got them and others to safety. She realized that, together, they had a chance.

For now, that would have to be enough.

Chapter 16

As they drove, Maddie noticed her mom kept looking in the rearview mirror, as if expecting to see the singing mob chasing after them.

The silence in the car was thick with tension until Jackson finally spoke up. "Are we going home now?"

Her mom didn't respond immediately, her eyes darting between the road and the mirrors. Suddenly, she made a sharp turn and pulled into the parking lot of another grocery store.

"Mom?" Maddie asked, confusion and alarm evident in her voice. "What are you doing?"

"I'm going to go in and get us more food." Her tone was determined as she maneuvered through the crowded lot and found a spot near the back.

"No, Mom. You can't. We have enough." She gestured to the packed SUV.

Her mom left the car running and turned to face them. She wiped something from her face—sweat, tears, or sprinkler water, Maddie wasn't sure—and smoothed her wet hair. Maddie reached for her own blond ponytail, suddenly realizing how soaked she was.

"Stay with Jackson. Get into the driver's seat. Keep it running and be ready to move if there's trouble."

"Mom, this is crazy. We barely got out of the last store alive!"

"I had a job here in high school," her mom continued as if Maddie hadn't spoken. "I'll use the back exit if needed and walk home. If things go bad, you get Jackson home. Don't wait for me."

She gave her mom a doubtful look. "It's two, maybe three miles home from here. Uphill."

"I'll get there. Don't worry. Pull the car into the garage. Unload in there. Stay inside."

"This is stupid," Maddie said, but Jackson cut her off.

"Go ahead." His voice was surprisingly firm. "Do what you need to. We'll be fine."

Their mom gave him a grateful smile before turning back to Maddie. "In the driver's seat, Maddie. Now."

As her mom hurried toward the store, Maddie reluctantly slid into the driver's seat. She turned to Jackson, bewildered. "What is the deal with you siding with her all of a sudden? You know how she is."

Jackson shrugged. "Did you see her in the store? She was awesome. She wasn't like . . . you know, not how she can be. She was tough."

"Yeah, well, maybe," Maddie conceded. "But she'll fall apart soon enough. And walking home? Ha. She can't even walk down the block."

"Then we'd better hope nothing happens while she's in the store."

The minutes ticked by agonizingly slow. She watched as more and more people streamed out of the store, their carts piled high. The parking lot was chaos, with cars jockeying for position and tempers flaring.

Just as Maddie was about to suggest they go look for their mom, she appeared, pushing a loaded cart. Maddie quickly got out to help her.

"I got what I could," her mom panted as they loaded groceries into the car. "They didn't want to let me shop. But I rushed around and, well . . . it helped I had cash from Grandma Bea's stash. I just kind of offered what I had to the manager, and he took it and waved me through. I remembered some of the things we lost in the cart we had to leave behind. It wasn't much, but every bit counts now."

"At least a little of Grandma rubbed off on you," Maddie muttered, thinking to herself that the manager had probably pocketed the cash.

As they finished loading, her mom looked around nervously. "Let's get out of here."

They joined the throng of cars trying to exit the parking lot, the atmosphere tense and urgent. Just as she thought they were headed home, her mom swerved into a gas station mini-mart.

"What now?" she asked.

"Maddie, fill the tank. I'm going inside."

"Let me guess. Cigarettes."

"Yes. And I'll grab more food too. They have a good selection at this store, you know that. And toilet paper. The way those Star Brights burned the toilet paper made me wonder why we didn't buy more."

"You bought a four-pack at each store," she pointed out.

Her mom shrugged. "Just fill the car."

As she began pumping gas, her mother disappeared into the store. She turned to Jackson. "Can you believe this?"

Jackson shrugged. "At least she's doing something. It's better than when she just sits around eating cookies, right?"

She had to admit he had a point. Still, she couldn't shake the feeling that this manic energy was just the calm before the storm. She'd seen her mother go through phases like this before, and it never ended well.

Was she taking her meds? Maddie closed her eyes as she thought. How much medication did she have on hand? She knew her mom used a mail-order pharmacy and was able to get three months at a time. When did she get the last order? She wasn't sure.

Without those meds, things would get rough for her mom. Being off her meds would for sure lead to her drinking again. She'd need to ask her mom how much she had left and hope it was enough to get through until things returned to normal.

Maybe her doctor would be willing to call in an emergency prescription to a local pharmacy. The insurance probably wouldn't cover it, but maybe they could figure something out. Her doctor knew she needed her meds. Nonadherence had resulted in terrible troubles more than once.

To her surprise, her mom came back with an impressive haul: bags full of canned and packaged food, more toilet paper, and even several packages of personal products. Maddie reluctantly acknowledged it was a good idea, even if she didn't say it out loud.

As they pulled out of the gas station, she asked, "So, what now? Are we going home, or . . .?"

Her mom was quiet for a moment, her eyes fixed on the road. "We're going home. But we need to be ready. Your father . . . he might be right about Cody."

Maddie and Jackson exchanged surprised looks. "You mean, you're considering it?"

"I'm considering it. But first, we need to get home and sort through all this. We need a plan."

As they drove, Maddie couldn't help but feel a mixture of relief and apprehension. Her mother was stepping up, taking charge in a way she hadn't seen in years. Not years. Ever.

But the world around them was unraveling fast, and it felt as if they were racing against time.

"What about Dad?" Jackson asked from the back seat. "Shouldn't we call him when we get home?"

Her mom nodded. "Yes, we should. And . . . maybe we should start packing. Just in case."

The rest of the drive home was quiet, each lost in their own thoughts. As they neared their driveway, Maddie noticed several neighbors outside, looking anxious and watchful.

"What are they doing?" Jackson asked.

"Not sure, but I think we should find out. As soon as we see what's going on, we'll unload. I think we need to be quiet about what we have," her mom said, her eyes darting around as if expecting someone to be watching them.

As they walked over to join the group in Tom's yard, Maddie felt a flicker of hope amid the fear. They weren't alone. And for now, that small comfort would have to be enough.

Tom waved and hurried over, concern etched into his features. "Are you guys okay? Did you hear what happened at Albertsons?"

Maddie's mom put an arm around her shoulders, her grip firm as she reached for Jackson's hand. "We drove by there. It looked like they had some trouble."

Maddie felt a slight pressure on her shoulder and suspected the same sensation was being delivered to Jackson's hand. An indicator to stay quiet about the fact they were actually in the store when the event went down.

Tom looked relieved, his tense expression softening as he glanced over the trio. Maddie, feeling exposed and vulnerable, raised her hand self-consciously to her hair, which was still damp around the ponytail holder from the fire sprinklers.

"Thank goodness you're okay," Tom said, his voice filled with genuine relief. "It's all over the internet. There're videos of what happened. Dozens dead. One of the women who worked there was . . . She was . . ."

Tom shook his head. "I'm sure you'll learn about what all happened soon enough. Listen, a bunch of us have been talking. With everything that's going on, we think it might be a good idea to set up some kind of neighborhood watch. Keep an eye out for each other, you know?"

Her mom's expression was thoughtful but wary. "That sounds like a good idea. Is that what you all are discussing out here?" She dropped her hand from Maddie's shoulder and motioned to the crowd gathered in Tom's yard. The group looked somber, their hushed conversations carrying a sense of urgency.

"Plus other things." Tom glanced across the street toward the Webers' home. His face darkened. "Peter Weber came home earlier. A police officer brought him. His wife . . ." Tom shook his head, his voice cracking. "She didn't make it. Peter said she'd come around and seemed like she might make it. But then she ended her own life."

"Oh, no!" Her mom's hand flew to her mouth.

Maddie stared at her shoes, the weight of the news pressing down on her chest. A sob welled up within her, but she forced it down, her eyes burning with unshed tears.

Jackson's eyes went wide with fear and confusion. "Why did she do that?"

Tom ran a hand through his hair. "Either she was a Star Bright, or she was scared. Upset over what had happened earlier in the day. Sometimes, when people get too scared, they do things they wouldn't normally do."

Heather pulled Jackson closer and wrapped her arms around both him and Maddie. "We're going to be okay," she whispered, though her voice wavered. "We're going to look out for each other. That's what neighbors do."

Tom's eyes met Heather's with a shared determination. "A neighborhood watch is a good idea, but I'm worried about how we can make it work. Until we know how this thing spreads, it's hard to know who we can trust. I'd socialized with Charla and Peter Weber on several occasions. I never would have thought . . ." He sighed as he shook his head.

"So, you think the neighborhood watch is a bad idea?" her mom asked, her voice barely above a whisper.

"I think it's a good idea. I really do. I'm just concerned about how we keep each other safe. These people, these Star Brights, they seem to just switch. One second, they're normal. The next, they're dead set on murder. At least, that's what the videos show. There's barely any warning before they go."

Maddie wanted to speak up, to tell him about the Star Brights at Albertsons and how they all acted like they knew the plan. Had they arranged it beforehand? It didn't look that way. Workers and customers alike seemed to understand they had to take part. Take part and burn it all down.

"They sing or hum," Jackson said. "Weird songs about stars."

Tom shrugged. "I guess that's something. Not much, but better than nothing."

"I'd like to hear what they have to say." Her mom lifted her chin toward the gathered group of neighbors.

As they walked into Tom's yard to join the others, a flicker of hope cut through Maddie's fear. They weren't alone. That was enough to bring a small smile to her face.

Chapter 17

Maddie stirred awake, the craziness of yesterday hitting her like a ton of bricks. She lay still for a moment and tried to wrap her head around the chaos at Albertsons, the mad dash through the aisles, and the shocking news about Mrs. Weber.

In the stillness of her bedroom, it all felt like a bad dream she couldn't shake off.

Glancing at her clock, she was surprised to see it was barely past seven in the morning. She'd always been an early riser, but after yesterday's ordeal, she could've benefited from sleeping in. It seemed she was overly exhausted lately. This whole end-of-the-world stuff was draining.

With a sigh, she pushed herself out of bed, determined to get a head start on organizing the groceries before her mom woke up.

"That'll be easy," she muttered to herself as she pulled on a pair of sweatpants. "Mom never gets up before noon when she doesn't have work."

She caught a glimpse of herself in the mirror and paused. The girl staring back at her looked older somehow, her eyes carrying a weight that hadn't been there just days ago.

She shook her head, trying to dispel the unsettling feeling her reflection brought. There was no time for self-examination now; there was work to be done.

As she made her way downstairs, her mind wandered to the treats they'd bought. She made a mental note to hide some of the cookies and other goodies. If she didn't, her mom would likely fully devour them in one of her stress-eating binges.

Jackson deserves cookies, she reasoned. *After yesterday, we all do. Maybe even Mom.*

But when she reached the kitchen, she stopped short and her jaw dropped in surprise. The room was immaculate. The granite countertops gleamed, dishes were neatly stacked in the drying rack, and there wasn't a crumb in sight.

Even more surprising, the groceries they'd purchased yesterday were all put away. They'd been so tired after yesterday's difficulty and the meeting with the neighbors that they'd left them in the kitchen to deal with today.

As she ran a finger along the breakfast island in disbelief, a voice startled her. "Oh, hey. You're up."

She whirled around to see her mom's head poking out of the walk-in pantry, a rare smile on her face.

"Mom?" She blinked, wondering if she was still dreaming. "I thought you'd sleep in after yesterday. Are you okay?"

Her mom stepped fully out of the pantry and wiped her hands on her jeans. "I thought you'd sleep in too. How are you feeling?"

She shrugged, still taken aback by the scene before her. "I'm . . . fine, I guess. How long have you been up?"

"Not too long," her mom replied, but the dark circles under her eyes suggested otherwise.

Maddie felt a pang of concern as she glanced around the spotless room, her mom's sudden burst of energy reminding her of past manic episodes.

Was Mom up all night? she wondered. It wouldn't be the first time during one of those phases. Swallowing her fear, she hesitantly asked, "Do you need any help?"

Her mom's smile widened. "Want to help me in the pantry? I've got a few things I thought should go up top. You can hand them up to me."

Nodding, she followed her mom into the pantry. As her mom climbed onto the step stool, Maddie began handing up cans and boxes. The familiar routine felt strangely comforting after the chaos of yesterday.

"The phones seem to be working better. I was able to text your dad. He got the message and called me right back," her mom said casually as she arranged items on the top shelf.

Maddie nearly dropped the can she was holding. "Your phone? And you answered?"

Her mom glanced down, a hint of her old defensiveness creeping into her expression. "Of course, silly. After all, I'd reached out to him. I figured he was worried. Besides, if I didn't answer, he'd call you, and I wanted you to be able to sleep."

Maddie stood there, momentarily speechless. It was one of the most mom-like things she'd heard in years . . . maybe ever. The simple consideration brought a lump to her throat as memories flooded back.

She remembered the good times, though they were few and far between—the rare moments when her mom was present, loving, and attentive. Those fleeting instances of normalcy were what she clung to, hoping they would last, but they never did.

She recalled the countless nights when Jackson was a baby, crying with hunger. Her mom, hungover and irritable, would wake four-year-old Maddie to fix a bottle before retreating back to bed, leaving them to fend for themselves.

Her dad had been around then, sort of. He worked on an oil rig and was gone for two weeks at a time. Even when he was home, he put in long hours at the machine shop his parents owned in Douglas, about forty-five minutes east of Casper. That was before they "retired" and opened the lodge near Yellowstone. Her dad tried to make up for his absences with bursts of "dad time," but it was never quite enough.

She remembered the excitement of his homecomings and the way Jackson's face would light up at the sight of him. Those moments made the long separations bearable, but also made the eventual breakdown of their family all the more painful.

Grandpa Dick and Grandma Ruth were selling the shop and moving to the North Fork. They had invited the whole family to go with them. Her dad had wanted to, even to try and work on the marriage, but her mom refused.

At first, her dad seemed willing to stay in Casper while his parents moved, but then her mom did things—things that made him realize the marriage was truly over.

After the divorce, her mom spiraled. She couldn't keep a job—Albertsons was just one in a long line of short-lived stints. They'd been on their own for about a year before the eviction notice on their apartment finally brought her grandma home from Arizona.

During that year, her mom put on weight, slept more than ever, and started eating, smoking, and drinking in excess. It was a nightmare, with ten-year-old Maddie trying to keep things together for herself and Jackson.

The bipolar diagnosis came after a three-day binge landed her mom in jail. Threats of social services taking Maddie and Jackson faded when her grandma stepped in.

Maddie shuddered at the memory of those dark days—constantly fearing separation from Jackson and the overwhelming responsibility she felt at such a young age. She'd grown up too fast, forced to be the adult in a situation no child should have to face.

"Whew, good thing we're almost finished," her mom's voice snapped Maddie back to the present. "This shelf is just about full." Looking down at Maddie, she smiled from the top of the stepstool, which groaned ominously as she shifted her weight.

Maddie forced a smile in return, but inwardly, she remained cautious. Sure, her mom might have gotten up early to put away groceries. She might have seemed like the put-together parent she'd always claimed she wanted to be.

But Maddie knew better than to trust it would last. She'd be ready to step in when needed, just like always.

"So," Maddie ventured, handing her mom the last can, "what did Dad say?"

Her mom's expression tightened. "He wanted to know if we'd made a decision about going to the lodge."

Maddie's heart rate picked up. "And? What did you tell him?"

Her mom climbed down from the step stool. "I told him we're still thinking about it. But . . ." She hesitated, meeting Maddie's gaze. "I'm leaning toward going."

She blinked in surprise. "Really? You want to go?"

"No, it's not what I want. But after yesterday, I don't know if what I want matters. It may not be safe in Casper."

A mixture of relief and anxiety washed over her. "But you think we might go?"

"I want to go to the meeting with the neighbors this afternoon, see if the things we discussed yesterday truly have a chance of working. I'd feel better knowing the neighborhood was secure, that our house will be watched over so we have something to return to. In the meantime, we should start making plans to leave. That's why I did all this." She motioned to the shelves.

"I thought if we had everything organized, we'd be able to better see what we should pack. There are some totes and boxes in the shed. We'll do things right. Keep things neatly together. That way, if we do go, we can contribute."

She felt a surge of pride at her mother's forethought. It was moments like these that reminded her of the capable, caring woman her mom could be when she wasn't battling her own demons.

She nodded, her mind already racing with all they needed to do. "Does Jackson know yet?"

"No, he isn't up yet. We'll let him sleep a bit, then we'll talk about it as a family. Perhaps, if the neighbors have a viable plan, we'll hold off on leaving. But I do think we should have things packed and ready to go at a moment's notice. Suitcases too. Anything we need to stay up there for weeks. Months, maybe."

"Months? Did something new happen?"

"Not that I know of. I was just thinking about last time and how two weeks to slow the spread became two years. Even afterward, things had changed."

Maddie was younger then, much younger, and her grandma had done her best to shield both her and Jackson from the turmoil. But she still knew what was happening. This felt different, more immediate and dangerous, but the lessons learned then could prove valuable now.

"I think I'll fire up my laptop, check and see if there is anything new. Plus, I want to see if Grandma responded on Chum Fun. I'm also going to message Eddie and email Dad."

As Maddie turned to go, her mom called out, "Maddie?"

"Yeah?"

"I'm . . . I'm sorry. For everything. I know I haven't been the mother you and Jackson deserve. But I'm trying. I really am."

Her throat tightened. She wanted to believe her, wanted to trust that this change was real and lasting. But years of disappointment had taught her to be cautious.

"I know, Mom," she said finally. "I hope . . . I hope you can keep trying."

As Maddie spoke the words, she realized how much she wanted them to be true. Despite everything, she still longed for the mother she'd always wanted, always needed. The mother her mom could be in her best moments.

As she headed upstairs, she couldn't shake the feeling that everything was about to change. Whether it was for better or worse remained to be seen. But for now, they had a plan, and that was something.

She just hoped it would be enough to keep them safe in the increasingly dangerous world outside their door.

She sat at her desk and opened her laptop. As she waited for it to boot up, she gazed out the window at the quiet street below. The world looked deceptively normal, but she knew better now.

Whatever came next, she was determined to face it head-on, protecting her family at all costs. It was a role she'd been preparing for her entire life, whether she'd realized it or not.

Her fingers hovered over the keyboard. Taking a deep breath, she began her search for updates on the growing crisis. The flood of information was overwhelming, each headline more alarming than the last.

"Wyoming Joins National Travel Restrictions," one headline blared. She clicked on the article, her heart sinking as she read about the new measures being implemented across the state.

Grocery stores were closing, replaced by armed food drop locations. Restaurants were also closed. While they weren't putting up roadblocks, the governor urged citizens to stay home, his plea echoing those of leaders across the country.

Gas stations were for official use only and were unavailable to the private sector. The governor assured them this was only temporary until they could put measures in place to help with safety. Once a plan was constructed, people would be able to shop or get gas on assigned days at specific times.

"Enjoy this time as a family," the article quoted. "Watch movies, play games, stay in contact with your friends and family via online methods and phone calls."

Maddie snorted. "Easy for them to say."

As she slid her chair back to go tell her mom about the latest info, a notification flashed on Chum Fun—a new message from her grandma.

Her heart raced as she clicked on it, hope surging within her. Could this be the good news she desperately needed? The uncertainty made her pulse quicken, literally leaving her on the edge of her seat as she waited for the message's contents to load.

Chapter 18

Maddie's breath caught as the message from her grandma appeared on the screen, her heart pounding with anticipation of the good news she so desperately needed.

"Hope you're all safe. We're stuck in Alaska. The ship docked, but they won't let us leave. We're still on the ship for now but will soon be moved to hotels as supplies onboard are dwindling. They say the port might reopen in a week, but who knows? While we're safe on the ship, we've heard there are Star Brights on land even here in Alaska. You need to go to your dad's lodge. I'm going to try to go there too. If there's any way I can, I will. Be careful. Love you all."

Maddie's throat tightened. She quickly typed a reply, assuring her grandma they were okay and promising to stay safe.

She hesitated a few moments after sending it, waiting for a reply. When nothing happened, she moved on to her email. She might as well check that, too, then she could let her mom know all the latest news.

Two new messages caught her eye: one from her dad and another from her grandma Ruth. She opened her dad's first.

Hey kiddo,

Just hung up after talking with your mom. I hadn't seen the news yet about the changes from the governor. The gas stations being closed is a problem. Were you able to get fuel in all the cars yesterday?

Things are getting worse by the minute. I know your mom said she'd think about coming up here. I hope she does. I know that you and her sometimes butt heads, but she will try her best, as she's able, to do the right thing. If you can make sure she stays on her meds, it'll help.

The lodge is the best choice. I think she knows that but worries about looking weak by leaving Casper. She told me this morning about her work building being destroyed. I know that's adding to her stress. Trust me when I say, her having a job is the least of her worries right now.

We saw a lot of traffic yesterday as folks left Yellowstone. Most of our guests also left or are leaving today. Grandma Ruth spoke with Uncle Rich and Aunt Beth yesterday. I think even they're going to come to the lodge, though Aunt Beth isn't yet convinced.

I'm sure you know that truly says a lot about Uncle Rich's concerns. I guess he saw some terrible things when he was stuck in Portland the other day. With just family here, we'll be safe. At least, that's the hope. Fewer people means less chance of . . . well, you know. Have you talked to your mom about it? Let me know what you decide. Stay safe.

Love, Dad

Maddie sighed and moved on to Grandma Ruth's email.

Maddie and Jackson,
I hope this email finds you well. Your grandfather and I are very worried about you all. The news from Casper is troubling. Please consider coming to stay with us. We have plenty of room and supplies. Your father is beside himself

Maddie stared at the screen. Her mind raced with thoughts about the lodge. It seemed like the safest option, but she couldn't help worrying about the potential conflicts that might arise.

Her mom and grandpa had never gotten along well; their arguments were legendary within the family. She could almost hear their voices now, bickering over the smallest things.

And if her aunt and uncle did come . . . Maddie sighed. They thought her grandpa was completely off his rocker. She'd overheard them once, whispering about how he'd "lost touch with reality."

She wasn't sure if her grandpa was a prepper or a full-on survivalist—the line seemed blurry to her. But she knew he'd been stockpiling supplies and spouting dire predictions long before the pandemic hit.

Now, with his warnings about the dollar failing and the country collapsing, she feared he might be right. The thought sent a chill down her spine. What if this really was the end of everything they'd known?

Despite the potential for family drama, the lodge seemed like their best option. At least they would be together, and her grandpa's preparations might actually save their lives.

Maddie knew she had to convince her mom that heading up there was the best and safest choice. And she needed to do it quickly—they had to leave soon.

A chat notification popped up.

Eddie: *Hey Maddie! You guys okay?*

Maddie: *Yeah, we're hanging in there. You?*

Eddie: *It's crazy here. Mom and Dad are fighting about whether to leave or not. Dad wants to go to the lodge. He thinks it'll be safer. My mom doesn't want to leave.*

Maddie: *Same here. Mom's actually considering it now though.*

Eddie: *Really? Wow. Hey, did you see that video of the cop and the girl?*

Maddie: *What video?*

Eddie sent a link, and Maddie clicked on it, her stomach churning as she watched the horrifying scene unfold.

A teenage girl, not much older than her, was screaming and crying as a police officer roughly handcuffed her. "Who did this? Who killed my parents?" the girl wailed. The cop shoved her to the ground, yelling, "You did!" before slapping her across the face.

Maddie felt sick. She quickly closed the video.

Maddie: *That's horrible. What's happening to people?*

Eddie: *I know. It's everywhere. That video is so sad. I found some backstory on it. The cop knew the family. Has known that girl since she was a toddler. Mom says we're safer staying put, but I'm scared. Things like that are happening everywhere.*

Maddie: *Me too. Listen, I gotta go. Talk later?*

Eddie: *Yeah, stay safe.*

Maddie leaned back in her chair, her mind reeling from everything she'd learned. The Star Brights were everywhere, and the violence was escalating. Even families weren't safe. She shuddered as she thought about the video Eddie had sent.

A knock at her door startled her. "Maddie?" her mom called. "Can you come downstairs? Tom's here. I-I think you should hear what he has to say. I'm going to wake up Jackson too."

Maddie hesitated. After everything she'd just read and seen, the idea of even talking with the neighbor bothered her. And a neighborhood watch seemed naive at best, dangerous at worst. How could they trust people when the Star Brights could be anyone?

"Coming," she called back, closing her laptop. As she headed downstairs, she knew she had to convince her mom that staying put wasn't safe. They needed to leave, and soon.

She found her mom and Jackson already in the living room with Tom. Their neighbor looked pale and agitated, his usual friendly demeanor replaced by a tense, worried expression.

"Maddie, good, you're here." Her mom gestured for her to sit. "Tom has some news."

Tom nodded, his hands fidgeting in his lap. "I just got off the phone with my brother in Cheyenne. He knows people who work for the governor. Things are . . . they're bad, guys. Really bad."

Tom recounted what he'd heard—most of it was information she'd already gleaned from her online searches: the travel restrictions, the armed food drops, the escalating violence. But hearing it from someone who'd gotten firsthand accounts made it all the more real and terrifying.

"They're saying it must be an airborne virus," Tom added, his voice barely above a whisper. "The Star Bright condition, I mean. That's why so many people are turning at once. It's the only explanation."

Jackson, who'd been quiet as he listened, suddenly spoke up. "We need to leave." His voice was firm despite the fear in his eyes. "Now. Today."

Their mom shook her head and wrung her hands. "I don't know . . . it's such a big decision. What if things get better? What if we're overreacting?"

Maddie couldn't stay silent any longer. "Mom, please. Dad's right. We need to go to the lodge. It's safer there. Fewer people means less chance of . . . of this happening to us."

Tom nodded in agreement. "If I had somewhere better to go, I'd be packing up right now. You folks are lucky to have that option."

Their mom still looked uncertain. "But what about our home? Our lives here? And my mom . . . what if she comes back and we're gone?"

"She responded on Chum Fun. I was going to tell you, sorry. She's okay but will be stuck there. They're going to move them off the ship and into hotels. She wants us to be safe. She wants us to go to Dad's place. And she'll go there, too, if she can get out of Alaska and things aren't back to normal. Mom, our lives won't matter if we're not alive to live them."

For a long moment, no one spoke. She could see the internal struggle playing out on her mom's face—the fear of leaving everything behind warring with the instinct to protect her children.

Finally, her mom took a deep breath. "Okay," she said quietly. "Okay, we'll go. But we need to be smart about this. We can't just rush out without a plan."

Relief washed over Maddie, quickly followed by a new wave of anxiety. They were really doing this. They were leaving Casper, possibly for good.

Tom stood up, looking both relieved and sad. "I'm glad you're going. I'll keep an eye on your house and let you know if anything happens here."

As Tom left, the reality of their decision began to sink in. Maddie looked around the living room, at the familiar photos and knickknacks that had been a part of her life for as long as she could remember.

How much of it will we be able to take? she wondered. *How much will we have to leave behind?*

"All right." Her mom's voice was stronger now that a decision had been made. "Let's make a list of what we absolutely need to take—clothes, medications, important documents. Maddie, can you start packing the food? Jackson, I need you to gather all the flashlights and batteries you can find."

As they dispersed to their tasks, Maddie knew their lives were about to change irrevocably. The world outside their door was growing more dangerous by the minute, and their only hope lay in fleeing to the relative safety of the lodge.

She just hoped they weren't already too late.

Chapter 19

The Reynolds house was a flurry of activity. Maddie, Jackson, and Heather moved with purpose, packing essentials and loading them into Grandma Bea's SUV. The air was thick with tension, but also with a sense of relief—they were finally taking action.

Maddie was in her room, carefully selecting which clothes to bring, when her phone buzzed with an alert. She grabbed it, hoping for a message from her dad or one of her friends. Instead, her heart sank as she read the notification.

"EMERGENCY ALERT: Governor's Proclamation—State Under Martial Law."

"Mom! Jackson!" she called out as she ran down the stairs. "You need to see this!"

They gathered around her phone as she read the proclamation aloud:

"By order of the governor, effective immediately, the state of Wyoming is under martial law. All residents are to remain in their current locations. No travel between cities. Effective immediately, Casper and Cheyenne are under a full security perimeter. No unauthorized travel in or out will be permitted. Violators will be subject to arrest and detention."

The room grew still. Their plans, so carefully made, were now impossible.

"What . . . what do we do now?" Jackson asked, his voice small and scared.

Her mom sank into a chair, her face pale. "We stay. We have no choice."

Maddie's mind raced as she stared at the proclamation. She remembered her dad's warnings, the fear in his voice when he told them to get out of Casper. The Star Brights weren't just a threat; they were a promise of chaos.

She could still see the videos showing all the trouble they'd caused. The confused girl who had killed her parents bothered her the most. How could she not remember killing them? What caused her to do that? Could she, or even Jackson, be like the girl and . . .

She hated to even think about it. But if they stayed in Casper, was that what awaited them? Fear and frustration welled up inside her. "But Dad said it wasn't safe here! We can't just sit around waiting for something to happen!"

"Maddie's right," Jackson chimed in. "What about the Star Brights? It's not safe in Casper."

Their mom took a deep breath and visibly pulled herself together. "Okay, let's think this through. We can't leave, but we can still protect ourselves. We'll go to that neighborhood watch meeting this afternoon. Some security is better than no security, right?"

Her mom's hands trembled as she reached for the pack of cigarettes on the table. She usually smoked on the back deck, away from everyone, but now she didn't seem to care.

Her unsteady hands reached for the lighter. She flicked it a few times, but the flame never touched the cigarette. If she was this shaken, things were worse than Maddie had thought.

"Yes, yes. That's what we'll do." Her mom glanced toward the back deck, cigarette in one hand and lighter in the other, but then shook her head as if dismissing the thought.

Maddie felt a surge of betrayal—was her mom really suggesting they rely on strangers? The walls seemed to close in around her as doubt gnawed at her. How could they just accept this? Surely, there was a way they could leave Casper.

"We can't. We can't trust anyone. We have to leave."

Jackson jutted his finger at her phone. "How? They won't let us out!"

"The neighborhood watch will work. We'll find a safe way to do it." Her mom's voice was steady but lacked conviction. "Maybe . . . maybe we can set up a system of signals or something. We'll figure it out at the meeting."

Maddie's arms flew out in frustration. "What good is that?" she snapped, her voice rising as she glared at her mom. "You really think some neighborhood watch is going to keep us safe?" Her breath came quicker, and her chest tightened. "What if they're part of the problem?"

"We have to trust someone, Maddie." Her mom dropped the lighter back on the table with a clatter, then hesitated before tucking the unlit cigarette back into the pack.

Maddie turned her attention to her phone, desperately trying to call her dad. He'd know what to do. He always did. But the call wouldn't go through. "Great. The phones aren't working again."

"Try the internet," Jackson suggested. "It was working earlier."

She navigated through the screens, her fingers shaking with frustration. Once in her email, she quickly replied to her dad's earlier message, making sure he'd heard about the martial law announcement and telling him how she'd tried to call but the phone wasn't working.

"I'll message Grandma Bea too." She swiped to the Chum Fun app and sent a near-duplicate message to her grandma.

"Bad news. Wyoming's under martial law. We can't leave Casper. Stuck here for now. What can we do to stay safe?"

After hitting send, she tossed her phone onto the table and began pacing the kitchen. "This is insane! We can't just sit here and wait for something bad to happen. What if the Star Brights find us first?" The thought sent a shiver down her spine, and her chest tightened with fear.

Tears pricked her eyes. She blinked them away, refusing to show weakness. "We have to fight back, not just sit here like . . . like sitting ducks."

Jackson shook his head. "You mean like leave anyway? Ignore the orders from the governor? But what if we get caught? What if we're put in jail?" His voice trembled, and his hands shook.

"Then at least we'll be doing something. I can't just sit here and wait for someone to come and . . . and attack us. That's not living. That's just surviving."

Her mom stepped in front of her and gripped her shoulders with both hands. The warmth of her mom's touch should have been comforting, but all Maddie felt was a growing frustration.

Just as their eyes locked, a deafening explosion shook the house. The windows rattled violently, and car alarms blared up and down the street. The air trembled around them, thick with the force of the blast.

Chapter 20

"What was that?" Jackson asked, his eyes wide with fear as another blast sounded, shaking the dishes on the kitchen counter.

Their mom rushed to the back deck. From their elevated location, they could see parts of the city. "Oh my! Oh no," she gasped, her voice barely audible over the noise.

Maddie joined her. In the distance, a plume of black smoke rose from the north. Even from this far away, they could see the orange glow of flames.

"What was it?" Maddie asked, her voice barely a whisper. "Was it Sinclair? The oil refinery?"

"My ears are ringing," Jackson said, his voice trembling.

Maddie tore her eyes away from the unfolding disaster and looked at her mom, seeking reassurance. In the distance, sirens began to wail, signaling the arrival of emergency responders.

"Will they be able to get the fire out?" Jackson asked.

Her mom shook her head. "I don't know. They have emergency procedures for trouble at the refinery, but this is— "

"Big," Maddie interrupted. "It looks like everything is gone. Or will be soon."

The Sinclair Refinery was the last refinery still operating in Casper. Maddie remembered her dad talking about how important the oil and gas industry was in Wyoming—how it even funded the schools. The refinery produced gasoline and diesel, and now it was gone. That explosion could mess up everything. Even though gas stations were closed, they'd need to refill eventually. Now, who knew if that would even be possible?

Her mom nodded, her face ashen. "I think you're right. This . . . this is big, kids. Much bigger than Mrs. Weber or the terrible event at Albertsons."

As they watched, additional explosions erupted. The fire was spreading beyond the refinery, threatening the surrounding area.

"Will it come this way?" Jackson asked. "The fire, I mean."

Their mom paused longer than Maddie thought she should, before finally shaking her head. "I don't think so. The wind doesn't usually blow in this direction. But there's a neighborhood not far from there. I'm . . . they . . ." She sighed. "It could be bad."

"How bad?"

She shrugged. "Several years ago, there was a fire that originated at the landfill. It burned many miles and destroyed over a dozen homes. Miraculously, there weren't any deaths. I only hope we can say the same after this."

"Will it burn to the river?" Maddie motioned toward the North Platte River, which was farther north of the refinery.

"Maybe?"

"This has to be the Star Brights," Jackson said, his voice trembling. "Right? Normal people wouldn't do this."

"I don't know. It could be intentional. Or, perhaps, it was an accident of some sort. Either way, we're safe."

Maddie's phone pinged—an email from her dad. She skimmed it before reading it aloud:

I know about the martial law and just saw the news about another explosion in Casper. They said it was the refinery. Are you all okay? Stay inside, away from windows. Board up ground-floor windows if you can.

Keep weapons handy—baseball bats, kitchen knives, anything. I wish you had something with some firepower, but I know that isn't something you keep in your home. Don't trust anyone outside our family. I'm trying to find a way to get to you.

Stay strong. I love you all.

"Okay, here's what we're going to do." Her mom's voice was determined and strong. "Jackson, you and I are going to gather anything we can use to board up the windows. Maddie, keep monitoring the news and messages, and watch the fire. We'll take shifts keeping an eye on it. Like I said, the wind isn't coming in this direction, but I want to keep an eye on things anyway. Understood?"

Maddie and Jackson nodded, both scared but grateful for their mom's sudden show of strength and leadership.

As her mom and brother headed to the shed in the backyard to gather materials, Maddie sat down on the deck chair and turned back to her phone. She kept refreshing her email and social media feeds while watching the fire, which was burning uncomfortably close.

Despite knowing her mom was right about the direction of the wind, the sight and sound of the blaze were unsettling. The internet was abuzz with panicked posts and conflicting information, with videos of the explosions and wild theories about their causes already circulating.

She was checking Chum Fun when a post from the neighborhood group caught her eye—it was from their next-door neighbor Tom:

Maddie wasn't sure if having the neighborhood watch meeting was a good idea, but since they had to stay, she figured they should probably do all they could. Of course, they still didn't know who they could trust and who they couldn't. Hopefully, the government truly was working to find a vaccine that would stop this mess.

She watched as her mom and brother struggled with a full-size sheet of plywood. As they worked, Maddie's mind raced with questions. *How long will this last? Will we run out of food? What if someone in our family gets sick or hurt?* The uncertainties piled up, threatening to overwhelm her.

"Maddie," her mom called, snapping her out of her spiraling thoughts. "Can you help me with this board?"

Grateful for the distraction, Maddie went down the stairs off the deck to assist her mother. As they worked together, she felt a small wave of hope. They were still here, still fighting. That had to count for something.

"Thanks. It was awkward to carry, especially with the wind picking up."

"That's going to make things bad for the fire." Jackson shook his head. "Should we nail this one up and then go back for more?"

"Let's bring out all the plywood—I think there are two or three more sheets—and the boards into the garage. We'll get everything we need staged and ready, then we'll start with the hammering. We won't have enough to do all the windows. We'll start with the ones facing the street."

"There was a message on Chum Fun from Tom." Maddie pointed in the direction of the neighbor's house.

"He said the meeting is on for this afternoon. It'll be held on his front lawn."

"I suppose it's best to go. I still worry about the others, but . . . Let's keep working."

By midafternoon, they had managed to secure the ground-floor windows facing the street. The house felt darker, more confined, but also safer. They gathered in the living room, exhausted but relieved to have accomplished something concrete.

"What now?" Jackson asked, voicing the question on all their minds.

Her mom ran a hand through her hair. "Now, we wait. We stay vigilant, we stay together, and we pray for the best."

Maddie raised an eyebrow. *Pray?* Her mom rarely mentioned praying or God. While the rest of the family attended church regularly, she never did, not even on Christmas or Easter.

Maddie's phone pinged again—another message, this time from Grandma Bea:

"I'm so worried about you all. Things are bad here, too, but at least we're somewhat isolated on the ship. Tomorrow they'll start moving us to a hotel on land. I'm sure it'll be fine. I've been keeping up on the news. The declaration of martial law in Wyoming is not only concerning but also shocking. So far, Alaska has not made that announcement. I'm going to do all I can to get back to the lower forty-eight and make my way home to you. Stay inside, stay together. Trust your instincts. Keep praying. I love you all so much."

Reading the message aloud, tears pricked Maddie's eyes. The thought of Grandma Bea, stuck far away, yet still worrying about them, made the situation feel even more dire.

Chapter 21

The afternoon sun beat down on Tom's front lawn as neighbors gathered for the community meeting. The smell of smoke from the out-of-control refinery fire filled the air, making everyone uneasy and turning Maddie's stomach.

Jackson kept complaining about a headache, and her mom had already smoked through her daily ration of cigarettes since they'd finished boarding up the windows.

They stood at the edge of the gathering, not just to avoid crowding but to keep her mom's smoke—from yet another cigarette—from bothering the others. Maddie glanced around and saw several other people also lighting up, clearly trying to cope with the stress.

She squinted against the bright sunlight, thinking about how summer used to mean freedom and fun. She wanted nothing more than to go to McKenzie Lake or, even better, Alcova Reservoir, to feel the cool water against her paddleboard and the breeze in her hair.

With a sigh, she shook off those desires and paid attention to the growing crowd, her eyes nervously scanning the faces around her.

Tom's usually neat lawn was now scattered with folding chairs and picnic blankets, creating a strangely normal yet uncomfortable scene. People had brought these items to make the situation more bearable, but they looked far from relaxed. The chairs and blankets were arranged with gaps between them, adding to the sense of separation and unease.

Maddie looked around and noticed the mix of people. A well-dressed older couple sat near the center, their designer clothes clashing with the tense atmosphere.

On the edge of the group, a young family huddled close, the parents' flashy Rolex watches catching the sun as they held their perfectly dressed twins.

She even spotted a local surgeon, known for advertising on billboards along the highway, who gave her a nod as he caught her gaze.

Seeing all the signs of wealth around her made Maddie feel uneasy. It was a reminder of how different things were now compared to before, when it was just her and Jackson trying to get by with a mom who was often drunk.

She remembered when Grandma Bea came in and changed everything. After becoming widowed and moving to Arizona, Bea had insisted that her daughter, Heather, had to manage on her own.

Even though Heather had inherited money from Grandpa Hank, it came with a lot of rules, and the monthly allowance didn't cover their needs after she started drinking.

Hank and Bea Logan both knew of their daughter's wild ways. They'd hoped marrying Brian Reynolds would settle her down, but it didn't.

They didn't know then about her bipolar disorder, and Maddie was sure her grandma didn't know just how bad the drinking was. Grandma Bea had assured her many times she never would have left had she known. She truly just thought they'd spoiled their only child and she needed tough love.

Heather, Jackson, and Maddie were living in a disgusting apartment when Heather disappeared and was arrested. Social services showed up and put Maddie and

Jackson in a foster home until Grandma Bea could get to Casper.

Everything happened fast after that. She found this house and bought it the same day. They were moved in within a week. She hired someone to pack up her life in Arizona, and she sold her home.

"We need a fresh start," Grandma Bea had said, her eyes twinkling with a mixture of sadness and determination. "Everything will be fine, you'll see."

It was several months before her mom was released from jail and treatment. The bipolar diagnosis happened during that time, and the meds, as long as she stayed on them, seemed to work.

Heather had been raised in luxury, but her children hadn't. They'd grown up living month to month and hand to mouth, eviction notices being a common occurrence.

Maddie recalled Jackson's shocked expression when they'd first driven down these tree-lined streets, past manicured lawns and sprawling mini-mansions— McMansions, as they were often referred to.

Even now, six years later, Maddie sometimes felt out of place among their wealthy neighbors. But as she observed the anxious expressions around her, she understood that money mattered less in the face of the current crisis. Regardless of their wealth, anyone could suddenly start humming or singing. Who knew what might happen next?

As her mom finished her cigarette, she motioned to a spot closer to Tom's house. They started to move when a booming voice cut through the murmur of conversation. "All right, folks, let's get this show on the road!"

Maddie turned to see a tall, broad-shouldered man striding to the center of the gathering. "I'm Elliot Blackwell," he announced, his voice carrying across the lawn. "And it's clear we need to get organized if we're going to survive this mess."

Tom stepped forward and raised his hands for silence. "Thanks, Elliot. I was just about to get us started— "

"No time for pleasantries, Tom," Elliot cut him off. "We need action, not chitchat."

Maddie's mom stiffened beside her; she could almost see her mom's internal struggle as she bit back a retort.

Elliot's gaze swept over the crowd, then landed on Maddie and her family. His eyes narrowed. "We need able-bodied men for patrols. Women and children should stay indoors."

Maddie's mom stepped forward, her chin lifted defiantly. "Excuse me, but— "

"Ma'am," Elliot interrupted, his tone patronizing, "I understand you want to help, but without a man in the house, you'd be better off focusing on your kids."

A ripple of discomfort went through the crowd. Maddie's face flushed with anger, but before she could speak, Tom interjected, "Actually, Elliot, Heather here is a nurse. Her skills could be invaluable."

Her mom opened her mouth, likely to correct Tom's assumption. While she was a nurse, sort of, as a certified nursing assistant, her duties mainly consisted of scrubbing bedpans and changing linens. Oh sure, she'd tried to tell Maddie about all the other things she did to help people, but Maddie knew she wasn't a real nurse.

Elliot spoke first before his presumption could be corrected. "A nurse, you say?" His eyebrows rose, and a hint of respect crept into his voice. "Well, that changes things. We'll need medical support."

Her mom closed her mouth and shot a grateful look at Tom.

Maddie shook her head. She hated deception. She shouldn't be surprised, though; her mom was a master at lying and manipulating. She'd do whatever she felt was needed to paint herself in a better light.

Maybe she'd never even told Tom how limited her skills truly were. After all, she'd pretended like she knew how to help Mrs. Weber after she was hit by the truck.

"Tom's got EMT training too," someone called out. "He used to work as one before he got into computers."

Elliot nodded approvingly. "Good, good. Heather and Tom, you'll oversee all things medical. Set up a station in one of your homes."

As Elliot continued outlining his plans, Maddie observed the reactions around her. Some nodded along eagerly, while others looked skeptical. One couple whispered to each other, worry lined their faces.

Martial law, and whether the governor could really do such a thing, was a hot part of the conversation. Elliot was in favor of the move, insisting it would make them safer overall.

Tom, who had heard from his brother moments before the declaration had been released, said it was an overstep on the part of the governor. The new rash of explosions included not only the refinery in Casper and another one along Interstate 80, but also the Capitol Building in Cheyenne. The governor was scared, plain and simple.

"Doesn't matter," Elliot declared. "It is what it is. Now we deal with it. We'll need round-the-clock surveillance. Window watchers and street patrols. That'll help increase our security."

A man raised his hand. "Isn't it dangerous to be out on the streets? With the Star Brights— "

"That's why we pair up," Elliot interrupted. "Known neighbors or family only. No strangers walking together."

A murmur of agreement rippled through the crowd, but Maddie couldn't shake her unease. She leaned closer to her mom and whispered, "But anyone can be a Star Bright, right? Even family members?"

Her mom nodded subtly, her eyes never leaving Elliot. "We'll discuss it later," she murmured back.

As Elliot began assigning roles and schedules, the neighbors formed into groups. Even the children seemed to sense the gravity of the situation; the earlier chatter was now gone.

Tom approached her family, his face apologetic. "Sorry about the nurse thing," he said quietly to her mom. "I didn't mean to volunteer you. I just hated the way he was acting. Of course, you are valuable. You don't need a man in your house to contribute."

"It's fine," her mom said, her voice tight. "I want to help."

Maddie marveled at her mother's composure. The old Heather might have lashed out or retreated into herself. This new, determined version of her mom was both reassuring and slightly unsettling.

As the meeting wound down, Elliot's voice boomed out once more. "Remember, people, trust your neighbors but verify. We can't be too careful."

The crowd began to disperse, an air of nervous energy permeating the gathering. Maddie overheard snippets of conversation as they made their way home:

". . . what if the food runs out?"

". . . what if the fire spreads?"

". . . should we board up the windows?" One man pointed to Maddie's house.

A woman replied with a look of disgust. "Dear Lord, no. I'm not going to live like a mole."

Back at their house, her mom sank onto the couch, exhaustion clear on her face. "Well, that was . . . something."

Jackson flopped down next to her. "Are we really going to do all that stuff? Patrols and everything?"

"I don't know. It seems like the best option we have right now. That man—Elliot—put us on the schedule for the day after tomorrow. We're to walk the streets together."

"I like the idea of closing off the street," Jackson added. "Since we live on a loop, they can put a car on either end to help keep other cars out. Of course, if there's no gas, I guess people won't really be driving around, right?"

"Right. Probably not."

Maddie perched on the arm of the couch. "But, Mom, what about what happened with Mrs. Weber? Anyone could be a Star Bright, even people we know."

They all knew the truth of Maddie's words, but acknowledging it meant facing a level of paranoia none of them were ready for.

Finally, her mom spoke, her voice soft but firm. "We'll be careful. We'll watch out for each other. But we can't live in complete isolation. We have to trust someone."

Maddie nodded, not entirely convinced but understanding the necessity. As the evening wore on, they found themselves falling into a new routine. Jackson took the first watch at the window, while Maddie and her mom prepared a simple dinner.

The distant glow of the refinery fire painted the sky in oranges and reds as night fell. It would be beautiful if it wasn't so deadly. Maddie couldn't shake the feeling that their world had shrunk to this house, this street, this fragile community they were trying to protect.

As she lay in bed that night, unable to sleep, her mind whirled with questions. *How long can we keep this up? What if the Star Brights infiltrate our neighborhood? What if one of them turns?*

She thought of her dad, sure that he would find a way to reach them; of Grandma Bea, stranded in Alaska, but also determined to return home to Wyoming; and of all the people out there facing the same fears and uncertainties.

In the quiet darkness of her room, she made a silent vow. She would stay strong, stay vigilant. For her family, for their neighbors, for the hope that somehow, someday, this nightmare would end.

But as she finally drifted off to sleep, a small voice in the back of her mind whispered a chilling thought. *What if this is just the beginning?*

Chapter 22

As Maddie sat up and rubbed the sleep from her eyes, she was surprised to hear movement in the kitchen. She glanced at the clock—6:30 a.m. Her eyebrows shot up. Once again, her mom was up early.

It had been three days since the refinery explosion and neighborhood meeting, and their new reality was slowly sinking in. The fires were still burning, having spread and caused widespread destruction and loss of life, driven by strong winds. The smoke and haze were almost unbearable.

Last night, Jackson asked if they could go to church today. He was certain there'd be a special service because of everything going on. Their mom had quickly said no, but Jackson had persisted, making Maddie consider agreeing.

However, after checking the Chum Fun page, she found out that, due to martial law, church services were canceled. Instead, families were encouraged to study and pray together.

Jackson thought that was a good idea, but their mom had dismissed it, saying, "We have a busy day tomorrow."

Padding quietly into the kitchen, Maddie found her mom at the stove, stirring a pot of oatmeal. The smell of coffee filled the air, a luxury they were rationing carefully. They'd managed to buy a few canisters on their disastrous shopping day, but it was an off brand. "Better than nothing," her mom had said, sounding less than convinced.

"Morning." Her mom gave her a tired smile. "Sleep okay?"

She shrugged, still wary of this new, responsible version of her mother. "As well as can be expected, I guess. You're up early again."

Her mom nodded as she poured a cup of coffee. "Figured I'd get breakfast ready before we head to the drop site. We all need to go today, remember? We'll get food and will also be able to get gas. Two gallons. We'll take your car since we didn't have a chance to put fuel in it the other day."

Maddie nodded. The thought of the food drop site, with a good portion of Casper meeting in one location, scared her. She'd heard from her friend Sonja that the whole thing was a disorganized mess and the guards were carrying automatic weapons or something.

She didn't want to go. Didn't think any of them should. But her mom insisted they needed the food that was being doled out because what they had wouldn't last forever. Anything they could add would help.

As they ate breakfast, Jackson joined them, his hair sticking up in all directions. "Is it drop day?"

Her mom nodded and pushed a bowl of oatmeal toward him. "Eat up. We need to be there early to avoid the crowds."

As they finished their meal, Maddie couldn't help but marvel at her mother's composure. No shaky hands reaching for a cigarette, no snapping at them for trivial reasons. It was . . . unsettling, in its own way.

"Mom," Maddie ventured, "how are you doing with the . . . you know, your meds?"

"Meds are fine. I'm taking them like clockwork. The cigarettes, though . . ." Her lips tightened slightly, but her voice remained steady. "It's tough, I won't lie. I'm down to one per day. And that'll only be for three more days.

I've been wanting to quit for years. This is as good a time as any, I suppose." She didn't sound convinced.

Jackson piped up, "Yeah, and you haven't even been sneaking cookies!"

A ghost of a smile crossed their mother's face. "Well, we need to make those last. Can't have your old mom eating them all, can we?"

As they prepared to leave for the drop site, Maddie caught her mother's eye and saw a flash of . . . something. Guilt? Regret? It was gone before she could be sure.

As they drove through the neighborhood, she saw how different everything had become. Many houses were boarded up, their darkened windows making them look like her own gloomy home. Living like moles seemed to appeal to many, maybe helping to control the residents' fear and uncertainty.

At the community barricade, a guard waved them to stop while his partner moved the roadblock car. "How long do you think you'll be gone, Heather?" he asked.

"No idea. It's our first time going to the food drop. Have you gone before?"

"Not yet. Tomorrow. But it could take a while. I heard yesterday it took the Smyths six hours to get their piddly amount of food and two gallons of gas. Your info is on the clipboard." He pointed to the board in his hand. "The next shift will know to let you back inside."

"Okay. Thanks." She nodded as he waved them through.

The streets were quiet, save for the occasional military vehicle rumbling by, its presence both reassuring and unsettling. A few stray pieces of litter blew across the road, carried by the ever-present wind. Maddie spotted a family huddled on their porch, their eyes following the military convoy with a mixture of hope and dread.

Her eyes were drawn to an old man hammering nails into his boarded-up window. Nearby, a group of kids played quietly in a fenced yard, their laughter hushed and cautious, as if they knew something serious was going on.

Passing by the Hilltop Shopping Center, where the once-bustling Eastside Albertsons was located, sent a ripple of sadness through her. Not only was the grocery store a burned-out shell but several cars in the lot had been affected. The buildings along the perimeter were all shuttered, and the parking lot was empty except for the abandoned vehicles.

The drop site was on the other side of town, at the fairgrounds. They were assured additional sites would be set up if needed, but for now, the one location was all they could handle.

With a population of over fifty thousand, she hated to think just how chaotic it was truly going to be. Even though the pickup was arranged based on her mom's driver's license number, she had no idea how many other people would be there at the same time. If it took the neighbors' family six hours yesterday, she suspected they should be prepared for something similar.

What about people who, for some reason or another, were on foot? It could take hours just to reach the fairgrounds. They definitely needed a better system and more locations throughout the small city.

The drive continued, each turn revealing more signs of a community bracing itself against an unseen threat. The tension in their car mirrored the uneasy calm outside, and a shared sense of foreboding settled over them.

As they approached the fairgrounds, her heart rate picked up. Armed guards stood at attention, their faces impassive behind dark sunglasses. Long lines of people snaked through makeshift barriers, each person clutching their identification cards.

"Remember," her mom said, "we each need to get our own bag. Stay close to me. And for heaven's sake, don't make eye contact with the guards."

They joined the line, the morning sun beating down on them as they slowly moved forward. Sweat trickled down Maddie's back, and it wasn't just from the heat. She was nervous and uncomfortable.

Nearby, a man's voice rose sharply, cutting through the quiet. His wife tried to calm him, her tone tight and urgent, while their baby's cries added to the chaotic scene. A little red-haired girl clung to her teddy bear, her wide eyes darting nervously between her father and the anxious crowd.

The man's desperate cries underscored the grim reality they all faced. Guards quickly surrounded the man and his family, and they were led away. The man's cries gradually faded. Maddie noticed that no one reacted or talked about what had just happened, as if the family had vanished from everyone's concern. As if they never existed in the first place.

"Next!" a guard barked, and she realized it was their turn. With shaking hands, her mom presented her driver's license. "I'm Heather Reynolds. This is my daughter Maddie and my son Jackson."

The guard scrutinized the ID with a curt nod, his eyes briefly flicking over Maddie and Jackson before gesturing them forward.

As they stepped toward the tables manned by armed guards, she couldn't shake the image of the distraught family being led away, the echoes of the man's desperate cries still lingering in her ears.

"You'll start here," the woman in uniform said, gesturing toward a table with cheap plastic grocery bags. "Bring empty bags with you next time. The throwaway kind, just like these. One sack per person, only."

Her mom nodded as she took the three bags she was handed. They'd been cautioned when they arrived in the parking lot not to take purses or anything with them. They'd even been patted down when they came into the distribution center.

The woman directed them to the next table, where the guard instructed them to each take three cans of vegetables. Maddie tried to select items they might like, but he hurried her along, saying, "Now! Move to the next table."

At the second table, they could pick two cans of fruit each. The third table held rice, beans, and flour, with a limit of one item per person. She noticed her mom grabbed beans, so she grabbed rice. Jackson hesitated before grabbing flour.

At the final table, they could grab five items from an assortment of boxes and cans. It was a grab-and-go situation with no time for choosing.

As they passed the tables, a woman handed them each an apple and directed them to the next person with fresh vegetables. Maddie quickly grabbed what she could identify as a cucumber or zucchini. The last station had a person in vinyl gloves who handed them two slices of bread from an open loaf.

With the food allocation complete, they were ushered out of the distribution area and directed to return to their car. They regrouped at the edge of the parking lot, each clutching their bags.

Her mom's face was grim, and her eyes filled with tears. "That was hardly worth the trip all the way over here. I don't— " She shook her head. "Okay. We know for next time."

"Maybe they'll have more things for us next time?" Jackson offered. "They're new at getting this organized, right?"

"Sure. Maybe. Let's get our gas and then get home." Her eyes darted around nervously. "This place feels like a powder keg."

There were nine gas stations open. The one they were to use was again assigned by her mom's driver's license number, based on the last digit. The line of cars snaked out into the road. "Well, at least it should go fast since we're only allowed two gallons."

Her mom's prediction wasn't accurate. It was two more hours before they were finally on their way home. Even though the guards at the roadblock had changed, getting back inside the semi-secured community was easy, due in part to Tom now being at the roadblock. He smiled and waved, seeming genuinely happy to see them.

Maddie noticed her mom subtly adjusting her hair and straightening her posture as they approached. She greeted Tom with a nervous smile, her voice slightly shaky as she exchanged pleasantries.

It was clear to Maddie that her mom was both flustered and trying hard to appear composed in front of him.

"Good to see you," Tom said as he leaned against the door frame. "How was it?"

"Overwhelming. They're going to need to figure something else out soon."

"They will. My brother says this is just to get people what they need quickly. They're already working on changes. In a few days, there will be multiple drop centers. They'll use both Walmart stores and both high schools, plus the old Parkway Plaza Hotel and a few other places. It'll be better. You'll see."

"Your brother sure has a lot of information. What'd you say he does?"

Tom shook his head. "That's not important."

"Well, maybe you can tell him something needs to be done about the gas lines. That was as bad, maybe worse, than the food."

He scrunched lower. With his voice barely above a whisper, he said, "I don't think we're going to need to worry about that. One of the reasons for the extra drop sites is so people can walk."

Her mom's expression shifted, her brow furrowing with concern. "No more fuel?" she asked, her voice betraying a mix of disbelief and worry.

Maddie and Jackson exchanged uneasy glances, the realization sinking in that their already challenging situation was about to become even more difficult without reliable transportation. It did make sense, though, that under martial law, they weren't allowed to travel outside the city of Casper. Why bother with gas?

"I'll see you later," Tom said, stepping back from the car. "Maybe tomorrow?"

Her mom smiled and dipped her chin. "I'd like that."

Once home, they spread the contents of their bags on the kitchen table. "Well, it's better than nothing," her mom said. "Plus, we still have plenty of food from our own shopping trips."

They had discussed whether they should even go to the drop site, considering they did have food in the house. In the end, they decided not going could raise questions among the neighbors about just how much food they had.

Even though they lived in an affluent neighborhood, there'd been plenty of talk at the neighborhood meeting about how low some people were on food. Were they truly low? Or were they putting up appearances like her family was?

"Let's have supper. I know it's early, but we missed lunch. And cookies. We're eating cookies tonight."

After a simple dinner of canned baked beans from their pantry stash, and canned carrots received in the day's allotment, they were sitting in the family room watching television and eating cookies. "So," Jackson said, licking crumbs from his fingers, "what's the plan now?"

His mom sighed and ran a hand through her hair. "We keep going. We stay vigilant. We help our neighbors where we can. And we hope . . . we hope this all ends soon."

"From what Tom said, it doesn't sound like it's going to end anytime soon. They don't even know what's causing it yet. How can they stop it if they don't know?"

Maddie nodded in agreement. She couldn't shake the feeling that this was far from over.

Later that evening, as they watched television, with the distant glow of the still-burning refinery fire visible in the windows overlooking the deck, her mom broke the silence.

"I know this is hard. And I know I haven't always been . . . well, I haven't always been the mom you kids deserve. But I want you to know, I'm trying. I'm really trying."

A lump formed in Maddie's throat. She wanted to believe her mother, wanted to trust that this change was permanent. But years of disappointment had taught her to be cautious.

Jackson looked like he wanted to touch their mom. To hug her. Instead, he gave a nod. "We're all trying."

Maddie felt a tiny spark of hope. They just might get through this. As a family.

Chapter 23

The mid-June sun beat down on the Reynolds's backyard, its warmth a stark contrast to the tension that had gripped their lives for the past few weeks.

Maddie stood at the kitchen window, her gaze wandering over the empty raised garden beds. Normally, by this time of year, they'd be bursting with life—tomatoes stretching toward the sky, cucumbers sprawling across the rich soil, and peppers adding splashes of color.

But this year was different. Grandma Bea's extended summer vacation had meant no garden, the beds lying fallow for the first time in years. As Maddie stared at the bare earth, an idea began to take shape in her mind.

"Hey, Mom? What do you think about starting a garden?"

Her mother looked up from the book she was reading, surprise etched on her face. "A garden? Isn't it a bit late for that?"

She shrugged, feeling a spark of excitement for the first time in days. "Maybe for some things, but we could still grow quite a bit. And it would give us fresh food to supplement the drop supplies. We don't get snow until . . . what? September or October?"

"It's not just snow that's a concern. Frost will kill a garden."

"Okay, but we could try. Grandma has a nice stash of seeds, and she always buys things that are fast growers, specifically for the frost."

She watched as her mother considered the idea, noticing how different she looked from just a few weeks ago. The constant tension in her shoulders had eased somewhat, and while she still looked tired, there was a steadiness to her that Maddie didn't remember ever seeing before.

"You know," her mom said slowly, a smile spreading across her face, "that's not a bad idea at all. It is late, but not terrible for some things. We can't do anything that needs to be started from seedlings. Not tomatoes. They'd take much too long. But we could grow stuff directly in the ground from seed. Zucchini, maybe. Cucumbers. It'll give us something to do besides watching movies and playing video games all day. Or fretting over the news channels."

Maddie grinned, her mother's enthusiasm infectious. "I can be in charge of it. I helped Grandma enough times to know what I'm doing."

"All right, then." Her mom nodded and set her book aside. "Let's see what seeds we have."

As they rummaged through the garage, looking for Grandma Bea's gardening supplies, Maddie felt a warmth in her chest that had nothing to do with the summer heat. For the first time since this whole nightmare began, she was starting to relax around her mother.

They found a dusty box filled with seed packets, some dating back several years. "I hope these are still good," Maddie mused as she sorted through them. "We've got peppers, squash, and even some flowers."

"I don't think the peppers will work. Those are best started inside and transplanted. What about that fast-growing lettuce your grandma always plants?"

Maddie rifled through the packets, her face lighting up. "Got it! And here's some spinach too. These will be perfect for quick harvests."

"Here's some radishes. They're fast growers."

As they spread the seed packets across the kitchen table, making plans and sketching out the garden layout, Jackson wandered in, his VR headset dangling from one hand.

"What's all this?" He eyed the colorful packets.

"We're starting a garden," Maddie explained, unable to keep the excitement from her voice. "Want to help?"

Jackson hesitated and glanced at his headset. "Maybe later. I promised Eddie I'd meet him in the game."

Her mom looked up. "You've been spending an awful lot of time in that game. Maybe it'd be good to take a break?"

"But it's the only way I can really talk to Eddie," Jackson protested, his irritation evident. "And things are even weirder in Oregon than they are here."

Maddie leaned toward him. "What do you mean? What's happening there?"

Jackson plopped down in a chair, his game momentarily forgotten. "Eddie says it's really bad. Only Uncle Rich goes out for food, and since he's alone and can't get food for anyone else unless they go with him, they don't get enough. Uncle Rich says it's too dangerous for the others to leave the neighborhood. They're super careful now. Something terrible happened."

Their mom's expression tightened. "What happened?"

Jackson shrugged. "Eddie won't tell me. He said it's too bad to talk about."

Silence fell over the kitchen as they absorbed that information. A chill ran down Maddie's spine, despite the warm day. She'd known things were bad elsewhere, but hearing about family members struggling brought it all into sharp focus. "But why are things so bad there? Astoria isn't that big of a place. It's smaller than Casper, even." She glanced at her mom. "Right?"

Her mom nodded. "Somewhere around ten thousand people. But Oregon has a much larger population than Wyoming. Four million or so compared to our six hundred thousand. And it's a hot spot for visitors over the summer, just like Cody is. That might be part of the problem."

Jackson bobbed his head. "Eddie said people left Portland when they could. Some of them went to Astoria and other beach towns. Others went to the mountain range between Portland and the ocean. I can't remember what it's called. I guess they thought that'd be better than staying in the city."

"I'm sure." Her mom reached out and squeezed Jackson's shoulder. "I'm glad you can stay in touch with Eddie. Just try to spend some time in the real world, too, okay? Maybe you can help us plant some seeds later?"

A small smile tugged at Jackson's lips. "Yeah, okay. But Eddie really does need me. He's scared. He tries to pretend he's not, but I know he is. At least Uncle Rich was able to pick up Alyson from Portland before everything happened. Eddie mentioned how happy his mom is about that."

"I can't imagine how upset I'd be if you both weren't here. Having your grandma gone is hard enough."

As Jackson headed to the family room, Maddie and her mom returned to their garden planning. They spent the next hour sorting seeds, checking germination times, and making lists of supplies they'd need.

"We'll have to be creative with some of this," her mom mused, tapping a pencil against her chin. "Be smart about what we plant."

Maddie nodded, her mind already racing with ideas. "Could we start seeds inside? Maybe grow them even after the cold and snow? We have the windows. We could use egg cartons and then transplant them into empty plastic containers as they grow. Would that work?"

"I'm not sure. Let's start with the outside stuff, then we can talk about other things."

As they worked, Maddie found herself studying her mother. The woman bent over the garden plans, focus sharpening her features, was a far cry from the distant, often irritable mother she'd known for so long. This mom was present, engaged, and . . . sober.

"Hey, Mom?" Maddie said softly, causing her mother to look up. "How are you doing? You know, with . . . everything?"

Her mother's face softened, understanding the weight behind the simple question. "It's . . . it's not easy," she admitted. "I miss my cigarettes something fierce. I found that half a pack I'd shoved in your grandma's glove box. They're old and stale, but . . ." She shrugged. "I'm savoring them. And there are moments when I'd give anything for a drink." She took a deep breath. "But I'm trying, Maddie. Really trying."

She covered her mother's hand with her own. "I know, Mom. I can see it." She hesitated, dreading the other thing she wanted to ask. In a rush, her words tumbled out. "How about your meds? Are you okay on them?"

Her mom bit her upper lip and gave a slow nod. "For now. I'd just received a new supply a few days before everything happened. Your grandma made sure I ordered them before she left. I'll be good for about three months. Then . . ." She sighed. "Then we'll figure it out. There are things I can do that will help. Gardening is something that will probably be good."

They shared a smile, the moment fragile but full of promise. Then her mom cleared her throat and turned back to the plans. "So, where should we put the beets?"

The rest of the day passed in a flurry of activity. They cleared the raised beds, turning the soil and removing weeds that were growing wild. Jackson joined them, his hands soon covered in dirt as he helped plant rows of lettuce and spinach seeds.

As the sun began to set, they stood back and admired their work. The beds were no longer bare, promise hidden beneath the dark soil. It would take time, but soon they'd have the beginnings of their own food supply.

"Not bad for a day's work." Her mom wiped the sweat from her brow. "What do you say we clean up and watch a movie? I think we've earned a night off."

Later, as they settled in front of the TV, Maddie found herself sandwiched between her mother and brother. On screen, an old comedy played out, the familiar jokes a welcome distraction from the world outside their walls.

Maddie glanced at her mom, noticing how her fingers twitched occasionally, likely missing the familiar feel of a cigarette. But she didn't complain, didn't snap at them. Instead, she laughed along with the movie, her arm draped casually over Maddie's shoulders.

It wasn't perfect. The tensions of the outside world still pressed in on them. The uncertainty of tomorrow still loomed. But at that moment, she allowed herself to hope. Hope that her mother's changes were real and lasting. Hope that their little garden would flourish. Hope that, somehow, they'd make it through this nightmare together.

As the movie ended and they prepared for bed, she paused at the window, looking out at their backyard. In the fading light, she could just make out the outline of the garden beds. Somewhere out there, seeds were nestled in the warm earth, ready to sprout and grow.

It was a small thing, starting a garden. A tiny act of defiance against the chaos that had engulfed their world. But as Maddie climbed into bed, she felt a sense of peace she hadn't experienced in weeks.

Tomorrow would bring new challenges, she knew that. The food drops would continue, each one a reminder of how precarious their situation was. The threat of the Star Brights still lurked, an unseen danger that could strike at any moment. And beyond their neighborhood, the world continued to struggle, with places like Oregon facing dangers they could only imagine.

As she drifted off to sleep, she found herself looking forward to tomorrow for the first time in ages. There were seeds to water, plans to make, and a family to hold together. And for now, that was enough.

Chapter 24

The morning sun barely showed itself as Maddie, Jackson, and their mom headed to Kelly Walsh High School. Maddie's school now served as a food distribution site, a stark reminder of how much things had changed.

They'd picked up supplies here last week, but back then they could drive and get another two-gallon fill-up. Now, as Tom had warned, gas was even more restricted. They wouldn't be able to get any until July 10, and it was only June 25. Her mom insisted they needed to conserve their gas in case of an emergency. Driving was no longer an option.

The walk to the school felt longer than ever, each step a reminder of how much their world had shrunk. Maddie's legs ached, unused to the extended trek. She noticed her mom's labored breathing and Jackson's sluggish pace, signs that their sedentary lifestyle of the past weeks was taking its toll.

As they approached the familiar building, Maddie felt a pang of nostalgia. She recalled walking these halls with her friends, laughing and gossiping between classes, the excitement of football games and school dances. Now the laughter was replaced by the murmur of anxious voices, and the school grounds were filled with rows of people waiting for supplies.

Jackson kicked a pebble along the sidewalk, his usual chatter replaced with a somber silence. She glanced at him, knowing he must be missing his friends and the sense of normalcy they once took for granted.

She had hoped some of her friends would be there, picking up their own supplies. But none she reached out to were scheduled. They had discussed the possibility of getting together. Even though gatherings weren't allowed, she'd heard they were happening. The soldiers were mainly focused on the interstate and highways, ensuring people weren't entering or leaving Casper.

There'd been a small party at Morad Dog Park, on the west side of town, just last night. Maddie found out about it too late to attend. Not that attending would be easy. Her mom watched them like a hawk. Going anywhere would be next to impossible. At least the guards knew her car now, so if she could slip by her mom, she'd be fine getting in and out of the neighborhood. Of course, using the precious gas would also be an issue.

Her mind wandered to potential routes, cataloging side streets and less-monitored areas. The thought of rebellion, of reclaiming even a small piece of her former life, was intoxicating. Yet, the memory of recent violence kept her rooted in place, the fear of consequences outweighing her desire for freedom.

Their mom walked ahead, her steps purposeful but her shoulders tense. Maddie could see the strain etched in the lines of her face. She was truly surprised her mom was doing such a good job of holding things together.

She was out of cigarettes now and insisted she didn't really miss them. "I feel good," she'd assured Maddie while they worked in the garden. Even so, she was much more irritable than she'd been only a few days ago, regularly snapping at both Maddie and Jackson.

Maddie wasn't sure if it was the lack of cigarettes or constantly being around each other, but whatever it was, she didn't like it.

Tomorrow would be exactly three weeks since the explosion that took out the building where her mom worked. The entire world had been in a downward spiral since then, with no end in sight. There'd been zero headway made on the source or treatment of the virus causing people to hurt others.

The only good thing was that there did seem to be fewer reports of the terrorist-style events, and there'd been no domestic disturbances in their immediate community. Nothing, in fact, since the Webers.

Last night, Maddie's family had roving patrol in the neighborhood. Her mom had been so on edge. She'd gotten after Jackson for not walking softly enough.

She'd hissed at Maddie when she accidentally kicked a can, the noise echoing through the quiet streets. "Are you trying to cause trouble for us?" she had snapped, her voice a harsh whisper.

Maddie had felt a hot flush of embarrassment and anger but held her tongue, knowing that arguing would only make things worse.

The memory of last night's patrol lingered and left a sour taste in Maddie's mouth. She watched her mom now, noting the twitching of her fingers and the darting of her eyes. The facade of control was cracking, revealing the frightened, addicted woman beneath. Maddie felt a mixture of pity and resentment, wondering how long this fragile peace would last.

A few hours away from her mom and her brother would do her good. Seeing her friends would be wonderful. Even if her mom wouldn't let her go, sneaking out would be worth it.

They joined the line, the crowd a mix of familiar faces and strangers. Maddie scanned the area, her eyes lingering on the building where she had spent countless hours studying and daydreaming about the future. So much for that. Now she wondered what kind of future she'd even have. What kind would Jackson have?

"Maddie, stay close." Her mom glanced back with both concern and determination.

Maddie nodded, her heart already racing. The crowd grew denser as they neared the school, a sea of anxious faces and tense bodies. Nervous energy crackled in the air, broken only by the sharp commands of the armed guards.

They joined the queue, shuffling forward inch by inch. Makeshift barriers funneled people toward the distribution point, while guards in full tactical gear stood at regular intervals, their faces emotionless behind dark visors.

"Look." Jackson nodded toward a familiar figure ahead. "It's Mr. Blackwell."

Elliot Blackwell from their neighborhood stood a dozen feet ahead, his broad shoulders tense, his eyes scanning the crowd. He caught sight of them and gave a curt nod before turning back to the front. They hadn't seen him at Kelly Walsh last week or at the fairgrounds the week before. Had he and his family not needed food before now?

Maddie studied Elliot, noting his rigid posture and vigilant gaze. Unlike many in the crowd, he seemed prepared, almost expectant. She wondered what resources he had, what knowledge he might possess that the rest of them didn't. The disparity between those who were prepared and those who weren't had never been more apparent.

As they inched closer to the distribution point, the crowd's restlessness grew. Whispers rippled through the line—rumors of dwindling supplies and of violence at other sites. Maddie felt her mom's hand on her shoulder, a gentle pressure meant to reassure her, but she could feel the tremor in her touch. And to be quite honest, even the touch was annoying.

It wasn't just the physical contact that bothered Maddie; it was the underlying tension that radiated from her mom. The worry and fear that had seeped into their lives made every small gesture feel heavy with unspoken anxiety.

Maddie knew her mom was trying to comfort her, but the constant closeness and the shared burden of their situation made it hard to find any real solace. Funny how she had longed for her mom to be exactly how she was acting now and Maddie couldn't stand it.

Maddie's attention was pulled to a commotion near the school's main entrance. A group of guards surrounded a middle-aged man who was waving his arms around and shouting, his voice cutting through the murmur of the crowd. Maddie's heart raced as she saw one of the guards reach for his weapon.

"Mom," she whispered, nodding toward the scene. "Look."

Her mom's grip on her shoulder tightened as they watched the tense standoff unfold. The man's face was red with anger or exertion, and even from their distance, Maddie could see the vein pulsing in his forehead. Was this the start of another Star Bright incident?

Just as Maddie was certain things were about to explode into violence, one of the guards stepped forward, his hands raised in a calming gesture. He spoke to the man in low, measured tones. Gradually, the man's posture relaxed, and his arms dropped to his sides.

Maddie realized she'd been holding her breath and let it out in a long, shaky exhale. The guards were now escorting the man away from the main entrance, but there was no roughness in their actions. It seemed the crisis, whatever it had been, had passed.

"False alarm," her mom murmured, but Maddie could hear the relief in her voice.

The incident served as a stark reminder of how fragile their situation was and how quickly things could turn dangerous. She scanned the crowd again, now hyperaware of every movement, every raised voice.

Out of nowhere, another disturbance erupted near the front of the line. Shouts rang out, followed by the sickening sound of flesh hitting flesh. Maddie craned her neck to see, her pulse quickening.

"What's happening?" Jackson asked, his voice tight with fear.

"Get down," their mother ordered, grabbing their hands and pulling them low.

A blood-curdling scream cut through the air. "Star Bright! The guard's a Star Bright!"

People began to push and shove, desperate to escape. Maddie was jostled and nearly lost her footing. She reached out and grabbed Jackson's sleeve, terrified of being separated.

Through the chaos, she spotted the guard. His face was twisted into a creepy smile, and his eyes were wide and unsteady. He started singing, his voice strangely calm and clear against the backdrop of the screams.

Chapter 25

The guard raised his weapon and fired indiscriminately into the crowd. The deafening cracks of gunfire sent a continued wave of panic through the masses. People scattered in all directions, trampling over each other in their desperation to escape.

"Mom!" Maddie cried out, unable to see her in the surging crowd.

"Here!" came the response, barely audible over the chaos. A hand grasped Maddie's arm, and her mom pulled her close. She tightened her grip on Jackson, forming a human chain as they struggled against the tide of fleeing people.

The singing guard advanced, his weapon spewing death with each pull of the trigger. Maddie saw people fall, their cries of pain lost in the commotion of terror. The scent of gunpowder filled the air, mixing with the metallic tang of blood.

"This way!" a gruff voice shouted. Maddie turned to see Elliot Blackwell, his face streaked with blood and sweat. He motioned toward a gap in the barriers. "Move!"

They followed him, ducking low to avoid the hail of bullets. Maddie's lungs burned as she ran, her legs trembling with each step. She could hear Jackson's ragged breathing beside her, feel her mom's iron grip on her arm.

As they neared the gap, a woman stumbled in front of them, clutching a bleeding arm. Without hesitation, Elliot scooped her up and carried her one-armed as they pushed through the opening.

They ran across the school grounds and crossed the side street, the sounds of shouting and commotion fading behind them. Thoughts tumbled through Maddie's head. *How many Star Brights are there? Are we being pursued?*

"In here," Elliot grunted as he led them behind an apartment building and toward a maintenance shed. He kicked the door open and ushered them inside before gently laying the injured woman down.

The shed was cramped and dark, smelling of oil and rust. They huddled together, chests heaving as they caught their breath. Outside, distant screams and sporadic gunfire could still be heard.

"Is everyone okay?" Her mom's voice shook as she checked Maddie and Jackson for injuries.

Maddie nodded, unable to speak. She looked at Jackson, his face pale and his eyes wide with shock. The injured woman whimpered as she clutched her bleeding arm.

After ensuring Maddie and Jackson were okay, Maddie's mom turned toward the woman and quickly assessed the wound. "We need to stop the bleeding. Maddie, find something we can use as a bandage."

Maddie frantically searched the small space, her hands brushing against rusted tools and old rags. She found a relatively clean cloth and handed it to her mom. "Will this work?"

"It'll have to," she replied, taking the cloth and pressing it firmly against the woman's wound. "It's not going to be enough. Jackson, give me your shirt."

Jackson, still in shock, stared at her for a moment as Elliot Blackwell said, "Use mine." He peeled it off and handed it over.

"Stay with me, okay?" her mom said to the injured woman, who nodded weakly as tears streamed down her face. She tied the shirt around the woman's arm, just above the wound, and twisted it tightly to slow the bleeding. "I don't want to make it too tight. If I do, you could lose your arm."

The woman whined. "It hurts."

"I know. Sorry. Maddie, help me hold her arm up."

Maddie moved to support the woman's arm, her own hands shaking. Her mom worked quickly and efficiently, her calm demeanor a stark contrast to the terror that still echoed outside.

"Keep the pressure on the wound," she instructed, looking at Maddie and Jackson with determined eyes. "We need to keep her awake and alert. Talk to her, distract her from the pain."

Maddie nodded and leaned closer to the woman. "What's your name?"

"Linda," the woman whispered, her voice barely audible.

"Linda, you're going to be okay." Maddie tried to sound reassuring, despite the fear gripping her heart. "Just keep talking to us."

Linda nodded weakly, her breathing ragged.

Maddie's mom continued to monitor the bandage, her focus unwavering despite the dire circumstances. "Looks like it's going to hold . . . for now, at least. I don't see any seepage."

Outside, the chaos continued, but in the cramped shed, a fragile sense of calm began to settle. Maddie and Jackson did their best to keep Linda engaged, while their mom kept pressure on the wound, her words soft and encouraging.

Maddie could hardly believe this pulled-together woman was the same one who, just a short while ago in the food line, was nervous and fidgety. Her mom certainly seemed to shine under pressure.

Her mom turned to Elliot. "We need to get home," she whispered. "It's not safe here."

"But how?" Jackson asked, his voice barely audible. "It sounds crazy out there."

Elliot met their gazes. "We wait," he said grimly. "Let the initial chaos die down. Then we move, fast and quiet." He turned toward Linda. "Where do you live?"

Maddie didn't recognize the street name she gave, but Elliot must have since he said, "Good. That's nearby. We'll get you home first."

"My husband. I don't know where he is."

"Was he with you in the line?"

"He was. We got . . . we were separated in the chaos."

"Well, hopefully he's at your home when we get there."

The minutes crawled by, each second punctuated by the rapid beating of Maddie's heart. The sounds outside gradually diminished, replaced by a deathly silence that was almost worse than the chaos.

Finally, Elliot stood. "It's time," he said, his voice low. "Stay close, stay quiet. If we get separated, head straight home. Don't stop for anything or anyone. I'll make sure Linda gets home. Understood?"

They nodded, fear and determination mingling in equal measure. Maddie and her mom helped the injured woman to her feet, supporting her weight.

Elliot cracked the door open and peered out. After a moment, he motioned for them to follow. They emerged into the sunlight, the school grounds now a wasteland of discarded belongings and scattered debris.

Maddie purposely avoided looking too closely. She was certain she saw more than one body.

They moved swiftly, keeping low and sticking to the shadows where possible. As they neared the edge of the apartment building, a figure stumbled into view. Her breath caught in her throat when she recognized the guard's uniform.

Elliot reacted instantly and pushed them behind a dumpster. They watched, hearts pounding, as the guard stumbled past, muttering incoherently. His uniform was splattered with blood, his eyes vacant.

Maddie was more than surprised to see him. With the other guards at the school and the crowd gathered for food, she was sure he'd be stopped. Yet there he was. At least he wasn't singing.

Once he was gone, they resumed their desperate journey home. The streets were empty, the usual sounds of life replaced by an oppressive silence. Occasionally, they'd duck into alleys or behind parked cars as military vehicles rumbled past.

It only took about ten minutes until they found the street Linda lived on. Maddie looked at Jackson; his face was pale, and his eyes were still wide with shock. The injured woman was quiet as she clutched her bleeding arm. Maddie's mom was still holding onto her, offering soft words of encouragement.

As they approached the woman's house, her husband came rushing out the door. "Linda!" His voice cracked with emotion. He sprinted toward them, fear and hope flickering in his eyes.

Linda, supported by Maddie and her mom, lifted her head and reached out with her uninjured arm. "David," she murmured as tears streamed down her face.

David enveloped her in a careful, yet desperate embrace as his body shook with relief. "I thought I lost you," he whispered, his voice choked with sobs. "I couldn't find you. It was . . . I was so scared." He kissed her forehead repeatedly, holding her as if afraid to let go.

Linda clung to him, her fingers digging into his shirt. "I'm here," she said softly, her voice breaking. "I'm here, David."

Maddie and her mom stepped back, giving the couple space, their own eyes misting at the raw display of love and relief. Jackson stood nearby, shifting awkwardly but clearly moved by the reunion.

David finally pulled back, and his eyes scanned Linda's injury. "We need to get you inside," he said, his voice steadying as he took on a more protective tone. "I'll take care of you."

"She needs to go to the hospital," Heather insisted. "I did what I could to stop the bleeding, but she needs proper treatment. I don't know the severity of her injuries."

The couple exchanged a glance before David said, "We have a friend who's a doctor. He'll help us."

"You have a doctor?"

He gave a nod as Linda said, "Please, keep quiet about it, but I'm sure if you needed help, he'd be willing. He's not just a friend. He's my brother. Come to my house, and we'll help you if we're able."

Linda leaned on David as they made their way to the house. She glanced back at Maddie and her family, gratitude shining through her pain. "Thank you," she whispered.

They stood there for a moment, catching their breath and steeling themselves for the remaining trek. Though sounds of the distant conflict had stopped, every shadow seemed to hold potential danger. The brief respite of the reunion was over, and the harsh reality of their situation set in again.

"Let's go." Elliot was already moving. They moved cautiously through the deserted streets, ducking behind parked cars at the slightest hint of movement. The adrenaline that had propelled Maddie that far began to wane, replaced by an aching exhaustion. Yet, the thought of home, with its fragile semblance of normalcy, kept her going.

As they turned onto their street, she felt a surge of relief. Their home was in sight, its familiar outline a beacon of safety in this nightmare landscape. Tom was one of the guards at the entrance.

"Heather? What happened?"

In place of words, her mom collapsed into his arms and sobbed. Elliot gave a brief accounting before saying he was going home. Tom escorted them to their house.

Her mom fumbled with the keys. "Come on, come on," she muttered.

Tom gently took the keys from her trembling hands. "Let me," he said softly. He quickly unlocked the door and pushed it open.

Maddie, Jackson, and their mom hurried inside, the familiar surroundings offering a semblance of security. Tom cast a quick glance around the street before stepping inside just long enough to ensure they were settled.

"Lock the door behind me, and don't open it for anyone," he instructed. "I'm going back to my guard position. Nobody will bother you. Nobody will bother *any* of us."

Her mom nodded, her eyes still glistening with tears. "Thank you, Tom. I don't know what we'd do without you. Without Elliot. He saved us today."

Tom gave a reassuring smile and stepped outside, closing the door firmly behind him. The sound of the lock clicking into place was a small comfort, a barrier against the chaos outside.

Maybe we'll be safe now. But even as she thought it, Maddie knew it wasn't true. They might be home, but they were far from safe. The world outside their door had become a deadly playground for the Star Brights. And they had no idea how long this nightmare would last.

Her mom took a deep, shaky breath, and her eyes darted around the room. "We need to check every window and door. Make sure everything is secure."

"We always keep everything locked," Maddie answered, peering out the front window.

"Don't argue. Just do it."

"Fine." Maddie rolled her eyes. "I'll take the upstairs."

"I've got the basement," Jackson chimed in, his voice steadier than Maddie expected.

Her mom was already moving toward the kitchen. Whether to check the door leading to the deck or to find solace from the pantry, Maddie wasn't sure. How could she be so calm and sure one minute and a blubbering mess the next? Maddie was just grateful her mom kept things together and helped Linda when she needed it.

As Maddie made her way through the upper floor, she meticulously checked each window, ensuring the locks were engaged and the barriers they'd installed were still in place. The familiar surroundings of her bedroom, once a sanctuary, now felt exposed and vulnerable.

She paused at the window overlooking the backyard, her eyes drawn to the garden they'd planted. The neat rows of seedlings seemed impossibly fragile in the face of the chaos they'd just escaped.

Downstairs, she could hear her mom's frantic movements, the sound of furniture being pushed against doors. Maddie furrowed her brow. *Mom's really shaken up,* she thought. The fear in those actions was unmistakable, and a knot formed in Maddie's stomach. She'd never seen her mom that scared before.

As Maddie descended the stairs, Jackson emerged from the basement. "All clear down there."

Her mom looked up from where she was wedging a chair under the doorknob of the front door. "Good. That was too close. We can't . . . we can't let our guard down like that again."

Maddie approached her mom and reached out to touch her arm. "Mom, we're okay. We made it home."

Her mom shook her head, her eyes wild. "You don't understand, Maddie. We were lucky. What if . . . what if next time . . ." Her voice broke, and she turned away, her shoulders shaking.

Maddie and Jackson exchanged worried glances. They'd seen their mom in various states over the years—angry, depressed, manic—but this raw fear was new and unsettling.

"What do we do now?" Jackson asked.

Her mom took a deep breath, visibly trying to compose herself. "We need to be prepared. For anything. We can't go to the food drops anymore. It's too dangerous."

They had food in the pantry, but they'd discussed this. Getting the food drop items, as meager as they were, would ensure they didn't face starvation later. With the whole world affected, food plants were either shut down or operating at the bare minimum. They needed this food now in case they couldn't get any food later. "But what about winter? We decided— "

"We'll figure it out," her mom cut her off, her tone leaving no room for argument. "As of right now, we do not leave our neighborhood." She paused for a moment, her face contorted in thought. "We don't leave the yard unless it's for patrol. No one goes anywhere alone."

As the adrenaline of their escape wore off, exhaustion set in. Maddie sank onto the couch, her body aching from the frantic run. Jackson joined her, leaning against her side in a rare display of vulnerability.

Her mom paced the living room, her nervous energy a stark contrast to her children's fatigue. "We need to inventory everything we have," she muttered, more to herself than to them. "Food, water, medical supplies . . ."

They'd already done that. Several times, in fact. But too tired to argue, Maddie just nodded. As she watched her mom's agitated movements, a new worry began to form. *How long can we survive like this, trapped in our home, jumping at every sound? And how long before the stress breaks us?*

She glanced at Jackson; his head was leaning back on the couch beside her, and his eyes were closed, his breath coming in gasps. Her mom was still pacing and muttering about supplies.

At that moment, Maddie realized that the greatest threat they faced might not be the Star Brights or the chaos outside, but the slow unraveling of their own minds.

Chapter 26

"How'd the garden look?" Maddie's mom asked as she wiped the kitchen counter.

"Fine, I guess. The weeds seem to grow faster than anything else, though."

"It rained overnight. That's good for it. Should help put the fire out too." Even though her mom was smiling, Maddie knew she was still upset about yesterday's close call at the food drop.

They had talked last night, and both had been surprised by Elliot's actions. He'd come off like a complete jerk when they first met him at the neighborhood meeting, but there was no denying he saved their lives.

Her mom clearly felt indebted to him and was searching for a way to repay him, though nothing seemed like enough. It was clear she was still dwelling on the near-death experience, but at least she'd slept instead of staying up all night worrying. Stress could trigger a hypomanic or manic episode, even with her medication.

This prolonged anxiety was bound to become an issue, and the severity of the incident could push her mom over the edge.

Maddie felt herself teetering on the brink too—and she wasn't even bipolar. As far as they knew, anyway.

Bipolar was often hereditary. Grandma Bea didn't have it, and neither did Grandpa Hank, but Grandma Bea said it was possible her own mother was bipolar and never diagnosed. There'd been things when she was growing up that were concerning, but her grandma didn't know any different and never considered her mother may be mentally ill.

Her mom had died young, shortly after Grandma Bea and Grandpa Hank were married. Had she lived longer, maybe there would have been a diagnosis.

Sometimes Maddie wondered if she'd get it. If she, too, would someday cause her own children all the pain she and Jackson had experienced. Then she realized she didn't need to worry about it because she didn't plan on having kids. Especially considering that even if she herself wasn't bipolar, she may still pass on the genes.

A knock at the door interrupted her thoughts.

Her mom's eyes went wide, and her lips drew tight. "Who could that be?"

"I'll go see," Maddie offered.

"Wait. I'll . . ." Her mom quickly grabbed the golf club, still tucked in the corner near the front door. Wyoming was a gun-friendly state, but they'd never had guns in their home. Since things had started falling apart and Star Brights were now around every corner, she sincerely wished they had better protection than a bag of golf clubs.

With her mom in position and the club at the ready, she gave Maddie a nod. "Go ahead," she whispered.

"Who is it?" Maddie called.

"It's Tom," the familiar voice called out softly. "Just checking in on you all."

Her mom sighed, and a smile covered her face. "Let him in," she said as she put the club back in its handy spot.

"How are you holding up?" Tom asked as his eyes scanned their tired faces.

Her mom gave him a weak smile. "We're . . . managing. Come in, please."

As Tom stepped inside, Maddie noticed how the morning light caught the silver strands in his dark hair and how his shoulders seemed to relax slightly as he entered their home. It was a stark contrast to the tense, vigilant posture he maintained during his guard duties.

"I actually came by with an invitation," Tom said, a hint of sheepishness in his voice. "I have the day off from neighborhood watch, and I know you're not on the schedule either. I thought . . . well, I thought you might like to come over for dinner. Maybe play some games afterward?"

Maddie perked up at that and exchanged a glance with Jackson, who had shuffled into the room, his hair sticking up in all directions.

"Games?" Jackson asked, his voice still thick with sleep but tinged with interest.

Tom nodded, and a smile spread across his face. "I've got a pretty impressive setup in my basement. Multiple players, VR, the works. Thought it might be nice to . . . you know, forget about everything for a while."

Her mom hesitated, her eyes darting to Maddie. Maddie gave a slight shrug, trying to keep her own eagerness in check.

After a moment, her mom's shoulders relaxed, and she nodded. "That sounds wonderful, Tom. Thank you."

As Tom left with promises to see them later, Maddie felt a flutter of excitement in her chest. It had been so long since they'd done anything remotely normal. The prospect of an evening of games and companionship was almost intoxicating.

It was exactly what she'd been thinking of yesterday. Of course, then she'd planned to go out with her friends. But after the trouble at Kelly Walsh, she knew leaving the neighborhood was a bad idea, even if she could figure out how to make it happen.

The day passed in a blur of anticipation. They tidied the house, more out of habit than necessity, and Maddie even spent additional time tending to their fledgling garden. As the afternoon sun began its descent, they prepared to head over to Tom's.

Tom's house, just next door, was a mirror image of their own from the outside. But as they stepped inside, she was struck by how different it felt. Where their home was filled with the accumulated clutter of family life, Tom's was neat and minimalist, yet somehow still warm and inviting.

"Welcome," Tom said, ushering them in with a smile. "Dinner's almost ready. I hope you like lasagna. It's from the freezer, but I hope you don't mind."

The rich aroma of tomato sauce and melted cheese filled the air, making Maddie's mouth water. From the freezer or not, it sure smelled like a proper home-cooked meal.

"It'll be ready in about fifteen minutes. Shall we have a seat in the living room while we wait? I'd offer you a tour, but as you can tell, my house is pretty much like yours. *Mi casa es su casa.*" He chuckled at his own joke.

Her mom laughed, too, while Maddie rolled her eyes. Jackson was busy looking at something on a shelf.

"Hey, Tom, what's with all the toys?" Jackson asked, pointing at a shelf lined with colorful action figures and model cars.

Tom picked up a G.I. Joe action figure. "They're vintage. Some are pretty rare. This one," he said, holding it up, "is a 1964 original. Mint condition, it could fetch a pretty penny."

Jackson's eyes widened with curiosity as he spotted a shelf of Matchbox cars. "And these? These are so cool!"

"Ah, those are classics." Tom gently picked up a miniature red Volkswagen Beetle. "This one's from the '70s. They're becoming quite sought after among collectors."

The two spent a few more minutes looking over the various toys while her mom stood nearby. While the toys were fine, interesting even, Maddie noticed a couple of paintings that caught her eye. She went over to check them out, not recognizing the artists' names but suspecting they were something special.

They'd yet to make it to the furniture in the living room when the timer on Tom's watch sounded. "Guess that's dinner," he said. "Everyone ready to eat?"

As they settled around Tom's dining table, the conversation flowed easily. For a while, it was almost possible to forget what was happening in the world. Tom regaled them with stories from his days as an EMT, his eyes lighting up as he described the more humorous calls he'd responded to.

"There was this one time," he chuckled, taking a sip of his sparkling water, "when we got called out for a 'man stuck in a tree.' Turns out, it was a grown man who'd climbed up there on a dare and couldn't get down. His friends were too drunk to help, so there we were, at two in the morning, trying to coax this guy down like a scared cat."

Laughter filled the room, a sound that had become all too rare in recent weeks. Maddie noticed how her mom's eyes crinkled at the corners when she smiled, how she leaned in slightly toward Tom as he spoke. It was nice to see her relaxed, even if just for a moment.

"When did you stop being an EMT?" her mom asked.

"When I moved here. The last place I lived was a small town, and all the firefighters and EMTs were volunteers."

"Why'd you move to Casper?" Jackson asked, a string of cheese dripping off his chin.

"My divorce. As I said, it was a small town. My ex-wife stayed there to help her folks. With my work, I can live anywhere. My brother lives in Cheyenne. I thought about moving there, but then I heard about Casper and the mountain. I like cross-country skiing, and when I learned about the trails on Casper Mountain, it just made sense. Last winter didn't disappoint. I'm happy to be here." His gaze met her mom's. "Plus, I like the people."

After dinner, Tom led them down to his basement, and Maddie couldn't help but gasp. The space was a far cry from their own classically decorated walkout basement where Grandma Bea lived. This was like stepping into a high-tech entertainment center.

A massive screen dominated one wall, surrounded by plush seating that looked like it belonged in a movie theater. On the other side, a state-of-the-art gaming setup awaited, complete with VR headsets and motion sensors.

"This is incredible," Jackson breathed. His eyes were wide as he took in the array of gaming equipment.

Tom grinned, clearly pleased by their reaction. "Shall we give it a go? I heard you say you like the VR game everyone's playing. I gave it a try a few days ago, and you're right. It's a great one. Don't know why I hadn't tried it before." He looked at Maddie's mom. "Heather? Have you played it?"

She motioned with her hands. "No. Not me."

"It's the one you tried before, Mom," Jackson stated.

"The one I couldn't play?"

"You could almost play it."

"C'mon, Heather." Tom smiled. "Give it a try again. I think you'll like it."

"Well . . . I guess. But isn't it for kids?"

"It's not for kids." Jackson looked hurt. "All sorts of people play it. From people my age on up to older folks. You just heard Tom say he likes it."

Tom furrowed his brow. "Yeah. Us older folks find it to be real fun."

Maddie and her mom laughed, but Jackson just shrugged, obviously missing out on his misplaced comment.

They started with the popular game, but Maddie and her mom quickly found themselves out of their depth. The complex controls and immersive VR environment were disorienting, and Maddie felt a wave of motion sickness after just a few minutes.

"Maybe something a little less . . . intense?" her mom suggested as she removed her headset with a sheepish smile.

Tom was quick to oblige, switching them to a more casual racing game that had them all laughing and shouting good-natured taunts at each other. Maddie couldn't remember the last time she'd seen her mom so carefree, her usual worry lines smoothed away by laughter.

As the evening wore on, they cycled through various games. Jackson, unsurprisingly, proved to be a natural at most of them, while Maddie found herself enjoying the simpler, puzzle-based games.

She noticed Tom and her mom often chose cooperative games, working together with an easy synchronicity that spoke of their growing comfort with each other.

During a break between games, Maddie wandered over to the small bar area, her eyes scanning the neat rows of bottles. She was surprised to see they were all nonalcoholic—various sodas, sparkling waters, and even some fancy mocktail mixers.

"Looking for something specific?" Tom's voice made her jump.

"Oh, no, I was just . . . looking," she stammered, suddenly feeling like she'd been caught doing something wrong.

Tom's smile was kind and understanding. "I don't keep alcohol in the house," he said softly. "Personal choice. But I've got some great mocktail recipes if you're interested."

Maddie nodded as relief washed over her. Whether Tom knew about her mom's history with alcohol or not, his choice to keep a dry house was comforting.

As the night wound down, she found herself on one of the plush couches, a warm contentment settling over her. Jackson was still engrossed in a game, his excited chatter filling the room. Her mom and Tom sat nearby, their heads bent close as they talked in low voices, occasionally breaking into soft laughter.

For the first time in weeks, Maddie felt a sense of hope again. Yes, the world outside was still dangerous and uncertain. But there, at that moment, they had found a pocket of normalcy, of connection. It wasn't perfect—the absence of Grandma Bea was keenly felt, and the specter of the Star Brights still loomed in the back of her mind—but it was something.

As they said their goodbyes and headed home, the cool night air on their faces, Maddie caught her mom's eye. There was a lightness there that she hadn't seen in a long time, a spark of something that might have been happiness.

"That was . . . nice," her mom said softly, her hand finding Maddie's and squeezing gently.

Maddie squeezed back. "Yeah, it was."

As they entered their house, the familiar surroundings felt different somehow. The shadows didn't seem quite as menacing, the silence not as oppressive. They had been reminded that even in the darkest times, moments of joy were still possible.

If only the darkness didn't always find a way to come back.

Chapter 27

The soft hum of the exercise bike filled the room as Maddie descended the stairs into the basement. She paused, watching her mom pedal with determination. Sweat glistened on her forehead, and a small smile played on her lips as she glanced at the fitness tracker on her wrist.

"Morning, sweetie," her mom called out, clearly out of breath. "Sleep well?"

Maddie shrugged. "I guess," she mumbled, glancing around. Grandma Bea's dumbbells were displaced from their usual shelf, and the weight bench gleamed faintly with a sheen of sweat left behind from recent use. She couldn't help but feel a twinge of annoyance at her mom's newfound energy.

It had been three days since their dinner at Tom's, and the change in her mom was startling. Gone was the nervous, chain-smoking woman who'd hover anxiously by the windows. In her place was this . . . stranger. A stranger who exercised, laughed easily, and seemed to have an endless well of patience for Jackson's video game chatter.

Maddie could hear Jackson in the family room, lost in his VR world. His excited shouts echoed through the house. Their mom had tried playing with him, though she didn't seem to enjoy it as much as she had at Tom's place. Maddie suspected it wasn't the game system her mom liked—it was Tom.

"Your brother's been at it for an hour already," her mom said, stepping off the bike and grabbing a towel. "I told him I'd join him for a racing game after my workout."

"Aren't you getting tired of those games?" Her tone was sharper than she intended.

Her mom laughed, a light, carefree sound that felt alien in their still-tense world. "Oh, I don't know, the racing games are fun. Tom showed me a few tricks the other night."

Of course he did, Maddie thought bitterly. Tom had been a constant presence over the past few days, stopping by each day, sometimes more than once, and even joining them for dinner again last night. His presence seemed to light up something in her mom, a spark Maddie hadn't seen in years. Hadn't ever seen, in fact.

"Well, have fun," she said, unable to keep the sarcasm completely out of her voice. "I've got some things to do upstairs."

Her mom's brow furrowed slightly. "Are you sure you don't want to join us? It could be fun, all of us playing together."

Maddie shook her head, already heading back upstairs. "Maybe later," she called over her shoulder, knowing full well she had no intention of coming back down.

In her room, she booted up her laptop, thankful the internet was still working. Several messages from Sonja and other friends awaited her—they were planning to meet at McKenzie Lake.

Maddie sighed and shook her head. She'd love to go, but she'd promised her mom she wouldn't wander off alone. Closing the app, she switched to her email, hoping for news from her dad or Grandma Bea. A wave of relief washed over her when she saw messages from both.

Grandma Bea's email was short but reassuring:

Dearest Maddie,

A lump formed in her throat. She missed Grandma Bea fiercely, missed the calm stability she brought to their household. She quickly typed out a reply, assuring her grandmother that the garden was doing well and that they were all safe.

Her dad's email was only slightly longer, and the worry was evident even through the screen:

Hey kiddo,
Things are okay up here. The lodge is secure, and we've got plenty of supplies. Your grandpa invited a few friends to come to the lodge, telling them, 'Load up your truck and bring everything you'll need to survive.' They took him up on the offer.

Sadly, we had some trouble. To prevent something like this from happening again, we set up the off-the-grid cabins along with a couple of outfitter tents for quarantine. We've decided on a two-week quarantine in hopes that will prevent us from getting the virus . . . or whatever it is. Every day brings new reports of Star Bright incidents, and it feels like we're no closer to understanding what's causing it or how to stop it.

How are you holding up? Is your mom doing okay? Give Jackson a hug for me. I miss you all terribly.
Love, Dad

Maddie stared at the screen, her fingers hovering over the keyboard. What could she say? That mom was suddenly Super Mom, exercising and playing video games? That she felt more alone than ever in a house full of people?

In the end, she told him how glad she was he was okay but sorry to hear they'd had trouble. She also assured him they were safe and managing as best they could. She didn't mention Tom or the changes in her mom. Somehow, it felt like a betrayal.

As she hit send, a burst of laughter erupted from downstairs. She crept down the stairs, making sure each step was as quiet as possible, and leaned carefully around the corner to get a glimpse into the family room. Her mom and Jackson were on the couch, VR headsets on, arms waving as they steered invisible cars.

Her mom laughed, her body swaying with the imaginary movement of her car. "I've got it! I've got it!" she cried, before letting out a groan. "Oh no! Did I crash?"

Jackson whooped triumphantly. "I win again! But you're getting better, Mo- um, you're getting better."

Maddie's chest tightened. When was the last time she'd heard that much joy in Jackson's voice? When was the last time her mom had shown that much interest in anything Jackson liked? And had Jackson almost called her *Mom*? He never called her Mom.

She retreated to her room and closed the door softly behind her. The muffled sounds of laughter and conversation continued to filter through, a stark reminder of the fun she wasn't part of.

Maddie flopped onto her bed and stared at the ceiling. She should be happy. Her mom was sober, engaged, and actually parenting for once. Jackson was thriving under the attention. Even Tom's presence was a positive thing, bringing a sense of normalcy and safety into their lives.

So why did she feel so . . . left out?

A soft knock on her door pulled her from her thoughts. "Maddie?" her mom's voice called. "Can I come in?"

Maddie sighed. "I guess."

The door opened, and her mom stepped in, still flushed from the game. "Hey, sweetie. We miss you downstairs. Are you sure you don't want to join us?"

Maddie shrugged, not meeting her mom's eyes. "I'm fine up here."

Her mom sat on the edge of the bed, her face creased with concern. "Is everything okay? You've been quiet. Are you still upset about what happened at Kelly Walsh?"

A surge of emotion welled up in Maddie's chest—anger, frustration, and loneliness all mingled together. "Oh, so now you notice?" she snapped, instantly regretting her tone but unable to stop. "You've been so busy with your new workout routine and bonding with Jackson and hanging out with Tom, I'm surprised you even remembered I exist!"

Her mom recoiled as if slapped, hurt flashing across her face. "Maddie, that's not fair. I'm just trying to— "

"To what?" Maddie interrupted, sitting up. "To be Mom of the Year? To impress Tom? Where was all this energy and interest when we really needed it?"

The words hung in the air between them, heavy with years of unspoken resentment and pain. Her mom's face crumpled, and for a moment, Maddie saw the fragile, uncertain woman beneath the new confident exterior.

"I'm sorry," her mom whispered, tears welling in her eyes. "I'm trying, Maddie. I really am. I know I've let you down so many times before, but I'm trying to be better. For all of us."

Maddie felt her own eyes stinging with unshed tears. "I know," she said softly. "I just . . . I don't know how to fit into this new version of our family. It feels like you and Jackson have this whole new bond, and Tom's always around, and I'm just . . . here."

Her mom gently took Maddie's hand. "Oh, sweetheart. You're not just here. You're the glue that's held this family together for so long. I know I've put too much on your shoulders, and I'm trying to change that. But I never meant to make you feel left out."

She nodded, unable to speak past the lump in her throat. Her mom pulled her into a hug, and for a moment, Maddie allowed herself to be held, to feel like the child she'd never really gotten to be.

"How about this?" Her mom pulled back to look Maddie in the eye. "Tomorrow, just you and I spend time together. We can work in the garden, maybe try out one of Grandma Bea's old recipes. She has that recipe book from World War II. What's it called? Eating for Victory? Yes. I think that's it. I'm sure we can find something to make in there."

"Maybe." Maddie shrugged.

"Or we could give each other pedicures. Whatever you want. No Tom, no video games. Just us. In fact, why don't we do pedicures now? How fun would that be?"

Maddie nodded, and a small smile tugged at her lips. "I'd like that."

"Give me just a few minutes to wrap things up with Jackson, then I'll be back."

As her mom left the room, closing the door gently behind her, Maddie felt a mix of emotions swirling inside her. Relief at finally voicing her feelings, hope for this new connection with her mom, and a lingering worry about how long it would last.

But at that moment, it was enough. A chance to bridge the gap that had formed. And in their uncertain world, that was something to hold on to.

Maddie was just starting to feel a bit better about things and had started to gather things for the pedis when she heard the doorbell ring. Her heart sank as she recognized Tom's voice greeting her mom. She crept to the top of the stairs, straining to hear their conversation.

". . . thought you might want to join me," Tom was saying, his voice low and excited. "I know it's not what you usually do, but I thought it'd give us some time together. To get to know each other better."

Her mom's reply was muffled, but Maddie could hear the hesitation in her voice. After a few more minutes of hushed conversation, the front door closed, and footsteps approached the stairs.

Maddie quickly retreated to her room, leaving the door slightly ajar. Her mom knocked softly. "Maddie? Can I talk to you for a second?"

"Come in," Maddie called, trying to keep her voice neutral.

Her mom entered, an apologetic look already on her face. Maddie's stomach dropped, knowing what was coming.

"Sweetie, about the pedicures . . ." her mom began, wringing her hands. "Something's come up. I know it's silly, but they've reworked the neighborhood watch schedule and Tom is without a partner on patrol. His shift starts in about twenty minutes. He thought . . . well, he thought it might be nice for us to walk together."

Maddie felt as if all the air had been sucked out of the room. "But . . . we had plans," she said, her voice small.

Her mom nodded, guilt evident in her expression. "I know, and I'm so sorry. We'll go ahead and do it tomorrow, as I originally suggested. Or you could come with us on patrol if you'd like?"

"Patrol? Thanks, but no," Maddie snapped, turning away to hide the tears stinging her eyes. "No, it's fine. Have fun with Tom."

"Maddie, please don't be like this. I promise we'll have our day together soon. It's just he needs my help— "

"I said it's fine," Maddie snapped, cutting her off. "Just go. It's what you want to do, anyway. Heather Reynolds always does what she wants to do."

"You know what, Maddie?" her mom said, her voice trembling with anger. "You're acting like a spoiled brat. You have no business talking to your mother that way. I'm trying to make things work, to keep us safe and do our part in the neighborhood, but all you can do is throw a fit."

Maddie's jaw clenched, defiance rising within her. "Help the neighborhood? Ha! This isn't about helping the neighborhood. This is about running off with Tom every chance you get!"

Her mom's face flushed red with frustration. "Tom is a good man, and he cares about us. He's trying to be a part of our lives, Maddie. Can't you see that?"

"Yeah, well, maybe I don't want him to be!" Maddie shot back, tears now streaming down her cheeks. "Maybe I just want my mom to care about what I want for once!"

Her mom's eyes filled with tears of her own, her voice breaking. "I do care, Maddie. I do. But I can't keep bending over backward to please you while ignoring everything else in my life. Especially not now. I know the timing is rough, but I'm . . . I'm . . . I like him."

"Whatever," she muttered, her voice barely audible. "Just go."

Her mom stood there, trembling with emotion, before turning and leaving the room without another word. The silence that followed was deafening, leaving Maddie alone with her thoughts and the weight of her words hanging heavily in the air.

Alone in her room, anger and disappointment washed over her. All the progress they'd seemed to make just moments ago felt hollow now. Her mom had chosen Tom and his stupid plans over their promised time together.

As she lay on her bed, staring at the ceiling, Maddie made a decision. If her mom could break promises and do whatever she wanted, why couldn't she? The invitation to her friends' gathering at the lake floated into her mind. Maybe it was time she stopped being the responsible one and had some fun of her own.

Chapter 28

Maddie glanced around as she loaded her paddleboard into her car. Her mom had left several minutes ago for patrol with Tom. By now, they'd be on the next street over.

Maddie had tried to be nonchalant, carrying the bag that held her swimsuit and other supplies as she slipped from the house into the garage. Not that she needed to be. Jackson was lost in his own virtual world, playing those stupid games of his.

A pang of guilt tugged at her heart, but she pushed it aside. They'd been fine without her lately; they probably wouldn't even notice she was gone. She climbed into the driver's seat, her heart racing as she started the engine.

She finally started to breathe easier after passing the barricade out of the community. The guard hadn't even questioned her, just motioned her to wait while the car blocking the road was moved before waving her through.

The drive to McKenzie Lake was surreal. The streets were empty, a stark reminder of the lockdown she was brazenly defying. As she pulled into the parking lot, she saw a handful of familiar cars. At least she wasn't the only one breaking the rules.

She shot off a quick text to her mom: *"Went for a drive. Be back soon."* While she'd considered not saying anything about leaving, she knew her mom would worry, and she didn't want that. Not really, anyway.

Well, maybe a little worry would be okay. Then maybe her mom would appreciate her more and not spend all her time thinking about Tom. With a mix of defiance and nervousness, she turned off her phone.

The small group gathered at the lake greeted her with obvious excitement. There were about ten of them, all classmates she hadn't seen in weeks.

"Maddie!" her friend Sonja called out, waving from the water's edge. "I can't believe you made it!"

Maddie grinned, already feeling the weight of the past weeks lifting. "Couldn't let you guys have all the fun, could I?"

"We've set up a changing room over there." Sonja pointed to a grove of trees with a sheet hanging off the front.

She quickly changed into her swimsuit, a black and orange tankini. She was unloading her paddleboard when a boy she recognized from her history class approached. "Need a hand with that?" he asked, a shy smile on his face.

"Thanks, um . . ." Maddie fumbled, realizing she couldn't remember his name.

"Ethan," he supplied, not seeming offended. "We sat next to each other in Mr. Henderson's class."

"Right, Ethan! Sorry, it feels like a lifetime ago."

They chatted, catching up on how they'd been spending their time during lockdown, as they took the uninflated board out of the duffel bag. Even though inflating it was a pain, it didn't take long, and they were soon carrying it to the water.

It felt wonderfully normal, like any other summer day at the lake. Of course, she made a point of not mentioning being at Kelly Walsh or Albertsons when the Star Brights attacked. Ethan made no mention of his experiences either, if he had them.

For the next couple of hours, she lost herself in the simple pleasures of swimming, paddleboarding, and laughing with friends. The troubles of the outside world seemed distant, held at bay by the sparkling water and clear blue sky.

As the afternoon wore on, she found herself sitting on the shore next to Ethan, watching their friends splash in the water.

"This was a great idea," she sighed, leaning back on her elbows.

Ethan nodded, his expression turning serious. "Yeah, it's nice to forget for a while. But . . ." He hesitated.

"But what?" Maddie prompted.

"I don't know. Don't you feel like we're tempting fate or something? With everything that's going on . . ."

Before she could respond, their friend Jake jogged up, his eyes bright with excitement. "Hey, guys! Did you see TalkZap? There's a protest against the lockdowns happening downtown. Who wants to go?"

Maddie felt a flutter of anxiety in her stomach. A protest seemed like a step too far, even for her rebellious mood.

Ethan shook his head firmly. "No way, man. This is one thing, but a protest? That's asking for trouble."

Jake shrugged, already turning to spread the news to others. "Suit yourself. Anyone who wants to go, we're leaving in ten!"

As a few of their friends began to pack up, eager to join the protest, Ethan turned to Maddie. "Hey, um, I know this is kind of weird, but . . . would you maybe want to go for a walk? Along the river path?"

Maddie hesitated and glanced at her watch. She should probably head home soon, but the thought of facing her mom's potential anger made her stomach churn.

"I've heard the police and military aren't really enforcing the lockdown for people just out walking," Ethan added quickly. "As long as we're obviously just exercising and not causing trouble. Besides, everyone will be focused on the protest. We'll be fine."

The idea was tempting. A quiet walk sounded perfect after the excitement of the lake. "Sure." She smiled. "That sounds nice."

They agreed to meet at the Lansing Field parking lot in half an hour, giving Ethan time to drop off a friend who had ridden with him and wanted to go home instead of joining in the protest.

As Maddie watched him drive away, she felt excited, yet nervous. This day of rebellion was turning out to be more adventurous than she'd planned.

She made her way to the changing area where Sonja was slipping into shorts. "C'mon, Maddie. Let's go show them how they're taking our freedoms away."

"Nope." She shook her head. "I'm not going to the protest." She took a step closer to Sonja. "Ethan asked me to go on a walk with him. I'm doing that instead."

Sonja wiggled her eyebrows. "Don't do anything I wouldn't do."

As Sonja drove away, Maddie took a few minutes in her car to fix her hair and makeup.

Thirty minutes later, she pulled into the Lansing Field parking lot, spotting Ethan waiting by his car. They set off down the river path and headed north, away from town.

"It's so quiet out here," she marveled, taking in the peacefulness of the river and surrounding trees.

Ethan nodded, his hands in his pockets. "Yeah, it's like the rest of the world doesn't exist. No Star Brights, no lockdowns, just nature."

They walked in comfortable silence for a while, occasionally pointing out interesting birds or plants. As they rounded a bend, they spotted another pair of walkers heading toward them.

"Should we . . .?" Ethan gestured off the path.

Maddie nodded, and they stepped into the grass, giving the other walkers a wide berth. The couple, an older man and woman, waved as they passed.

"Have a great walk!" the woman called out cheerfully.

As they continued, she felt a sense of normalcy she hadn't experienced in weeks. Just two people out for a stroll, enjoying the summer day. It was almost possible to forget the chaos that awaited them back in town.

But as the afternoon wore on and the sun began to dip lower in the sky, reality started to creep back in. She knew she'd have to head home soon, and the thought filled her with dread.

"We should probably start heading back," she said reluctantly.

Ethan agreed, and they turned around, retracing their steps along the river. As they neared the trailer park across the water, a chorus of barking erupted.

"They don't sound too happy." Ethan frowned. "Sounds like every dog in the park is barking. Wonder why?"

A chill ran down Maddie's spine, despite the warm evening air. Her eyes darted around, suddenly alert for any sign of danger. "Maybe we should cut across," she suggested. "Get off the trail and head straight for the parking lot."

"Probably a good idea," Ethan agreed, giving her a reassuring smile.

They had just stepped off the path when someone started shouting. It was followed quickly by even more shouting. A dog yelped, the sound high and pained.

Ethan reached for her hand. "Let's go," he said urgently, his earlier calm replaced by obvious fear.

Maddie froze, her heart pounding. Something was terribly wrong.

Chapter 29

As Maddie's fingers brushed against Ethan's, a sudden jerk rocked his body. The sharp crack of a gunshot shattered the evening air. Time seemed to slow as Ethan's eyes widened in shock and his gaze dropped to his chest. Maddie followed his look, her breath catching in her throat.

Another shot rang out. Ethan's body crumpled, and a crimson bloom spread across his shirt. Without thinking, she dropped to the ground beside him, her heart pounding in her ears. More shots followed, the air filled with the deafening sound of gunfire.

She pressed herself close to Ethan's motionless form, using his body as a shield. The metallic tang of blood made her stomach churn. She squeezed her eyes shut and prayed for it to end.

The cacophony of barking dogs that had warned them earlier had ceased, replaced by a deathly silence broken only by the occasional pop of gunfire. She didn't know how long she lay there, her cheek pressed against the rough gravel of the path, before the shooting finally stopped.

In the sudden quiet, she could hear her own ragged breathing. Slowly, she raised her head and scanned the area for any sign of the shooter. The river path was deserted, and no movement was visible in the fading light.

She turned her attention back to Ethan, her hands shaking as she touched his shoulder. "Ethan?" she whispered, her voice cracking. There was no response, no rise and fall of his chest. The reality of the situation hit her like a physical blow.

"I'm so sorry," she choked out as tears streamed down her face. "I'm sorry this happened. I . . . I wish I didn't have to leave you here."

Her eyes fell on the phone peeking out of his pocket. With trembling fingers, she pulled it out and quickly scrolled through his contacts. When she found "Mom," she hesitated only a moment before hitting call.

The phone rang twice before a worried voice answered. "Ethan? Where have you been? I've been worried sick!"

Maddie swallowed hard, struggling to find her voice. "I . . . There's been a shooting," she managed, her words tumbling out. "He's . . . I couldn't help him. He's gone."

The woman on the other end of the line let out an anguished cry.

Maddie winced and pulled the phone away from her ear for a moment before continuing. "Listen," she said, raising her voice over the woman's sobs. "He's on the trail near the river. Across from the trailer park. His car . . . his car is parked by Lansing Field."

His mother's cries intensified, her speech becoming almost incoherent. Maddie felt her own composure slipping.

"He needs a proper burial," she said, her voice breaking. "I'm sorry. I'm really, really sorry."

Unable to bear the sound of his grieving mother any longer, Maddie ended the call. She stared at the phone for a moment, then carefully wiped it down, removing any traces of her fingerprints. The last thing she needed was the police tracking her down.

With a final, sorrowful look at Ethan's still form, she pushed herself to her feet. Her legs felt weak, threatening to give way beneath her. But the need to get away, to get home, propelled her forward.

She ran toward her car, her footsteps echoing in the empty parking lot. Her hands fumbled with the keys, and she dropped them once before managing to unlock the door. As she slid into the driver's seat, a wave of nausea washed over her. She leaned out and retched on the pavement.

Wiping her mouth with the back of her hand, she started the car. The engine's rumble seemed unnaturally loud in the quiet evening. She threw the car into reverse, her tires squealing as she peeled out of the lot.

The drive home was a blur as she replayed the horrific events over and over. The touch of Ethan's hand, the sound of the gunshot, the look in his eyes as he fell. She gripped the steering wheel so tightly that her knuckles turned white, then she forced herself to focus on the road.

As she neared the barricade, reality began to set in. *What do I tell Mom? How can I explain where I was and what I saw?* The thought of facing her family after everything that had happened made her stomach churn again.

They waved her through, and she made the final bit of the drive to her house. When she pulled into the driveway, she killed the engine, not bothering to move the car into the garage. For a long moment, she sat there, staring at the familiar facade of her home. It looked exactly the same as when she'd left earlier that day, but everything had changed.

Taking a deep, shuddering breath, she stepped out of the car. Her mom and Tom were at the edge of the driveway, their expressions a mix of relief and concern. She could sense her mom's anger simmering beneath the surface, visible in the tightness of her jaw and the tension in her posture.

"Maddie," her mom began, her voice strained and clipped. "Where have you been? We've been worried sick. Do you have any idea— "

Maddie cut her off, her own emotions raw and unchecked. "I sent you a text. I told you I'd be fine."

Her mom's eyes narrowed, hurt and frustration mingling with her anger. "That doesn't excuse you disappearing. We were supposed to stick together, to keep each other safe."

"Yeah, well, maybe I needed to do something on my own for once," she retorted, her voice rising despite herself.

Her mom's face flushed with indignation. "You are a child, Maddie! You can't just run off whenever you feel like it, especially not now!"

Tom stepped forward, his voice calm but firm. "Are you injured?" He pointed at her shirt. "Is that blood?"

Maddie glanced down as her mom made a whimpering noise deep in her throat. "Maddie. Oh, no, Maddie."

"I-I'm fine." Tears filled her eyes. "Something . . . something terrible happened." Her voice trembled as she struggled to find the words, her composure cracking under the weight of her emotions. "I saw . . . I saw . . ." She choked on her words, unable to continue.

Her mom's anger seemed to evaporate, replaced by a deep concern as she rushed forward and enveloped Maddie in a tight embrace. "Oh, sweetheart," she murmured, her voice thick with tears. "Are you sure you're not hurt?"

Tom stood nearby, his expression conveying both worry and understanding. "Maddie," he said gently, "can you tell us what happened? We're here for you."

Maddie leaned into her mom's embrace, drawing strength from her touch. "It was . . . it was awful," she managed to say, her voice barely above a whisper. "There was a shooting. My friend Ethan . . ."

Her mom held her tighter, her own tears mingling with Maddie's. "It's okay, sweetheart," she whispered. "You're safe now. We'll figure this out together. Does Ethan need help?"

"No. No. He's . . . he's dead."

Tom appeared behind her mom, his face grim.

"Let's sit down." He guided them toward the house. They stepped inside, the familiarness of the living room offering only brief comfort. Tom motioned toward the couch, and they all took their seats. "Maddie, take a deep breath. Tell us what happened."

Slowly, haltingly, she recounted the events at the river path. She left out the earlier part of her day, the fun she had at McKenzie Lake, focusing on the walk with Ethan and the horrific shooting. As she spoke, her mom's face paled, her grip on Maddie's hand tightening.

When Maddie finished, everyone was quiet. She could see the shock and disbelief on their faces, mirroring her own feelings.

"Oh, Maddie." Her mom pulled her into another tight hug. "I'm so sorry for your friend, but I'm grateful you're safe."

Tom stood up, his expression serious. "We need to report this. The authorities need to know what happened."

Maddie felt a flash of panic. "But I wasn't supposed to be out there! I broke the lockdown rules." She dropped her gaze. "I snuck out of the house. Besides, I called his mom. Told her about how he was . . ." She shook her head. "The authorities can't do anything, anyway."

Tom sat back down. "I suppose you're right. Sometimes, I forget about the world we're now living in.

The old societal rules no longer apply. It was good thinking on your part to call his mom. You're right that she needed to know."

"I'm sorry," she murmured into her mom's shoulder. "I'm so sorry for leaving, for worrying you. I never thought . . ."

"Shh," she soothed, stroking Maddie's hair. "We'll talk about that later. Right now, I'm just thankful you're home safe."

Maddie closed her eyes, allowing herself to be comforted by her mom's presence. She knew there would be consequences for her actions and difficult conversations to be had. But for now, she was home; she was safe.
If only she didn't feel so responsible for Ethan's death.

Chapter 30

The soft hum of the refrigerator suddenly ceased, plunging the kitchen into eerie silence. Maddie looked up from her bowl of cereal and exchanged a glance with her mom across the table. It was the third time this week that the power had cut out unexpectedly.

"Here we go again." Her mom sighed. "I wonder how long it'll be out this time."

Maddie pushed her half-eaten breakfast aside, no longer hungry. The past few days had been a blur of tension and unspoken words.

After the incident at the river, she'd made a conscious decision to stop arguing with her mom, to swallow her rebellious urges and play along with this new family dynamic. It was easier than facing the alternative—the guilt, the fear, and the memory of Ethan's lifeless body.

Jackson wandered in, rubbing sleep from his eyes. "No power again? How am I supposed to play my games? I haven't been able to talk to Eddie in days. He wasn't on last time I played."

Their mom ruffled his hair affectionately. "Maybe we could do something together instead? Board games, or cards?"

Maddie watched the exchange, noting the easy affection between them. It still felt strange, this new version of their mom and the way Jackson welcomed the interactions. But she had decided to stop questioning it. In this crumbling world, maybe pretending was all they had left.

The day dragged on, the house was uncomfortably warm without air conditioning. They tried to distract themselves with card games, but the atmosphere remained tense. Everyone was acutely aware of the changing world outside their walls.

When the power flickered back to life at two in the afternoon, there was a collective sigh of relief. Maddie immediately went for her laptop, hoping to check her emails, but the internet refused to connect.

"Mom," she called out, frustration evident in her voice. "The internet's not working."

Her mom appeared in the doorway with a worried frown creasing her forehead. "The cell signal's weak too. I can barely get one bar."

As if on cue, the house phone rang, startling them all. Her mom rushed to answer it, and Maddie's face lit up when she realized who it was.

"Brian? I'm so glad you got through."

Maddie and Jackson crowded around, straining to hear their dad's voice. Their mom fumbled with the handset for a moment before switching it to speaker.

"Heather, listen to me," their dad's voice crackled through the speaker. "Things are getting worse. These blackouts, the communication issues—I'm really worried now. I think it's time you guys came up here."

"How do you think we can do that with martial law in place?" Her mom's grip on the phone tightened. "Besides, we're managing, Brian. It's not ideal, but we're okay. We've been pooling resources with the neighbors."

"And what about food? I've heard the drop sites are giving out less and less."

There was a pause before her mom replied, her voice less certain. "We . . . we haven't been back to the drop site. Not since . . . well, you know. But we're making do. Combining forces with Tom next door has helped."

Maddie could hear the frustration in her dad's voice. "That's not enough, Heather. You need to think long term. Up here, we have space and resources. We can hunt, fish— "

"And how exactly are we supposed to get there?" her mom interrupted. "The roads are closed. There are checkpoints everywhere."

"We'll figure something out. I could come get you— "

"No. It's too dangerous. We're staying put for now."

The conversation continued for a few more minutes, but it was clear neither side was willing to budge.

Finally, his voice soft and pleading, her dad said, "Please. Please think about it. If you're willing, I'll come down there. I've got a few ideas about how I can make it work. In fact, I'm confident I'd have little trouble. The National Guard is spread thin. They aren't even in the smaller towns between here and there. Meeteetse, Thermopolis, and Shoshoni don't have military roadblocks, at least that's what I'm hearing. The town folk are doing what they can, but I think I can get through."

"What about Cody?"

"There's some patrolling happening there, but it's limited. They're just checking people as they enter town and escorting them through. They just don't have enough people to go around, so they're focusing on the larger towns—Cheyenne, Laramie, Gillette, and Casper. I've heard that even the larger towns are escorting people through now."

"I haven't seen anything about that on the internet," Maddie interjected. "The governor said all towns are under lockdown."

"True. He did. And they are . . . but it's not exactly as he presented it. Not really. If we can get you out of Casper, we'll be fine getting back here. I'm confident about this. Let me come get you."

Heather glanced at her children. Maddie gave a nod while Jackson said, "I'd rather be up the North Fork with Dad and Grandpa Rich. Dad's right about hunting and fishing."

"We can hunt and fish here," her mom said, her tone uncertain. "There's antelope and deer, plus the North Platte River."

"We don't own any guns," Jackson reminded her.

She let out a sigh, her expression tight with hesitation. "I'll think about it."

"That's all I'm asking." Maddie could practically hear the smile in her dad's voice. "How about I try to call you again tomorrow?"

As her mom hung up, Maddie could see the worry on her face.

"He means well," her mom said softly, more to herself than them. "But I think he's underestimating just how dangerous it could be between here and there. Besides, we're doing okay, right?" She didn't sound convinced. Not even close.

The rest of the afternoon passed in a haze of restless energy. The electricity remained on, but the internet was still out. Jackson checked it many times to get on to play games with his friends. "I really need to get on. I want to talk to Eddie and ask him where he's been."

When the internet finally sputtered to life, Maddie pounced on her laptop, relieved to see an email from Grandma Bea.

"Mom!" she called out. "Grandma sent an email."

They gathered around the screen and she read Grandma Bea's words:

My darlings,

I'm resigned to being stuck here for now, but please don't worry about me. I'm safe and well cared for. But I miss you all terribly. I've been thinking, you should seriously consider going up to the North Fork to be with Brian.

I know it seems impossible with the lockdown, but surely there must be some way to slip past the guards. It would be safer there, with fewer people and more resources. Brian can hunt; there's game aplenty. Plus, with the river nearby, there's fishing.

Please consider it. For your safety, for your future. I love you all so much.

Maddie looked up at her mom, hope rising in her chest. "Grandma's saying almost the exact same thing Dad said. Maybe we should— "

"It's not possible," her mom cut her off, but her voice lacked conviction. "Even though your dad thinks it is, it's just not. The roads are closed. We don't have enough fuel. It's just . . . it's not possible."

Maddie bit back her frustration, remembering her vow to stop arguing. Instead, she turned back to the computer and quickly typed a reply to her grandmother detailing her mom's concerns. To her surprise, a response came almost immediately:

Maddie, my brave girl. You need to find a way. Call your father, have him come get you if necessary. I'm sure he has a plan for fuel. This is about survival now. Get everyone packed and ready.

Tell your mother that Jackson says she's been doing great and that he feels like he has a new mom now—the one he always knew she could be. This is something she must do to keep you children safe.

I don't know how much longer communication will be possible, but please, let me know when you're on your way. I believe in you all.

Maddie read the email aloud, her voice growing stronger with each word. She watched her mom's face and saw her fear warring with determination.

"She's right," Jackson said quietly. "You have been different. Better. Like . . . like the mom I always wanted you to be."

Tears welled in her eyes. She pulled Jackson into a tight hug and reached out to include Maddie as well. "Oh, my babies," she whispered. "I'm trying. I really am."

They stood there for a moment, holding each other. When they finally pulled apart, there was a new resolve in her mom's eyes.

"Okay," she said, her voice steady. "Okay. We'll try to reach your father and see if we can come up with a plan."

Maddie's heart leaped. She dialed their dad's number. It rang once, twice, then cut to a busy signal. She tried again, with the same result.

"The cell signal's gone again," Jackson reported, holding up his phone.

"Try the landline," her mom said. "He got through on that before."

Even though it had worked earlier, this time the line was completely dead. There wasn't even a hum when she lifted the receiver.

"Text?" Maddie asked.

Her mom grabbed her phone, fingers flying as she typed out a text to their dad. "I'll tell him we're considering coming up there and ask him to call when he can."

Just as she hit send, the lights flickered and went out. The hum of electronics died, leaving them in sudden, oppressive silence.

"Well," her mom said, her voice sounding unnaturally loud in the quiet house. "Let's start packing, just in case. And I . . . I want to talk to Tom. Tell him we're going to leave. I hope he'll understand."

Maddie felt a flash of irritation at her mom's concern for Tom. It seemed misplaced, almost as if her mother cared more about him than their own safety. She clenched her fists, fighting back the urge to snap at her.

Instead, she forced a tight-lipped smile and nodded, though inside, she seethed with frustration. Her vow to not pick a fight with her mom was again put to the test.

Chapter 31

Maddie paced the living room, her footsteps echoing in the quiet house. She glanced at her phone for the hundredth time, wondering how long her mom would be at Tom's. The thought of them together made her stomach churn with a mixture of anger and anxiety.

"Would you stop stomping around?" Jackson called from the couch, where he was fiddling with his phone, playing some sort of puzzle game that didn't require the internet. The soft beeps of the game were the only sounds breaking the silence. "You're acting like a kid."

Maddie whirled toward him, her frustration finding a new target. "Oh, I'm sorry. Should I be thrilled that Mom's over there with Tom while we're supposed to be planning our escape?"

Jackson set his phone down and fixed his eyes on her with a surprisingly mature look. "You're being selfish, you know that?"

"Excuse me?" Maddie sputtered, taken aback by his tone. She'd expected him to back down, not challenge her.

"You heard me." He sat up straighter, looking more like their father than Maddie had ever noticed before. "Whatever Mom did before, however she was, she always loved us. Even if she didn't know how to show it sometimes. And now that she's finally doing better, you're acting like a brat about it."

She felt her face flush with anger. The words stung, hitting too close to home. "I'm not— "

"You are," Jackson cut her off, his voice rising slightly. "And you'd better stop, or I might decide I don't like you very much."

She stared at her little brother, seeing him in a new light. *When had he grown up so much? When had he become so . . . perceptive?*

Jackson patted the couch next to him, inviting her to sit. "Grandma and Dad are right about leaving. We need to go to the lodge. It'll be safe up the North Fork. Mom knows it too. That's why she's talking to Tom. He gets news from his brother in Cheyenne. He'll know if Dad's right about the smaller towns and how it's easy to get through them. He may even know how to get out of Casper."

She sank onto the couch, and the fight drained out of her. She suddenly felt tired, the weight of the past weeks pressing down on her. "What does Tom's brother do, anyway? He never says. Just that he knows things."

Jackson shrugged, his shoulder brushing against hers. It was a familiar, comforting touch. "He didn't tell me either. But I think he may work for the governor. Maybe she'll ask Tom to come with us. He could help us get there."

"That's a terrible idea!" The thought of Tom joining them, of him being there when they reunited with their dad, made her skin crawl. "She can't take another man up there. Not where Dad is."

"Sure she can. They've been divorced for years." Jackson's tone was matter of fact, lacking the emotional charge she felt.

"It's just wrong, that's why." She struggled to articulate the complex emotions swirling inside her. How could she explain the loyalty she felt toward their dad or the fear of this new dynamic disrupting their family further?

Jackson rolled his eyes, looking every bit the annoyed little brother. "Dad wants Mom to be happy. He's always said so."

Before she could respond, the front door opened. Her mom walked in, followed closely by Tom. Maddie felt her defenses rise again, but she bit her tongue, remembering Jackson's words. She watched as Tom held the door, the gesture intimate in its casualness.

"Kids," her mom said, her voice both determined and nervous, "we need to talk." Her mom and Tom took their seats, and an awkward silence fell over the group.

"I've been talking with Tom," her mom began, her fingers twisting together in a familiar nervous gesture. "And . . . well, he agrees that leaving might be our best option."

Maddie felt a surge of conflicting emotions—relief that they were finally taking action, anxiety about the journey ahead, and a lingering resentment toward Tom's involvement. She glanced at Jackson and saw an "I told you so" look in his eyes.

"It's not safe here anymore." Tom's voice was gentle but firm. He looked at each of them in turn, his gaze lingering on Maddie as if sensing her resistance. "The rations are getting smaller, and with so many people in Casper, it's only a matter of time before things get worse."

Her mom nodded and met Maddie's eyes. There was a plea in her gaze, a request for understanding. "I know you're not thrilled about this, but Tom has offered to help us. He has a conversion van we can use. It'll hold all of us and a lot more supplies than our cars will."

Maddie opened her mouth to argue, but Jackson spoke first. "That's great! We'll be able to take so much more food and stuff." His enthusiasm was palpable, and Maddie felt a pang of guilt for her own reluctance.

"Exactly." Tom smiled at Jackson, the corners of his eyes crinkling. "It even has a luggage rack, and the van has some modifications that might come in handy on the road."

Maddie couldn't hold back any longer. "So, what? You're just coming with us? Up to Dad's place?" She heard the accusation in her voice and saw her mom flinch at her tone.

The room fell silent, tension thick in the air.

Her mom took a deep breath before responding, her voice steady but with an undercurrent of pleading. "We're going to try to call your father again and make sure it's okay. But yes, if he agrees, Tom will come with us."

"And if Dad says no?" Maddie challenged, crossing her arms over her chest.

"Then I'll help you get as far as I can," Tom said quietly. His calm demeanor in the face of her hostility made Maddie feel childish. "Your safety is what matters most. I've heard the same things your dad did about the smaller towns not having the National Guard securing them. And I might have an idea how you can get out of Casper. People are being escorted through town, but you have to show your identification and prove you live elsewhere. They let people through twice per day. As soon as the phones start working again, I'll try to reach my brother and see if he can help us."

Maddie's anger deflated, replaced by a confusing mixture of gratitude and uncertainty. She looked at her mom, saw the hope and fear battling in her eyes, and made a decision. It wasn't easy, but she knew it was necessary. "Do you think he can?"

"Maybe. If the plan I'm working on is possible, he'll know how to help us."

"Okay," she said softly as she uncrossed her arms. "If . . . if this is what we're doing, then I'm in. All the way."

The relief on her mom's face was evident. She moved to Maddie and pulled her into a tight hug, whispering, "Thank you, sweetheart. We're going to get through this together."

As they broke apart, Jackson piped up, "So, when do we leave?"

"As soon as we can reach your father and figure out a way to get out of town," her mom replied, running a hand through her hair.

They spent the next hour trying to get through on the phones. Tom and her mom took turns dialing, while Maddie and Jackson attempted texts, only to get a failure-to-send notice. The internet was still out. Nothing seemed to work. The atmosphere grew more tense with each failed attempt.

"The cell towers must be down again," Tom muttered. He paced the room, phone in hand, trying to find even a single bar of signal.

"My phone's dying," Jackson added, tossing it aside with a sigh.

"You can charge it in the car," his mom offered.

A knot of anxiety formed in Maddie's stomach. The reality of their situation was sinking in, bringing with it a host of new fears. "What if we can't reach him? What if we get all the way there and he's . . . he's not . . ."

"Don't think like that," her mom said firmly, though Maddie could see the worry in her eyes. "We'll keep trying. And if we can't reach him, we'll figure something out."

As the evening wore on, they began the task of gathering supplies. Tom's van was indeed spacious, and they were able to pack far more than Maddie had initially thought possible. She watched as Tom efficiently organized the space, his experience with the vehicle evident in every move.

"We'll empty the fuel from all the cars," Tom explained as they worked, wiping sweat from his brow. "I've got some gas cans we can strap on the luggage rack. Every little bit will help."

As Maddie helped load boxes of canned goods into the van, Jackson nudged her side. "Told you so," he whispered with a smug grin on his face.

"Told me what?" she hissed back, though she couldn't muster any real annoyance.

"That Mom would figure it out. That Tom would help."

She rolled her eyes, but she couldn't help the small smile that tugged at her lips. "Yeah, yeah. When did you get so smart, anyway?"

Jackson shrugged, his grin widening. "Someone has to be the mature one around here."

She snorted and gave him a playful shove. For a moment, it felt like old times—just her and her annoying little brother, teasing each other like the world hadn't fallen apart around them.

As night fell, they gathered in the living room. They'd packed almost all the food from the pantry. They planned to empty Tom's pantry and take it, too, provided he was invited to go.

He'd brought over another frozen dinner, this time enchiladas, cooking it on the grill. With the power out, the house felt off, so they ate on the deck.

"I hope the power comes back on soon," Tom said. "I've got more stuff in the freezer. I've been running the generator to keep it frozen, but I'm almost out of fuel, except for what we set aside for the cars. If things are still frozen solid, we can put everything in coolers to take with us."

"We'll keep trying the phones," her mom said, her voice tinged with worry. She sat on the couch, Tom beside her, their shoulders touching. "If we still can't get through . . . we'll have to make a decision."

"About whether to go without talking to Dad first?" Maddie asked, voicing the concern they all shared.

Her mom nodded, her eyes distant. "It isn't ideal, but we might not have a choice. The longer we wait . . ."

"The more dangerous it gets," Tom finished for her. His hand found her mom's, and he gave it a reassuring squeeze.

They sat in silence for a moment. Finally, Jackson spoke up, his voice small but determined. "We'll be okay, right? As long as we're together?"

Their mom wrapped an arm around his shoulders. "That's right, honey. We've got each other. That's what matters most."

Maddie watched them, feeling a complex mix of emotions. Part of her still rebelled against this new family dynamic, against Tom's presence in their lives. But a larger part recognized the truth in Jackson's words from earlier. Their mom was trying, really trying, to do what was best for them.

After a rather quiet dinner, Tom said his goodbyes.

"I'm exhausted," her mom said after closing the door behind Tom. "I'm going to bed."

As she prepared for bed, the house still dark and quiet without power, Maddie found herself hoping that tomorrow would bring answers. That they'd reach their dad and that they'd find a safe path to him.

That somehow, in this broken world, they'd find a way to be a family again—whatever that might look like now.

Chapter 32

Maddie jerked awake to the low buzz of the electricity flickering back to life. The room was lit up, and she groaned—she must've left the light on before crashing.

Outside, it was still pitch dark, way too early for anyone to be awake. She sat up and rubbed her face, still groggy. Faint noises drifted up from downstairs, and her stomach twisted. *Who's up at this hour?* she wondered. *Mom, of course.*

Going softly down the stairs, Maddie found her mom in the kitchen, huddled over a steaming cup.

"Still no luck with the phones or internet," she said, noticing Maddie's questioning look. "But at least we have power again."

Maddie leaned against the doorframe and studied her mother's face. The lines of worry seemed deeper than ever, etched into her skin like a map of their troubles. "Have you been up all night?"

She shrugged and took another sip of her coffee. "Couldn't sleep. Too much on my mind."

"Yeah. The lights coming back on woke me up." Maddie moved to the cabinet and grabbed a mug for herself. As Maddie poured her coffee, she stared into the mug, her thoughts tangled.

The silence between them stretched on, thick and uncomfortable. After several more minutes, Maddie said softly, "Are you worried about leaving or . . .?"

Her mother's eyes met hers over the rim of her mug. "I am. Are you?"

Maddie stirred her coffee slowly, buying time as she considered her response. "Yeah," she admitted finally. "But not for the same reasons as you, I think."

Her mom raised an eyebrow, inviting her to continue.

Maddie took a deep breath, steeling herself. "I'm worried about Dad. About how he'll react when we show up with . . . with Tom."

Her mother's face tightened, and a flicker of defensiveness crossed her features. "Your father and I have been divorced for years, Maddie. He's moved on, and so have I."

"Have you?" The words slipped out before she could stop them, sharper than she intended.

The kitchen fell silent; the only sound was the soft ticking of the clock on the wall. Her mom sat her mug down with a deliberate slowness that spoke volumes about her restrained anger.

"That's not fair, Maddie. You have no idea what I've been through, what I'm still going through."

"And whose fault is that? You brought it all on yourself. You think it's been easy for Jackson and me? You've never talked to us, never explained— "

"Because you were children!" her mom interrupted, her voice rising slightly. "You still are! It wasn't your job to understand or to fix my problems. Problems I didn't even know I had for years. I always knew there was something . . . different about me. But I had no idea I was sick. Mentally ill."

"No, it was just our job to live with those problems, with your supposed illness," Maddie shot back, immediately regretting her words as she saw the hurt flash across her mother's face.

Her mom turned away, her shoulders slumping. "I've made mistakes, Maddie. So many mistakes. But everything I've done, everything I'm doing now, is to try to make things better. For you and Jackson."

The anger drained out of Maddie, leaving her feeling hollow and tired. She moved closer to her mom and hesitantly placed a hand on her arm. "I know, Mom. I know you're trying. It's just . . . it's a lot to process."

Her mother turned back to her, eyes glistening with unshed tears. "I'm scared, too, you know. Scared of leaving, scared of facing your father, scared of what might happen if we stay. But we have to do something, Maddie. We can't just wait for things to get worse."

Maddie nodded, feeling the truth of her mother's words. She thought about Jackson, still sleeping upstairs, blissfully unaware of the tension between them. She thought about her dad, waiting for them in the lodge up the North Fork, unaware of the changes heading his way.

"I'm sorry," Maddie said softly. "I shouldn't have said those things. I know you're doing your best."

Her mom pulled her into a tight hug, and for a moment, Maddie felt like a little girl. Like the little girl she'd always wished she could be. Safe in her mother's arms. "I'm sorry, too, sweetie. For everything."

As they pulled apart, Maddie silently renewed her vow. No more arguments, and no more pushing back against her mom's decisions. Whatever lay ahead, they needed to face it as a united front.

"So," Maddie said, forcing a lightness into her tone, "what's the plan for today?"

Her mom smiled, a genuine smile that reached her eyes. "We pack, we prepare, and we pray either the phones start working or the internet comes back so we can let your father know we're coming."

"Sounds like a plan. I'll start breakfast if you want to grab a shower. Take advantage of it while the power is on and everything is working."

As her mom headed upstairs, Maddie pulled out pans and ingredients. They'd packed most of the food yesterday, but they'd left out a package of pancake mix for breakfast this morning, along with a partially empty bag of chocolate chips. Chocolate chip pancakes sounded delicious.

The sun was just beginning to peek over the horizon, painting the sky in shades of pink and gold. A new day was dawning, bringing with it the promise of change and the hope of a fresh start.

It wasn't long before her mom returned. The exhaustion was still evident in her eyes, but she appeared more refreshed. Jackson was behind her, waving his tablet. "Still no internet, and I haven't heard from Eddie in forever. I want to tell him we're leaving. Did you notice the date?"

"The date?" Maddie said in a mocking tone.

He stuck his tongue out at her before turning to their mother. "It's the Fourth of July. Independence Day. You know, barbecues, fireworks, and stuff."

Her mom gave a sad smile and a shake of her head. "If only things were still that simple."

"Maybe, if the power stays on, we can watch the movie? The one about the aliens attacking on the Fourth of July. Grandma has it on DVD."

"I do love the end where the pilot tells the aliens he's baaaaaack," her mom snickered.

"I like the president's speech." Jackson grabbed the bottle of syrup and moved it to his mouth like a microphone.

"We're fighting to be free, not from mean, brain-sucking aliens who blow things up—but from innocent-looking folks who suddenly start humming . . . and then blow things up.

"We're fighting to keep on living, to leave the city and go to the country.

"And if we win today, the Fourth of July won't just be an American holiday anymore. It'll be the day the whole world said together: We're not afraid of your songs! We won't let you beat us with golf clubs! We're going to show you! We're going to survive! Today, we celebrate our Independence Day!"

Maddie shook her head and whispered, "Dork," with a wide smile on her face.

Their mom clapped. "Bravo! Bravo!"

Jackson took a bow, then poured syrup on his pancakes. "Thank you, thank you. I'll be here all week."

Maddie giggled. "Or at least until the syrup runs out."

Their mom's smile faded slightly, and she glanced out the window, the laughter momentarily eclipsed by the reminder of their reality. "All right, eat up, everyone. We've got a long day ahead of us."

Jackson's grin faltered, but he quickly recovered and looked at Maddie. "Last one done eating washes the dishes?"

"Loser washes everything," she replied, her eyes sparkling.

"Deal!" Jackson said as he shoveled pancakes into his mouth.

For a brief moment, the worries outside the walls of their home seemed a little less daunting, replaced by the warmth of family and the simple joys of a morning breakfast.

The day unfolded in a flurry of activity. Boxes were packed. Decisions were made about what to take and what to leave behind. Food, toiletries, and heavy-duty clothes would be needed at the lodge. While they had electricity there, in most of the cabins, the main lodge also had a whole-building generator, along with a solar electrical system.

Jackson suggested they bring the DVD player and all of Grandma Bea's DVDs too. Her mom didn't want to waste the limited space they had on movies. "I'm sure your grandparents have movies. Don't they keep a stash of books, games, and movies for their guests?"

"They do," Maddie agreed.

"But not the same ones Grandma Bea has," Jackson added.

"Go ahead and grab some. You can use that small box." She pointed to a midsized box.

"We should bring some of Grandma's books too. She'll go straight there as soon as she can get out of Alaska. She'll want to have books."

Jackson was probably right about that. Their grandma loved to read. Even more than watching movies, she read. Usually, she used her eReader, but she kept her favorite books in paperback, too, saying she needed backups in case her battery was dead or the eBook broke.

Tears filled their mom's eyes. "When your grandma is able to get out of Alaska, she'll appreciate having a few of her favorites. That's good thinking, Jackson."

Maddie, like her mom, knew the chances of her grandma making it to the lodge were slim. Beyond slim—practically nonexistent. She'd be stuck in Alaska until the situation with the Star Brights was figured out and stopped. How that was going to happen, Maddie did not know.

In the early days, the president and his medical advisers held regular press conferences. Now they were suspiciously silent on the entire thing. They'd even stopped mentioning a vaccine or how they thought the illness was being spread. The official silence was concerning.

As the packing continued, Maddie found herself lost in thought. She recalled a few summers ago when she and Jackson had gone up to the lodge.

Grandpa Dick and Grandma Ruth had only bought the lodge the previous year, just before hunting season. While it had been sold as a turnkey operation, they'd planned many upgrades and improvements, which they'd begun over the winter.

Grandma Bea had driven them up and, at her dad's invitation, stayed a couple of days. Maddie's mom was in treatment then, at an inpatient facility after she stopped her meds and went on a binge . . . again.

Being at the lodge was nearly perfect. It had been a simpler time, filled with hikes, fishing, and stories by the campfire. Her dad had always known how to make them laugh, even when things got tough.

"Hey, remember that summer at the lodge when Grandpa Dick tried to teach us how to fish?" Maddie asked, smiling at the memory. "He ended up catching his own hat instead of a fish."

Jackson laughed. "Yeah, and then he blamed it on the 'legendary hat-stealing trout.' He kept that story going all summer."

Their mom chuckled, a soft, bittersweet sound. "Your grandfather always did have a way of turning mishaps into adventures. Grandma Bea got a kick out of retelling that story."

"Do you think there will be times like that when we go up there now? Will things be closer to normal? Can we enjoy things like fishing, or will it only be for survival?"

Her mom sighed as she folded a sweater and placed it in a box. "I don't know, Maddie. But I'd like to think we'll be safe . . . safer, anyway. The lodge and the cabins are in such a remote area. Cody's almost an hour away, and we know Yellowstone was closed down and evacuated. There's nothing else around, so . . . Besides, we don't have many options left."

The hours slipped by as they packed, each item a piece of their lives being carefully wrapped and tucked away. When lunchtime rolled around, Maddie's stomach growled loudly, breaking the silence. "How about a break? I'm starving."

Her mom wiped her forehead with the back of her hand. "Sounds good. I left out some soup, a mixture of single cans. Should I mix them all together into . . . well, something that may be interesting? Or should we heat each can individually?"

"There's four cans," Jackson said, pointing to the counter.

"Um, yes. Tom should be here anytime. He had guard duty at the barricade this morning, but that ended at noon. It's ten after now."

The warm feelings of family Maddie had been experiencing as they packed and reminisced faded abruptly.

She knew her mom wanted Tom to go with them. But even though they'd tried calling and texting many times, plus checked the internet to see if it was working, they hadn't been able to reach her dad to make sure bringing Tom along would be okay. Maddie thought it was a bad idea, but she knew she was outvoted.

Maddie's smile wavered, and the earlier laughter was replaced by awkward glances. She took a deep breath and plastered on a forced smile, trying to bridge the gap. "Let's just mix them all together. Might be fun to see what we end up with."

Jackson gave a halfhearted chuckle. "Soup roulette. Sounds adventurous."

Their mom nodded, trying to keep the mood light. "All right, then. Soup roulette it is."

As they opened the cans and poured the contents into a pot, Maddie glanced out the window, the sky now overcast and gray. The sense of impending change loomed over them, a constant reminder of the uncertainty ahead.

Chapter 33

The aroma of their experimental soup roulette wafted through the kitchen as Maddie stirred the peculiar concoction. It was a medley of vegetables, pasta, and various broths swirled together, creating an oddly enticing scent.

The doorbell cut through the simmering sounds, prompting her mom to hurry toward the entrance, her fingers combing through her hair in a last-minute attempt at tidiness.

Maddie couldn't help but roll her eyes as she heard Tom's voice drift in from the entryway, its familiar timbre tinged with an eagerness that grated on her nerves.

"I hope I'm not too late for lunch," Tom said, his easy smile visible as he entered the kitchen. He wore a plaid button-down shirt tucked into well-worn jeans, looking every bit the friendly neighbor he'd become.

"Your timing is perfect," her mom replied, her voice a touch too cheerful for Maddie's liking. "We're having a . . . unique soup today."

Tom raised an eyebrow and peered into the pot with genuine curiosity. "Looks interesting. What do you call this culinary creation?"

"Soup roulette," Jackson said, grinning from ear to ear. "We mixed four single cans together. It's like a flavor adventure in every spoonful!"

"Adventurous indeed." Tom chuckled and settled into a chair at the table. "I'm always up for a good food experiment."

Maddie ladled the soup into bowls, trying to ignore the awkward energy permeating the room. The soup was a bizarre mixture of colors and textures: chunks of chicken, beans, and vegetables floated alongside noodles and pieces of tomato.

As they ate, the conversation felt forced, each of them searching for safe topics that wouldn't stir up the underlying tension.

"So, uh, how was guard duty?" Maddie asked, breaking a silence that had stretched a bit too long. She stirred her soup, watching the various ingredients swirl together. It certainly didn't look very appealing, but the taste wasn't too bad.

Tom swallowed a spoonful before answering, his expression thoughtful. "Quiet, thankfully. No incidents to report. People seem to be hunkering down and staying out of sight."

Her mom's eyes darted between Tom and her children. "That's good to hear. We made a lot of progress with the packing today. It's amazing how much stuff you accumulate over the years. We're bringing a few things for my mom too." She pointed to the boxes marked *Bea*, which held not only books but practical shoes and clothing along with keepsakes and photos.

"We'll start loading the SUV after lunch," Maddie declared.

"About that," her mom said, setting down her spoon with a soft clink against the bowl. Her voice took on a more serious tone. "Even if we can't reach your father, Tom will be coming with us."

Maddie's stomach tightened, and the soup suddenly became less appetizing. She forced herself to nod, remembering her promise to stop arguing. The spoon felt heavy in her hand as she lifted another mouthful to her lips.

Jackson, on the other hand, seemed pleased by the news. His face lit up, a stark contrast to Maddie's carefully neutral expression. "That's great! Tom can help us if we run into any trouble on the road. Plus, he knows all those cool survival tricks!"

Tom smiled, though Maddie noticed a flicker of uncertainty in his eyes. It was brief, but it made her wonder if he was as confident about this arrangement as he appeared.

"I'll do my best. I've gone camping quite a bit, but I'm not sure I have survival tricks," he said, his voice warm but with an undercurrent of seriousness. "Most of what I know, I learned in video games. Just like you, Jackson. That said, roads might be challenging, but together, I think we stand a good chance. We'll make it a convoy."

As they continued eating, Maddie found herself studying Tom more closely. She had to admit, grudgingly, that he had been a stabilizing presence in their lives over the past weeks. His calm demeanor and practical knowledge were invaluable during the neighborhood watch meetings and in helping them prepare for their journey.

"This soup isn't half bad," Tom commented, scraping the bottom of his bowl. "It's like a culinary tour of your pantry."

Jackson laughed. "Yeah, who knew chicken noodle and bean with bacon could be friends?"

As lunch wound down, Tom stood to leave, straightening his collar. "I should head home soon to work on my own packing. There's a lot to sort through."

"Do you need any help?" her mom offered, a little too quickly for Maddie's liking.

Tom shook his head, a small smile playing on his lips. "I appreciate the offer, but I think I can manage. However," he paused, his eyes brightening with an idea, "why don't you all come over for dinner tonight? We can make an evening of it before we leave in the morning."

Her mom agreed enthusiastically, her face lighting up at the idea. "That sounds wonderful. What time should we come over?"

"Let's say around six? That'll give me time to pack and prepare something for us."

As they walked Tom to the door, Maddie couldn't help but feel a mixture of emotions. Part of her was grateful for his help and the sense of security he provided, but another part still resented the change he represented in their family dynamic.

"See you at six," Tom said, giving them a wave as he headed down the driveway.

As Tom disappeared from view, Maddie felt a sudden heaviness in the air. She glanced up and down the street, taking in the profound quiet that had settled over their once-bustling neighborhood.

Driveways that used to be filled with cars were now empty. The Webers' house across the street, where Charla had attacked her husband just weeks ago, was dark and lifeless. They'd heard Peter Weber had left town a day or so after his wife's death.

No one saw him go and didn't even know he'd gone until Elliot Blackwell and a few others broke down his door, fearing the worst. They were relieved to find the home abandoned. Food and useful supplies were organized and even passed around.

Maddie's family received a small grocery bag. She crinkled her brow. In fact, she thought one of the cans of soup they'd eaten today may have been part of that allotment.

"It's so strange," Jackson murmured, following Maddie's gaze. "Remember when we used to have block parties every summer? Now it's like a ghost town."

Their mom placed a hand on each of their shoulders, her touch gentle but firm. "Things change, but we adapt. That's what we're doing now."

As soon as the door closed, her mom turned to them, her eyes shining with a determination Maddie hadn't seen in years. "All right, team. We've got a few hours to finish packing and tidying up. Let's make the most of it."

The afternoon passed in a whirlwind of activity. Maddie found herself moving from room to room, helping Jackson sort through his belongings and assisting her mom with the shared spaces. The atmosphere was charged with a mixture of tension and unexpected moments of levity.

Their main goal was to take things that could be of use in their life up at the lodge. The challenge was that they didn't exactly know what that life would hold.

"Hey, remember this?" Jackson held up a battered Monopoly box. "Remember how Grandma Bea always let us team up against her?"

Maddie couldn't help but smile at the memory. "Yeah, and she'd still manage to bankrupt us both."

Their mom paused in her sorting, and a wistful expression crossed her face. "My mom always did have a knack for strategy games. Maybe we should bring it along?"

The moment hung in the air, fragile and bittersweet. Maddie felt a pang of guilt for her earlier resentment.

Despite everything, they were still a family, trying their best to navigate an impossible situation.

As they worked, Maddie found herself studying her mom and brother more closely. Jackson, usually so carefree, moved with a new sense of purpose. He carefully packed his favorite books and games, occasionally asking for advice on what was truly necessary.

Her mom seemed to be drawing strength from the task at hand. Her movements were decisive, her instructions clear. It was as if the act of preparing for their journey had awakened something in her—a resilience Maddie had almost forgotten existed.

Eventually, Maddie found herself in her room, sorting through the remnants of her childhood. Each item sparked a memory—the stuffed bear her dad won at a carnival, the friendship bracelet from her best friend in elementary school, the dog-eared copy of her favorite book about a boy who survived a plane crash. She hadn't read it in years but remembered it had some excellent survival tips in it. She'd bring it along, just in case there were tips in there that could help them.

As she packed, her mind wandered to the uncertain future ahead. The thought of leaving behind everything she'd ever known filled her with a mixture of fear and strange excitement. She thought about Tom joining them on their journey, and her stomach twisted with conflicting emotions.

On one hand, she couldn't deny that his presence made her feel safer. He had been a steady, calming influence over the past weeks. But on the other hand, the thought of him potentially becoming a permanent part of their family made her uneasy.

What will Dad think? And Grandpa Dick? How will this change the dynamic between all of us? Those thoughts swirled in her mind, leaving her feeling unsettled and torn.

She wanted to be supportive of her mom, to be the mature, understanding daughter. But a part of her still clung to the hope of her parents reconciling, of their family being whole again. Tom's presence complicated that dream, and she wasn't sure how to feel about it.

"Maddie?" her mom's voice drifted in from the hallway. "Can I come in?"

"Sure," she replied as she hastily wiped away her tears.

Her mom's eyes softened as she took in the scene. "It's hard, isn't it? Deciding what to take and what to leave behind. Especially since we have such limited space."

Maddie nodded, not trusting her voice.

Her mom sat down beside her on the bed and picked up the stuffed bear. "You know, it's okay to be scared. To be angry, even. This isn't how any of us imagined our lives would go."

Maddie looked at her mom, really looked at her for the first time in what felt like ages. She saw the lines of worry around her eyes, the gray strands peeking through her hair. But she also saw strength there, and love.

"I know I haven't always been the mom you deserved. But I want you to know that everything I'm doing now, including asking Tom to come with us, is because I want to keep you and Jackson safe."

Maddie felt the walls she'd built up start to crumble. "I know, Mom. I just . . . I worry about Dad. About how he'll react when we show up with Tom."

Her mom nodded, understanding in her eyes. "Your father and I may have our differences, but he wants us to be safe. We'll figure it out together, okay?"

Maddie leaned into her mom's embrace, drawing comfort. Had she ever felt so vulnerable and yet so secure at the same time? Had her mom ever been the one to provide that security? Not that she could recall. It was definitely a first. And she liked it.

As they sat there, surrounded by the remnants of her childhood, she felt a shift in her perspective. The journey ahead was still daunting, the future uncertain. But at that moment, wrapped in her mother's arms, she found a glimmer of hope. Whatever challenges lay ahead, they would face them as a family—a family that was changing and evolving, but still bound by love.

With renewed determination, Maddie pulled away gently and reached for another box. "We should finish packing. We've got a long day ahead of us tomorrow."

Her mom smiled, a mixture of pride and gratitude in her eyes. "That's my girl," she said softly, reaching for a stack of clothes. "Let's do this together."

Chapter 34

As they walked the short distance to Tom's house, the evening air was hot and stifling. Exactly as every Fourth of July Maddie could remember. Only this one was quiet. Too quiet.

People should be in their yards laughing and barbecuing. Children should be in the streets, throwing Poppers and jumping back at the bang. As darkness approached, they'd use sparklers to write their names.

Would those things ever happen again? Maddie had her doubts.

Tom greeted them at the door, the smell of grilled chicken wafting from inside. "Come on in! I've got a surprise for you all."

They stepped into Tom's living room, which had been transformed into a cozy dining area. The coffee table was laden with plates of food—grilled chicken, roasted vegetables, and what looked like homemade bread.

"Wow, Tom!" her mom exclaimed with wide eyes. "This looks amazing."

Tom beamed, clearly pleased with their reaction. "I figured we could use a good meal before our journey. But that's not the only surprise."

He gestured to his laptop on a side table. "The internet's back up. Just happened a minute ago. I've already messaged my brother, and I thought you might want to send some messages. You're welcome to use my computer or your phones . . . whatever you need."

Maddie's heart leaped. She pulled her phone from her pocket and quickly navigated to her email. With trembling fingers, she pecked out a message to her dad, explaining their plans to come to the lodge and asking if it was okay for Tom to join them.

She followed with a message to her grandma via Chum Fun, ensuring her they were working on a plan to get out of Casper and hoped to leave the next morning.

"I'm messaging Eddie," Jackson said. "Letting him know we're going to Grandma and Grandpa's place. I hope he's okay. It's been forever since I talked to him."

As Maddie hit send, she heard her mom gasp. "Tom! A message just popped up. It looks like your brother responded already!"

They gathered around Tom's computer and read the message. "Yes, there's a way out of Casper," Tom read aloud, his voice filled with excitement. "You need to be at the check station at six tomorrow morning. Use the code word 'Yellowstone Sunrise' and they'll let you through. With that code, you won't have to provide your identification and won't have to prove where you're traveling to."

A collective sigh of relief filled the room. The tension that had been building for weeks seemed to dissipate slightly, replaced by cautious optimism.

Tom continued reading, "The small towns between Casper and Cody won't be a problem. If you reach Cody by 7:00 p.m., they'll provide an escort through town. If you don't make it by 7:00, you'll need to camp outside of town and try again at 7:00 a.m. Those are the only times you can go through town."

"This is really happening," Maddie murmured, the reality of their impending journey sinking in. She glanced at Jackson, who was practically bouncing with excitement.

"Yellowstone Sunrise," Jackson repeated, testing the words. "Sounds like something out of a spy movie."

As they sat down for dinner, the mood was lighter than it had been in weeks. The chicken was delicious, as were the vegetables, even though Tom said they would've been better if he'd had fresh instead of frozen.

"I didn't think frozen veggies would hold up in the cooler too well, anyway," he said. "Same with the bread. It's also from the freezer."

They discussed the route, double-checking their supplies and going over the timeline for the morning.

"We should leave here by five," Tom suggested as he took a bite of chicken. "That'll give us plenty of time to get to the checkpoint. It's just on the other side of the airport. My brother mentioned it to me before."

Her mom nodded, her fork paused midway to her mouth. "Agreed. We'll need to be up by four at the latest to finish loading up. We have the SUV almost finished, but we'll need to add things to your van. I'll admit, we've probably packed more than we should have."

"Maybe we should take my car," Maddie suggested, her voice holding little conviction. They'd already had this conversation and decided two cars were plenty. She knew her mom was worried about her driving on her own with the way things were. Truth be told, she worried about it herself.

"No, no." Her mom shook her head. "Two cars are enough. We need you as an extra driver in case . . . in case one of us gets tired or something."

"Which reminds me," Tom said, "I have the walkie-talkies I told you about. They'll allow us to stay in contact in case the phones don't work . . . which is what we expect to happen."

"Walkie-talkies?" Jackson said, his eyes lighting up. "That's cool."

As they ate, Maddie found herself actually enjoying Tom's company. His calm demeanor and practical approach to their situation were reassuring. She could see why her mom had been drawn to him.

After dinner, as they helped clear the table, Jackson said, "Hey, since the internet's working, let's get in a few games. Who knows when we'll be able to play again? I packed mine, but I'm not sure we'll have electricity. Besides, I'd really like to see if Eddie's on."

Tom's eyes lit up. "Great idea! I was planning to bring my system too. My computer, too, in case I can work again. Might as well get in one last session here."

Maddie hesitated, memories of her past experiences with the game flooding back. The immersive world, the strange pull it seemed to have on people . . . she didn't really care for it.

Seeing the eager looks on Jackson's and her mom's faces, she found herself nodding. "Okay, why not?"

They gathered in Tom's basement, where his elaborate gaming setup awaited them. The room was dimly lit, with soft LED lights creating a cozy atmosphere. Like upstairs, he had more collectibles, but these were all sports focused—footballs, hockey sticks, baseballs, and bats. All were properly displayed, and all seemed to be signed.

The gaming chairs looked inviting, each with its own VR headset resting on the seat. "All right, everyone," Tom said, his voice taking on the tone of an excited tour guide. "Let's get you all set up."

He walked them through the process of adjusting the headsets and reminding them of the basic controls. Maddie watched as her mom fumbled with the equipment, a mixture of confusion and determination on her face.

"You sure you want to try this, Mom?" Maddie asked, a hint of teasing in her voice.

Her mom grinned, looking younger than she had in years. "Don't worry. I've been playing with Jackson, and I'm getting pretty good. Just watch, I'll probably win it all."

"Let's try to stay on the rug." Tom pointed to the bright circle on the floor. "This game is best experienced while standing. Remember, it can be a bit disorienting at first. If you need to take a break, just let me know."

Maddie took a deep breath as she slipped on the headset. The familiar loading screen appeared, the game's logo floating in a sea of stars. As the world began to materialize around her, she felt excited yet apprehensive.

The game opened in a bustling virtual city, filled with players from around the world. Avatars of all shapes and sizes moved about, some clearly new to the game, others decked out in high-level gear.

"Wow," she heard Jackson's voice through the headset. "This is so cool! Your system is so much better than mine. Everything is brighter."

Maddie had to agree. Despite her reservations, she couldn't help but be impressed by the detail of the virtual world. Every building, every character, even the leaves on the trees seemed to pulse with life.

"All right, team," Tom's voice came through, his avatar appearing beside them. "Ready for an adventure?"

As they took their first steps into the game world, Maddie felt a strange sense of freedom. Here, in this virtual space, the troubles of the real world seemed far away. No Star Brights, no food shortages, no constant fear.

For a moment, she allowed herself to get lost in the game, to forget about the journey that awaited them in the morning. Tomorrow would bring new challenges, new fears. But for now, in this digital realm, they were just a family, enjoying a moment of normalcy in a world turned upside down.

As they embarked on their first quest, Maddie couldn't help but wonder what adventures—both virtual and real—lay ahead of them. The code word "Yellowstone Sunrise" echoed in her mind, a beacon of hope in the uncertainty that surrounded them.

As they navigated through the virtual city, Maddie noticed something peculiar in the corner of her screen. A small, glowing symbol caught her attention. She remembered seeing it the first time she'd played, the day Jackson was over at his friend's house and she'd been bored out of her mind. So bored, she decided a video game would help pass the time.

That was the same day the explosion took out her mom's work and Casper—the entire world—began its downward spiral.

"What do I do about that thing in the corner?" Maddie asked, her voice laced with curiosity.

"What thing in the corner?" Jackson replied, confusion evident in his tone.

"The orange ball, down on the bottom," Maddie explained, her eyes fixed on the unfamiliar icon.

Tom's avatar turned toward her. "I see it too," he confirmed. "It looks like a sun. Sunshine."

"I don't," Jackson said, a hint of frustration in his voice. "I never see it. I've heard others talk about it, but it doesn't come up for everyone."

Her mom's avatar spun around, clearly searching. "Where's the sun? I don't see anything like that."

Tom's avatar reached out, seemingly interacting with something invisible to the others. "Let me just click on it and see what happens."

Suddenly, the virtual world exploded into a blinding light. Maddie gasped, the intensity overwhelming her senses. She ripped off her headset and blinked rapidly to clear the spots from her vision. Jackson and her mom had done the same, their faces mirroring her shock and discomfort.

But Tom hadn't removed his headset. He stood in the middle of the room, swaying gently with a serene smile on his face. And then, to Maddie's horror, he began to hum.

Chapter 35

The familiar melody of "Twinkle, Twinkle, Little Star" filled the air, Tom's voice eerily calm and content.

"It's so beautiful," he murmured, his body moving in a slow dance. "Yes. Yes, I understand now."

Maddie, Jackson, and their mom exchanged terrified glances. The realization of what was happening washed over Maddie. The game, the humming—it was all connected to the Star Brights. And now, Tom had become one of them.

The serene smile on Tom's face twisted into something unnatural as he swayed to the melody. Maddie's heart raced as she watched the transformation unfold before her eyes.

Her mom raised a finger to her lips, signaling for silence. Her eyes, wide with fear and disbelief, darted between her children and Tom. She motioned toward the stairs, her movements slow and deliberate.

Maddie felt her muscles tense, ready to bolt at any moment. The basement, once a cozy gaming haven, now felt like a trap. The soft glow of the LED lights cast sinister shadows, making Tom's silhouette seem more menacing with each passing second.

As they began to inch away, Tom's hand reached up to remove his headset. The trance-like state that had gripped him seemed to be lifting, replaced by something more threatening. He stepped away from the VR rug, gravitating toward his collection of sports memorabilia, seemingly lost in his own world.

The collection, once a source of pride for Tom, now cast a threatening presence in the dim light. Signed baseballs, previously intriguing, seemed like potential projectiles. The sight of vintage wooden bats, their polished surfaces reflecting the faint light, sent a shiver down Maddie's spine.

They had barely reached the bottom of the stairs when a blood-curdling cry echoed through the house. "Heather!" Tom's voice was filled with a manic excitement. "It's so beautiful. You have to see. You have to see!"

The cry reverberated off the walls, seeming to come from everywhere at once. Maddie's breath caught in her throat, and her heart pounded so hard she could feel it in her fingertips.

Her mom grabbed her and Jackson by their arms, practically dragging them up the stairs. Their feet pounded against the steps, each thud matching the frantic beating of Maddie's heart.

"Do we go home?" Jackson gasped as they reached the top landing.

Her mom shook her head, determination flashing in her eyes. "Go directly to the garage. We're leaving now. We can't stay. We'll find someplace to hide until morning when we can go through the checkpoint."

As they burst into the main-floor hallway, Tom charged up the stairs behind them. The door, once locked to keep them safe from the outside world, had become a barrier, trapping them with the very danger they were fleeing— Tom, whose presence had suddenly turned from trusted ally to imminent threat.

The irony of their safety measure now working against them wasn't lost on Maddie. The heavy locks were supposed to keep danger out, but instead, they'd become a trap, sealing them inside the house that had turned from a sanctuary to a battlefield in an instant.

Maddie's heart raced as she glanced back, seeing Tom's determined expression as he reached the landing with the baseball bat gripped tightly in his hands. The bat, usually a symbol of leisure and sport, now seemed menacing in the dim light of the staircase, its polished wood catching glints of light. She could almost make out the signature on it. Was it the one he said he'd gotten at a Dodgers game?

Maddie's thoughts flashed to Tom's animated tales of getting it signed, memories that now seemed distant, belonging to another lifetime.

He swung the bat casually at his side, a smile playing on his lips. She exchanged a quick glance with her mom, their fear reflected in each other's eyes. The air around them felt charged with tension, the hallway suddenly feeling claustrophobic as Tom's presence loomed over them like a shadow.

"Heather, honey," Tom called out, his voice calm. "You didn't really think you could leave without me, did you?"

Maddie froze. She exchanged a quick, uneasy glance with her mom, who stood beside her, eyes wide with fear. Tom's calm demeanor sent a shiver down Maddie's spine, the baseball bat in his hand now seeming like a weapon poised to strike.

The disconnect between Tom's soothing tone and the menace in his eyes made Maddie's skin crawl. It was as if two different people were occupying the same body, battling for control.

Her mom took a step forward and placed herself between Tom and them, her voice shaky but determined. "Tom, please . . . you don't have to do this."

Tom's smile widened, but it held none of its usual warmth. "Oh, but I do, Heather. I really do. You'll understand soon. You'll thank me. We'll be together. Together forever. We can have the family you've always wanted. You can be the mom you said you wished you could be. There will be no distractions."

He glanced at Maddie. "No bratty teens misbehaving. It'll be perfect. Utopia. You told me. You told me you wished you could go back and do it all over again. You can let me show you how."

Each word felt like a knife twisting in Maddie's gut. The intimate knowledge Tom possessed and the secrets her mother had shared were now weaponized against them.

Maddie's mind raced as she tried to make sense of what was happening. It didn't feel real. The way he was playing the game one minute, happy, kind, helpful Tom. A neighbor they trusted. Now, his presence filled the hallway with an unsettling tension, turning their safe haven into a trap. He was a Star Bright.

"Tom," Jackson's voice quivered from behind Maddie. "What are you doing?"

Tom's gaze flicked to Jackson, his expression momentarily softening before hardening again. "Just making sure no one leaves without me," he replied casually, as if discussing the weather.

"We're going to be a family. A loving family. A family where you can call her— " He pointed at Heather. "Where you can call her mom. That's what she wants, you know. She wants you to call her mom. To allow her to hug you and tell you bedtime stories. To share in your life."

The words landed hard, rattling Maddie to her core. The betrayal in her mother's eyes, the hurt on Jackson's face—it was all too much. The family dynamics they'd struggled with for so long were being laid bare in this moment of crisis, adding another layer of pain to an already unbearable situation.

"Tom," her mom hissed out his name. "Please. I told you about those things in confidence."

Maddie's thoughts raced. They needed a plan, an escape route. The hallway stretched ahead, seemingly endless, and Tom stood between them and the front door. She glanced at her mom, silently urging her to do something, to find a way out of this nightmare.

Maddie's eyes darted around, cataloging potential weapons. A vase on a side table, a framed photo that could be used as a shield—her mind whirred with desperate possibilities.

"We can talk about this," her mom pleaded, her voice trembling. "We can figure this out, Tom. Please . . ."

But Tom shook his head, the smile never leaving his face. "No more talking, Heather. It's time for action. It's time to be the family you've always wanted." Tom took a step forward.

The haunting melody of "Twinkle, Twinkle, Little Star" filled the air as Tom advanced, the bat swinging lazily at his side.

The nursery rhyme, once innocent and comforting, now felt like a twisted mockery of childhood. Each note seemed to hang in the air, building a suffocating atmosphere of dread.

Her mom stepped forward, her hands raised in a placating gesture. "Tom, please," she pleaded, her voice trembling. "This isn't you. Remember us, remember what we have. The relationship we're building. We can start a new life. Away from here, away from this . . . this trouble."

For a moment, Tom's advance slowed and a flicker of recognition crossed his face.

"I–I'm falling in love with you," her mom continued, her voice barely above a whisper. "I do want to be a family with you, but it has to be the normal way. N–not whatever it is you have in mind. Whatever *they* want you to do."

Maddie felt a surge of conflicting emotions at her mother's words. There was hope that Tom might be reached, along with fear of what might happen if he wasn't, and a pang of something else. Jealousy? Betrayal? The complexity of their family dynamics seemed to crystallize in this moment of crisis.

Tom's grip on the bat loosened, but it was short-lived. "Not *they*, Heather. Not they. It is one. Just one. The One who knows what is best for us." In an instant, Tom's features twisted back into that terrifying grin, and he lunged forward with shocking speed.

Her mom ducked just in time, the bat whistling through the air where her head had been moments before. "Run!" she screamed. "Get out through the garage!"

Time seemed to slow as she turned, her mother's anguished expression searing into her memory. Beside her, Jackson froze, his eyes wide with fear and indecision, his hand gripping the hall table like he wasn't sure whether to keep running or turn back.

Her mom was on the ground. Tom stood over her with the bat raised high. Acting on instinct, Maddie grabbed a heavy vase from a nearby table and threw it at Tom. It felt like it weighed a ton in her hands, but once released, it flew straight toward him. The crash against his back was both satisfying and terrifying.

The vase shattered on impact, causing Tom to stumble. It gave her mom just enough time to roll away and scramble to her feet.

Jackson sprang into action. He darted forward, grabbed a picture frame from the wall, and swung it at Tom's knees.

The unexpected attack threw Tom off balance. He toppled backward, and the bat clattered to the floor.

Her mom seized the opportunity, snatching up the bat and backing away, her children flanking her on either side.

"Tom, please," she tried one last time, her voice breaking. "Don't make us do this."

But the man they had known was gone. The thing wearing Tom's face lunged forward, hands outstretched and teeth bared in a snarl.

At that moment, Tom ceased to be human in Maddie's eyes. He became something else entirely—a creature of nightmares, driven by an incomprehensible force. Something from the game had changed him. Turned him into a killer.

What happened next was a blur of movement and sound—the sickening thud of the bat connecting, Jackson's terrified scream, the warm splash of something wet on her face.

When it was over, Tom lay still on the floor. The house was quiet. The only sound was their ragged breathing.

Her mom dropped the bat, her hands shaking violently as tears ran down her blood-covered face. "We have to go," she said, her voice hollow. "Now."

They stumbled out of the house, the still too-warm night air a welcome change to the suffocating atmosphere inside.

Chapter 36

They hustled down the sidewalk, not running but moving fast. Her mom fumbled with the key to their front door, muttering under her breath until it finally opened.

"Inside, quickly," her mom hissed, her voice tight with barely contained panic. She ushered them through the front door and locked it behind them with shaking hands.

The familiar surroundings of their home felt surreal after what they'd just experienced. The ticking of the grandfather clock in the hallway, usually a comforting sound, now seemed to mock them with its normalcy.

"Upstairs, both of you," their mom instructed, her eyes darting nervously to the windows. "Change into your sleeping clothes and . . . and wash up."

Maddie caught sight of herself in the hallway mirror and gasped. Flecks of blood dotted her face and clothes, a gruesome reminder of the violence they'd just escaped. She stumbled up the stairs, her legs feeling like lead.

In the bathroom, Maddie scrubbed her skin, watching as the water in the sink turned red, then pink. She changed into clean clothes and took her bloodied outfit to the bathroom. She dropped it in the tub and started the water.

When she emerged from the bathroom, she found Jackson sitting on the top stair, his face pale and drawn. He'd changed clothes, too, but his hands still bore faint traces of blood.

"You okay?" Maddie asked softly, knowing full well that none of them were okay.

Jackson shook his head, his eyes distant. "I keep seeing it, Maddie. Tom's face when he . . . when he changed. It wasn't him anymore."

Maddie sat next to her brother and wrapped an arm around his shoulders. She could feel him trembling slightly. "I know," she whispered. "I see it too."

He leaned his head against her shoulder. "Did you see her? See what she did? What Mom did to protect us?"

Tears filled Maddie's eyes at her brother's words. The fact that he called her *Mom* . . . that so rarely happened. "I saw it. She was amazing."

"Beyond amazing. Do you think . . . did she really tell him those things? About how she wanted to be a better mom?"

"I think she did. I know she did. He wouldn't have said those things otherwise." They sat in silence for a long time before Maddie asked, "Where are your clothes? I'll add them to the tub to soak with mine. And you should probably wash your hands a little better."

After taking care of his clothes, and supervising his hand washing, they made their way downstairs, finding their mom in the kitchen. She stood at the sink, scrubbing her hands with such force that her skin was turning red. Tears streamed down her face, mixing with the water.

"Mom?" Maddie called out softly.

Her mom turned, her eyes wild with a mixture of fear and grief. "I . . . I killed him," she choked out. "I killed Tom."

Maddie rushed forward and enveloped her mother in a tight hug. "You had to, Mom. He would have killed us. He wasn't Tom anymore. He was a Star Bright."

For a moment, they stood there, clinging to each other as if their lives depended on it. Then Jackson's voice broke the silence. "I need to call Eddie."

Her mom pulled away and wiped her eyes. "What? Why?"

Jackson was already pulling out his phone. "He needs to know about the game. He's seen the ball. Seen it before in the game. I have to warn him not to click on it."

"The ball?" her mom asked, her brow furrowing in confusion.

"Didn't you see it?" Maddie asked, remembering the bright orange ball. Only to her, it didn't look like a ball, but a sun.

"In the game," Jackson explained, his fingers flying over the phone's screen. "There's this ball that appears sometimes. I've heard of it but have never seen it. Tom was talking about it . . ."

"I saw it," Maddie said with a nod. "You and Mom both asked about it."

"Right," Jackson said, his brow furrowed. "The text failed. I'll try calling. I've heard about it before. Some people see it. Tom clicked on it, and then . . . well, you saw what happened. Good thing Maddie didn't click on it."

Their mom's face paled. "So, the game is causing this? The Star Brights? Are you sure? I mean . . . it makes sense." Their mom moved to a kitchen chair. "But how could it happen to so many people? And it's not like they are playing and then . . . I mean, remember? The people at Albertsons didn't have a game up. And the day of the explosions, there was a man who worked at the restaurant. He was . . . was one of them. He didn't have a VR set with him or anything like that."

"Maybe it's long lasting?" Maddie suggested.

Jackson nodded grimly. "Eddie's told me about seeing the ball before, but he hasn't clicked on it. I have to make sure he doesn't."

They watched anxiously as Jackson tried to make the call, but it wouldn't go through. "I hope the internet's still up," he muttered, switching to a social media app.

After a tense moment, Jackson's face lit up. "It's working! He isn't online, but I'll send him a message. He'll get it soon. I hope he does anyway."

Maddie and her mom huddled around Jackson, reading over his shoulder as he typed out a frantic message: *"Don't click on the ball in the game. It's dangerous. It turns people into Star Brights. My mom's boyfriend clicked on it and he tried to kill us."*

Jackson hit send, then said again, "I sure hope he sees this soon."

Replaying the events of the game in her mind, a chill ran down Maddie's spine. "Mom, we saw the bright light when Tom clicked on the ball. Do you think . . . could we be affected too?"

The question seemed to suck all the air out of the room. Her mom's face went pale, her eyes widening with horror. "I . . . I don't know," she whispered. "But we can't take any chances." She cleared her throat. "Tell Eddie not to even play that awful game. I need to talk to his parents. Give them my number and tell them to keep trying."

Jackson quickly typed out a message to Eddie, relaying his mom's request. "I wish we could talk to them in person," he said.

"So do I," their mom agreed. "Maddie, send your dad and grandma messages too. Let them know what we know. Tell them to spread the word. Who else can we tell?"

"The neighbors?" Jackson said.

Her mom's face fell. "Yes, we will, but . . . I can't do that tonight. We'll need to let everyone know about Tom. Tomorrow morning . . . we'll do it first thing. Elliot will probably have an idea of how to get this information out to everyone."

"I hope so," Jackson muttered. "It still doesn't feel real. I played the game so many times. I used to be jealous I never saw the ball."

"I'm just grateful you didn't," her mom said softly, reaching out for his hand.

Jackson took her hand, hesitated, then stepped closer. In an instant, he was wrapped around her, clinging tightly as tears fell. She extended a hand toward Maddie, silently inviting her into the embrace.

They remained that way for many minutes until Jackson asked, "Do you think we can stop this?"

"I don't know, but we're going to try." She gave them a teary smile.

Maddie nodded her agreement, feeling a small sense of accomplishment amid the fear. They would do what they could to warn others about the danger.

"While I think we're fine since none of us clicked on the ball, we'll stay up in shifts tonight and watch each other for any signs of change. Everyone will sleep in the living room. And tomorrow, we leave for your grandparents' lodge as planned."

Maddie nodded, feeling a mixture of fear and relief at her mother's decisiveness.

Her mom ran a hand through her hair, her expression troubled. "We'll tell the people stationed at the barricade on our way out of the neighborhood, and we'll tell those at the roadblock on the way out of Casper. I hope the code word truly will allow us to leave Casper." She let out a noisy breath. "We'll worry about all that tomorrow. Right now, we need to focus on keeping ourselves safe."

"Who do you think *The One* is?" Maddie asked.

Her mom tilted her head and crinkled her forehead. "The One?"

"Remember what Tom said? You asked what they wanted. He said, 'It is one. Just one. The One who knows what is best for us.'"

"I-I don't know. I guess whatever happened in the game must have . . . must have affected his mind. It's not a virus after all." She made a snorting sound. "Not a flu virus, anyway, but more like a computer virus that somehow affects humans in the real world. It doesn't even make sense how that could happen."

"Will they believe us? The people guarding the neighborhood and the town?"

Her mom's lips went into a tight line. "I don't know. If I wouldn't have seen it myself, I'm not sure I'd believe it."

"Maybe they already know," Maddie said. "The doctors. The government. Maybe that's why they've stopped talking about a vaccine. Maybe— "

"If they already know, why is the game still available?" her mom interrupted. "Surely, they'd take it offline and . . . and maybe even take down the internet."

"Is that why the internet is out so much?" Maddie asked. "Are they trying to take it offline, but the game's creators are fighting it? It must be the creators of the game responsible for this, right?"

"Why would they do that?" Jackson's eyes were heavy, and dark circles underlined his weary expression.

"We'll talk more about this tomorrow," their mom said. "Let's get ready for bed. We'll use the blankets we have piled up to take with us. I'm going upstairs to change into sweats, then I'll take the first watch. I'll wake one of you up when I need to sleep."

Jackson nodded, barely able to keep his eyes open as he moved toward the living room sofa. Maddie squeezed his shoulder, sharing a silent understanding. They all needed rest, but the night ahead would be long and uncertain.

Chapter 37

The soft glow of predawn light was just beginning to seep through the blinds of the living room when Maddie's phone buzzed insistently. She jolted awake, her heart racing as she fumbled for the device.

The events of the previous night came flooding back, and for a moment, she was disoriented, unsure of where reality ended and nightmares began. She remembered her mom said they'd share the watch last night, but here it was, almost daylight, and she hadn't been woken up.

As her eyes focused on the screen, she saw a flood of messages, all from her dad. Her breath caught in her throat as she read the same words repeated over and over:

"I got your text. Stay where you are. I'm coming for you."

When had they texted him? The last she remembered, all their attempts to reach him had failed. But now, somehow, he had received their message and was on his way.

Without hesitation, she scrambled out of the recliner and nearly tripped over Jackson, who had somehow ended up on the floor.

"Mom," Maddie whispered urgently, looking around for her. She found her in the front room, peering out the curtains, her phone in hand. "Did you get them too?"

Her mother nodded, her eyes wide. "Yes, just now."

Jackson stirred, his own phone buzzing near his head. He blinked sleepily, then sat up straight as he read the messages. "Dad's coming?" he asked, his voice a mixture of excitement and uncertainty.

The three of them huddled together in the dim light, their phones clutched tightly in their hands.

"When will he be here?" Jackson asked, voicing the question they were all thinking.

Her mom's fingers moved swiftly over her phone screen. "I'll see if I can get a text to him," she said, her brow furrowed in concentration.

The seconds ticked by, feeling like hours as they waited for a response. Then, suddenly, her mom's phone buzzed. She let out a small gasp as she read the message aloud: *"I'm five minutes away. See you soon."*

Maddie nodded, unable to find words. The realization that their father was coming, that help was on the way, was almost too much to process after the horrors they'd faced.

"He's really coming." Jackson's smile was wide, but then a shadow crossed his face. "The barricade. Will they let him in?"

Her mom's hand went to her mouth. "I'll go and make sure they do."

"I'm coming with you," Maddie said.

"Me too," Jackson added.

They rushed down the street toward the barricade, the warm morning air promising another hot day. As they drew closer, the sight of the makeshift barrier loomed ahead, guards stationed with tense postures, their eyes scanning the surroundings.

"Look!" Jackson shouted, excitement sparking in his voice as he pointed down the road. In the distance, a small figure on a dirt bike roared toward them, the whine of the engine reaching their ears.

Her mom waved her arms and called out to the guards. "That's my ex-husband! Please, let him through!"

The guards exchanged glances, clearly uncertain. One of them stepped forward, his hand on his weapon. "Ma'am, we can't just— "

But before he could finish, the dirt bike skidded to a stop on the other side of the barricade. Brian Reynolds pulled off his helmet, his face a mixture of relief and urgency.

"Heather! Kids!" he called out. "Are you all right?"

"Dad!" Maddie and Jackson shouted in unison.

The guard looked from her dad to them, and then back again. "I guess it's okay."

After a tense moment of scrutiny, the second guard nodded. "Just walk it around, okay?"

"Yes, sure. That's fine," her dad said as he walked the dirt bike around the barricade. As soon as he was on the same side as them, he popped the kickstand and ran to Maddie and Jackson. Without a word, the three of them embraced, clinging to each other tightly. When they finally pulled apart, his eyes were wet.

He turned to their mom, his voice husky with emotion. "Are you okay, Heather?"

She nodded firmly. "We're already packed. We need to hurry. Let's go."

As the sun teased its arrival, painting the sky in brilliant shades of orange and pink, Maddie closed her eyes. Hope surged through her.

Whatever the day might bring, they would meet it head-on. As a family. As survivors. With hope for a world teetering on the brink of chaos.

The journey was just beginning.

The adventure continues in The Greater Light: Lights of the Collapse Book 2.

The Greater Light: Lights of the Collapse Book 2

An ordinary day turns out to be her worst nightmare.

Alyson Reynolds is living her best life in Portland, Oregon, attending college and rooming with her best friends. As unexplained events turn ordinary people into killers, nicknamed Star Brights online, Alyson is forced into a deadly struggle.

After narrowly escaping certain death, she and her family hunker down at their coastal home, intending to wait out the weirdness. Soon, the entire state of Oregon is in lockdown. But then it becomes too dangerous to stay, not just because of the Star Brights but because a corrupt police officer targets Alyson's dad. They eventually make the only choice they can . . . sneak out of Oregon and head for Alyson's grandparent's cabin in Wyoming.

But the trip won't be easy with the threats of Star Brights and other hostiles. It might even be deadly.

Can Alyson and her family make it to Wyoming? Or was leaving Oregon the worse decision they could make?

Thank you for spending your time on our new Star Bright adventure.

If you have five minutes, you'd make this writer very happy if you could write a short review on Amazon, Goodreads, Bookbub, or your favorite review site.

I appreciate you!

Join my reader's club!
As part of my reader's club, you'll be the first to know about new releases and specials. I also share info on books I'm reading, preparedness tips, and more.

Please sign up on my website:
MillieCopper.com/Freebie

Also by Millie Copper

The Havoc in Wyoming Series

When a series of coordinated attacks devastate the United States, the people of Bakerville, Wyoming, must come together to survive. Unfortunately, not everyone has the town's best interest at heart. Some are striving for personal gain during the apocalypse.

The Montana Mayhem Series

A group from Bakerville, Wyoming strikes out on their own while searching for the desires of their heart. Unfortunately, the road will not be easy, and sometimes the heart is hardened and deceitful. When things don't work out as they hoped, will they become stranded in the wilderness? Or will each be able to find their way home?

The Dakota Destruction Series

After a series of coordinated attacks devastate the United States, Katie and Leo sacrifice everything to help their country. But some things aren't as they seem. Is it time to go home and start fresh, or can something good come out of this terrible situation?

In The October Fall World

In the blink of an eye, an EMP changed everything for Lauren and her family. Now they are in a fight for survival, trying to keep their loved ones alive as society collapses around them. Their once peaceful town of Cody, Wyoming has turned into a powder keg. And with law enforcement a thing of the past, evil lurks around every corner.

Nonfiction Books

Millie has penned seven nonfiction, traditional food focused books, sharing how, with a little creativity, anyone can transition to a real foods diet without overwhelming their food budget. Many of her books also include preparedness and food storage tips.

Find these titles at:
MillieCopper.com

Acknowledgments

Thanks to:

Ameryn Tucker, my editor, beta reader, and daughter wrapped in one. I had a story I wanted to tell, and Ameryn encouraged me and helped me bring it to life.

Dee from Dauntless Cover Design.

My husband, who gave me the time and space I needed to complete this dream and was very patient as I'd tell him the same plot ideas over and over and over.

Three more adult daughters and a young son, who willingly listen to me drone on and on about storylines and ideas while encouraging me to "keep going."

My amazing Beta Readers! Thanks to Barbara, Christine, Christy, Jim, Melonie, Tammy, and Tracy for your help in creating the final story. Your insights and abilities to see the things I miss are very much appreciated!

And also, a special thank you to Tim, a specialist in all things that go boom, for always answering my questions and pointing out things I wouldn't even think about.

And to you, my readers, for spending your time on our new Star Bright adventure. If you have five minutes, you'd make this writer very happy if you could leave a review. I appreciate you!

About the Author

Millie Copper, writer of Cozy Apocalyptic Fiction and preparedness mentor, was born in Nebraska but never lived there. Her parents fully embraced wanderlust and moved regularly, giving her an advantage of being from nowhere and everywhere.

Millie Copper lives in the wilds of Wyoming with her husband and young son, tending chickens and attempting a food forest on their small homestead. After living off the grid for several years, they've recently gone back on the grid. Four adult daughters, three sons-in-law, and six grandchildren round out the family.

Since 2009, Millie has authored articles on traditional foods, alternative health, homesteading, and preparedness-many times all within the same piece. Millie has penned seven nonfiction, traditional food focused books, sharing how, with a little creativity, anyone can transition to a real foods diet without overwhelming their food budget.

The *Havoc in Wyoming, Montana Mayhem, Dakota Destruction, Wyoming Fall, and Yellowstone County Fall* Christian Post-Apocalyptic fiction series use her homesteading, off-the-grid, and preparedness lifestyle as a guide. The adventures continue with the *Lights of the Collapse* series.

Find Millie at www.MillieCopper.com
Facebook: www.facebook.com/MillieCopperAuthor/
Amazon: www.amazon.com/author/milliecopper

BookBub: https://www.bookbub.com/authors/millie-copper
Instagram: https://www.instagram.com/cozyapoc
YouTube: https://milliecopper.com/Youtube

www.ingramcontent.com/pod-product-compliance
Lightning Source LLC
Chambersburg PA
CBHW061655190726
48289CB00006B/1879